A Midnight Masquerade

Copyright © 2023 Mirror Press
Print edition
All rights reserved

No part of this book may be reproduced or distributed in any form whatsoever without prior written permission of the publisher, except in the case of brief passages embodied in critical reviews and articles. These stories are works of fiction. The characters, names, incidents, places, and dialog are products of the authors' imaginations and are not to be construed as real.

Interior Design by Cora Johnson
Edited by Meghan Hoesch and Lorie Humpherys
Cover design by Rachael Anderson
Cover Image Credit: Arcangel / Matilda Delves

Published by Mirror Press, LLC

A Midnight Masquerade is a Timeless Romance Anthology® book.

Timeless Romance Anthology® is a registered trademark of Mirror Press, LLC.

ISBN: 978-1-952611-34-6

Timeless Georgian Collections
Her Country Gentleman
A Lady's Wager
A Midnight Masquerade

Timeless Regency Collections
Autumn Masquerade
A Midwinter Ball
Spring in Hyde Park
Summer House Party
A Country Christmas
A Season in London
A Holiday in Bath
Falling for a Duke
A Night in Grosvenor Square
Road to Gretna Green
Wedding Wagers
An Evening at Almack's
A Week in Brighton
To Love a Governess
Widows of Somerset
A Christmas Promise
A Seaside Summer
The Inns of Devonshire
To Kiss a Wallflower

Timeless Victorian Collections
Summer Holiday
A Grand Tour
The Orient Express
The Queen's Ball
A Note of Change
A Gentlewoman Scholar
An Autumn Kiss

Timeless Western Collections
Calico Ball
Mercer's Belles
Big Sky
A Wyoming Summer

Table of Contents

A Double Masquerade by Elizabeth Johns _____ 1

Their Masked Secret by Jen Geigle Johnson _____ 95

Masquerade A-la-Mode by Annette Lyon _____ 181

A DOUBLE MASQUERADE

Elizabeth Johns

One

PHOEBE CARTWRIGHT WAS NOW RELEGATED to the life of a poor relation, though she was not precisely poor. Her mother had died giving birth to her, and her father had died nine months ago. His baronetcy, estate, and all that went with it passed to a distant cousin she had never met. She had nowhere to go but to her mother's sister, and with only a small competence that would not be considered a dowry to Society, according to that aunt.

Normally, this would not have been such a terrible thing, but Phoebe looked much like her first cousin, Lady Fanny, daughter of an earl . . . except prettier. The main difference was in their eyes—Fanny's being hazel to Phoebe's blue, and more closely drawn together into a permanent scowl. They both had golden hair and slim figures, but that was where the similarities ended. They could not be more opposite in nature.

Fanny was being brought out this Season, and Phoebe was still in mourning. Her Aunt Millicent had made it clear that Phoebe was to remain in the shadows to honor her dear father, of course. Phoebe did not expect them to mourn along with her, but it was clear why she needed to stay out of the way. It was not as though she could expect to make a grand match anyway. When she was out of mourning and Fanny was wed, they would take her back to the country and find a squire or some such country gentleman for her there.

Phoebe did not mind. She had little inclination to make a splash in Society, but she disliked playing second fiddle to her cousin. It had always been thus. Phoebe could hardly blame her cousin, for her superiority had been schooled in her, just as the pianoforte and watercolors had been. However, it was still not pleasant to endure, and now she had to live with her. Phoebe's evening prayers included that of a swift marriage for Fanny.

While Phoebe knew she was not completely unwanted, she still felt as though she needed to earn her keep and not cause trouble. Often, she did little tasks that a lady's maid would have done in order to keep the peace. However, they were removing to London and the countess intended to engage a proper maid for Fanny. Phoebe was grateful, for the girl was near impossible to please. She did not quite feel like Cinderella, though she could empathize with the character a little.

As they arrived in London, her aunt spoke to her as though she were old and seasoned about Town, and that Phoebe was a country bumpkin. Perhaps she was, but she was too excited to be there to pay much mind to her aunt's superiority. Mercifully, her cousin had slept most of the journey, on account of feeling ill when traveling.

It was near dark when they arrived, but she took note of everything as they passed, hoping to see it again on her own. The buildings were much larger and there were many, many more of them. There were new, not terribly pleasant smells of smoke, excrement, and dirty river, but that was to be expected in so large a city. She had never been to London and fully intended to take advantage of the museums and parks while Fanny was away at Society events. If her aunt's intentions came true, Phoebe might never have the opportunity to visit London again.

When they finally arrived in Mayfair, she saw that the earl's townhome was a beautiful estate on the edge of town, standing three stories high of white stone, with a double-pile, hip-roof, and a recessed center. The carriage pulled to a stop inside of the courtyard surrounded by three sides of the house.

Phoebe had not known what to expect, but it seemed most peers had such residences. Her father had not been a peer, but she had grown up on a large estate in Northumberland as the apple of her father's eye, yet lonely for friends and occasionally dreaming of what London had to offer.

The first morning after their arrival, Fanny had an appointment at the modiste, and Phoebe had plans to visit the Tower of London with her old nurse-now-companion who had been allowed to stay with her. Having Sully made all of it bearable somehow—even though she was getting on in years—but she was the last tie left with her former life.

She arose to the sunlight entering her bedchamber and threw back the curtains, smiling at her prospects. Despite the strangeness and hum of the city, she was feeling excited for the first time since before her father's unexpected death.

Phoebe dressed herself, having become accustomed to doing for herself. Sully would help if her dress required it, but usually her countrified day dresses did not. She opened her door to go downstairs to breakfast, only to hear commotion two doors down coming from her cousin's room.

"Fanny. You are not, no could not possibly be, ill!" she heard her aunt scold. "It is only being in the city air. Once you are up and about, you will feel better. Now rise and prepare yourself for Madame Celeste. I had to make this appointment months ago. You will never have your wardrobe in time otherwise!"

Phoebe had gained the open doorway enough to hear her cousin's pained murmurs. "Mama, I cannot."

"Phoebe, please come and talk sense into your cousin! Convince her to get out of her bed at once!" her aunt pleaded once she saw Phoebe in the doorway.

Phoebe approached cautiously and could see her cousin shaking with chills. She touched her cousin's head with the back of her hand, like Sully and the doctor had when she'd been ill before. Her cousin was burning with fever.

"I do think she is quite unwell, Aunt."

"But she cannot be!" Her aunt threw up her hands and began to pace the room. "If she misses this appointment, she will not secure another! And we have just received invitations to the masquerade ball. It is the most coveted invitation of the Season. I had not hoped to have such good fortune already with just arriving in Town!"

"Perhaps we should call for the doctor, ma'am? And have his opinion?" Phoebe suggested, though she did not know how her aunt would react.

Fanny muttered, "Mama, I cannot," through chattering teeth.

Phoebe could see the indecision on her aunt's face. She was certainly glad she'd never experienced her parents' worrying over her health versus her place in Society.

"Very well, we shall call the doctor. But Phoebe, you must go be fitted in Fanny's place."

Her aunt must be desperate indeed, Phoebe thought with an inward groan, but knew it was the only way to maintain peace. "Very well," she agreed. The Tower of London would still be there tomorrow.

A DOUBLE MASQUERADE

ARTHUR JONATHAN EILING MILLS, EIGHTH Marquess of Claremont, was now in need of a son. Leopold, his cousin and only heir, had been taken by a fever while stationed in India, along with his wife and unborn child. He placed the letter with the unfortunate news down on the desk. How could such a life-changing event come in the form of a small piece of paper? Now the inevitable could no longer be prolonged. He had never truly considered taking a wife—why should he when he had a perfectly competent cousin as his heir? He was not opposed to marriage in and of itself for the sake of companionship, but he had always disdained it for wealth and position. He had always been sought after when foolish enough to attend *ton* events, but he'd long since made it clear that he was not on the market.

No one seemed interested in Arthur Mills, merely Claremont.

How was he to go about it, then? Or should he let his distinguished family tree die with him?

He poured himself a glass of brandy, then stared out of the window at the garden.

"Bad news, my lord?"

Arthur had forgotten his secretary was still present.

"You could say that, Ridley. My heir has died."

"My condolences, my lord."

Arthur raised his glass in acknowledgment. Condolences did not begin to cover the emotions he was feeling, but that was hardly his secretary's fault.

"Is there anything you wish me to do?"

"Keep quiet about the news."

Ridley looked at him with surprise. Arthur drained his glass then set it down. "I suppose I must now seek a wife."

If his secretary was shocked, he kept any sign of it from his face. Ridley had been raised almost as a brother, son to the steward of his father before him.

"Are there any invitations that I might accept without advertising my change in circumstances to the entire *ton*?"

Ridley looked down on the stack of correspondence he had thrown in the bin and retrieved it. "I did not think you would be interested," he explained sheepishly.

"Rightly so," Arthur agreed. He still was not interested, but it seemed fate was to determine his social agenda for the nonce.

"There is a musical evening at Lady Worthing's, a come-out ball for Lady Jane Rutherford, and the Midnight Masquerade at Knighton's."

Arthur groaned. "No musical evenings or come-out balls."

"The masquerade? You could always disguise yourself there," Ridley said as a bit of a jest. "Survey the crop, so to speak."

"A disguise," he muttered. "Tell me more about that one. Is it a true costume masquerade or one where people wear dominoes, and the women are of ill repute?"

"No, my lord, this one includes debutantes. It is all aboveboard. The Knightons began the tradition several years ago for their daughter, and it is now quite the coveted invitation by the debutantes who are not otherwise allowed costume balls." He handed the invitation to Arthur.

"One wonders why they bother sending invites here when I never attend."

"They will not expect you there," Ridley agreed, "but will hope, nonetheless."

"Then should I bother to accept the invitation? Subterfuge would be much more effective if people are guessing who I am." He tapped the invitation on the mahogany desk.

"I believe you need only present the invitation, not proclaim who you are. It would defeat the purpose, would it not?" Ridley glanced over his spectacles with raised brows.

"Indeed. Very well. I shall see if I can discover any potential brides at this masquerade, though they may not quite be themselves either."

"I think that is much the fun of it, but there is an unmasking at midnight if you should choose to do so."

"If only you could go in my stead, Ridley. At least narrow down the field for me." The type of female he would wish for a wife likely did not exist anyway. He had never met one, at any rate.

"I can make you a list of those available ladies, if you wish."

"It certainly could not hurt, since I have intentionally kept myself away from such people."

"Are there any qualities in particular I should be searching for?" His ever-efficient secretary was ready to write the dictated list.

"I would think you know my taste rather well by now, Ridley. You know me as well as anyone."

Ridley cleared his throat. "I remember your tastes from Oxford, but I would not think it would signify for what you seek in a wife."

Arthur cast him a withering look, which Ridley ignored.

"Beauty? Lineage? Dowry?" Ridley suggested.

"I have no need of any of those things, as you well know. Someone able to carry on a discussion, perhaps?"

"That will be difficult to ascertain for you, but I shall try. I always find the ability to converse with someone very personal. Shared interests and experiences usually determine such things."

"I certainly prefer to discuss more than the weather over the dinner table. Perhaps a bluestocking," Arthur reflected. "I know it is out of fashion, so it will be harder to discover, but I cannot abide an empty-headed female."

"Most mamas try to discourage such propensities in their daughters," Ridley agreed.

"That is another thing. I would prefer not to look at the brand-new crop, as you put it. Someone with a few more years on them, perhaps one or two Seasons behind them, and hopefully some maturity."

"Very well. I will ask around—discreetly, of course."

"Now, what shall I disguise myself as?" Arthur asked, switching topics.

Ridley sat back and looked at him critically as if he had never taken note of him before. "You would never be able to pull off Henry VIII."

"Thank you," Arthur responded dryly.

"Shepherds, gods, knights are all popular choices. Do you wish to blend in with the crowd?"

"I would not want to look too dashing," Arthur agreed. "But not too boring. Neutral—so that I may not repulse fair maidens yet not overly encourage them either."

"You ask for so little, my lord," Ridley rejoined.

Arthur rewarded his old friend with a grin. "Remember, Ridley, you have a vested interest in my wife as well. You must suffer the lady almost as much as I."

"Touché. You truly do not care about beauty?" he asked doubtfully.

"I suppose it would help if she were tolerable, but I have no need for an Incomparable."

"A knight in armor might be the most effective disguise," he suggested.

"But it would make dancing most difficult, which is essentially the only time I can converse with most maidens."

Ridley inclined his head, then scribbled down some notes. "The grim reaper will also send the wrong message, though a long cloak and mask would allow for ease of movement."

"A shepherd is too blasé. What of a pirate? I quite fancy playing the rogue." Arthur wagged his brows.

"You would have to do something about that hair. You would have just enough time to grow a beard, but it would have to be darkened with kohl."

His most distinguishing feature was his golden-blond hair. It would be hard to disguise without a wig. He loathed wigs and only wore them when required. "It will need to be covered," he agreed.

"I will see what I can come up with."

"I have given you much to do, Ridley. Shall I take on some tasks myself?"

His secretary shot him the long-suffering look of one who had been his playmate since childhood. "This work is out of the norm and I will enjoy doing it."

Arthur smiled. It would be fun to him as well if it were not for such a dreaded purpose. He could feel the shackles tightening around his ankles already.

Two

"Do not tell anyone who you are, remember? I trust you can do this much for your cousin," her aunt reminded as though she had not already done so a dozen times that morning.

"Of course, Aunt," Phoebe answered quickly as they rode to the modiste, leaving Fanny with a maid to await the doctor.

"What costume would be best?" her aunt seemed to wonder out loud. Phoebe did not fool herself that her opinion was wanted. "A shepherdess will be very common, you know, but it does favor your coloring and gives off the appropriate air of innocence. However, I would wager, if I were not a lady, there will be a dozen shepherdesses. We need something original."

"I have never been to a masquerade," Phoebe remarked, but still tried to think. "A goddess?"

"A goddess might show off your figure to advantage, but would the costume look too fast? But a nun would never do—it would hide your assets, and black does not favor your coloring."

Phoebe remained quiet, trying to follow her aunt's logic. She had exchanged her mourning gown in favor of one of

Fanny's day dresses of pale blue muslin for the modiste. It would not do for Lady Fanny to be seen in black. Phoebe had thought it acceptable to tell the modiste she was standing in for her cousin, but Aunt Millicent did not want it known there were two of them. She turned her mind back to the matter at hand. What would she want to be if she were able to attend and hide behind a costume?

"What about a swan or a peacock? It would be a very beautiful costume."

Her aunt looked at her for the first time as though she had said something right.

"I believe that would be perfect, Phoebe. It will be extravagant, but worth it in the end when everyone sees Fanny in it." Her aunt's face took on a dreamy look. "You are of the same build and coloring—I suppose it is a blessing. I had not thought so before now. I had thought perhaps you would feel competition, but you do seem to have your cousin's best interests at heart. As soon as Fanny is settled, we will find someone for you." She reached over and patted Phoebe like a small child as they pulled before the modiste's shop.

Phoebe had had dresses fitted before, of course, but this was nothing like she expected. For one, the amount of pandering to the aristocracy was nauseating. For two, the countess insisted on silly, unflattering colors and gowns. Phoebe remained quiet. Perhaps this was how upper echelons comported themselves. She was grateful not to worry about it. She was merely there as a mannequin for measurements.

When Madame Celeste would drape fabrics over her and hold them up to her eyes, Phoebe had to bite her tongue. She would smile and agree with whatever the lady said.

When they had settled on their day dresses, walking costumes, riding habits, and several ball gowns, her aunt requested a costume.

"But there is so little time, my lady!" Madame Celeste exclaimed. "My other customers ordered them some time ago."

"I will pay your fees," the countess said with a sniff, ignoring the slight.

"Perhaps, if it is something simple," the modiste said, hesitating.

Her aunt looked at Phoebe, pleading.

"I had hoped to be a swan or a peacock," she said sweetly, hoping to bring the modiste to her side with honey.

"*C'est magnifique!* But I do not know if there is time," she said, shaking her head. "The design alone would take days I do not have."

"What if I designed it myself?"

Madame Celeste pursed her lips. "Perhaps, but the feathers!"

"Is there somewhere we might procure them ourselves?" Phoebe did not bother looking at her aunt. She was rather enjoying the prospect.

"*Oui.* There is an emporium near the docks. I will give you the address."

The countess gasped. Phoebe gathered the docks were not a place frequented by ladies.

"Let me take some measurements again. I will begin on the bodice and skirts. They should be simple enough."

The modiste led her to a table with a sketchpad and pencil. "Can you give me an idea of what you have in mind? The masque is but three days away. It will take a miracle to make the costume in time."

Phoebe sat dutifully at the table and began to sketch. It had been one of her favorite things to do in Northumberland—walking around the hills and lakes, sketching the scenery and the wildlife.

She indicated the back with panels of skirts sweeping down like the drawn feathers. The mask and headdress were what would make the costume truly spectacular.

As the sketch began to take shape, the modiste ran away and came back with fabrics.

There was one of celestial blue, and a shimmering fabric of Prussian that seemed to change to almost green in the light.

"What if we cannot find the feathers?"

"Hopefully, there will be enough for the headdress. The skirt we may cover with embroidery and crystals," the modiste replied, looking at the sketch with a gleam in her eyes as though time no longer mattered. She waved for Phoebe to stand and draped the fabric with pleats at the back.

"If we make a straight skirt in front, we can bustle these in the back and perhaps embroider eyes down the back as if the tail were closed. Then the headdress can feather out." She marked on the sketch pad what she meant. "If you work on the mask and the headdress, I will set my girls to the dress."

Phoebe smiled widely, feeling as though London might be more fun than she'd hoped. Until she remembered Fanny would be the one in the costume. Though if it helped her to be married sooner, then it would be worth the effort.

Once in the carriage, her aunt positively refused to go to the emporium.

"May I go with Sully? During the day, it should be safe enough."

"Only if you dress as a maid and wear a bonnet down over your curls. You cannot be recognized! People might mistake you for Fanny!"

Phoebe did not bother to remark that no one had seen either of them yet except the seamstress this morning.

They arrived to find the doctor speaking with the earl. He bowed to the countess, then took his leave. Phoebe began to make her way up the stairs, but she could not help but hear her aunt's shriek. "Measles!"

Phoebe frowned. Had her cousin already been ill for a couple of days? Phoebe tried to think back to her own case. There had been fever and spots in her mouth before the rash began. Perhaps her cousin had had such signs. She certainly had the fevers. She shook her head. This would not bode well for Fanny's entrance into Society. Would her aunt still wish her to make the elaborate costume?

She turned and went back down the stairs to ask, but stopped short when she heard her aunt and uncle conversing.

"We cannot miss the masquerade!"

"But dearest, we can hardly send Fanny with fever and spots!"

"No, but we can send Phoebe in her stead. This is an opportunity not to be missed, and I found my niece to be very compliant today."

Phoebe frowned. It was one thing to pretend to be Fanny at the modiste, quite another to pretend amongst the *ton*!

"Besides, what better place than a masquerade? No one acts like themselves anyway," her aunt insisted.

"I do not see the harm, I suppose, as long as Phoebe is agreeable," the earl conceded. Phoebe could tell her uncle did not see the utility in arguing with her aunt. Phoebe was not sure she could blame him. It looked like she might have the chance to wear the costume after all.

A DOUBLE MASQUERADE

ARTHUR WAS READING THE PAPERS and sipping on his coffee when Ridley joined him for their morning ritual.

"Good morning, my lord," Ridley greeted before he sat down to his own cup of coffee.

"How proceeds the research?" Arthur asked, even though he was not sure if he wanted to know.

"Not as well as I would like," his extremely efficient secretary admitted.

Arthur looked up at the confession. "Something has you stumped for once?"

"The thing is, my lord, I am not encouraged. There are several new young ladies out this year, but those I was to strike from my list. The ones who are two or three Seasons out, who also meet your qualifications, are apparently spoken for, and the other bluestockings are either widows who already have children or are proclaimed Wollstonecraft followers who are staunchly against the institution of marriage."

"I see." Arthur had always thought it would be difficult to find the right person.

"Perhaps you should not rule out the ladies new to Town? Sometimes they are not just out of the schoolroom."

"Ridley, do I detect doubt in your statement?"

Ridley sighed. "Perhaps you could ask your mother?"

"Absolutely not. I forbid you to mention anything should that esteemed lady cross your path. It would be like a pack of hounds catching the scent if the marchioness were to hear of my heir's passing or so much as any consideration of me marrying. I suppose you can leave off the list of ladies, but how comes the costume?"

"Speaking of hounds, I was wondering if it might not be amusing to be an animal such as a fox?"

"A predator?" Arthur considered. "Would it send subconscious messages?"

"Methinks you overthink too much. I was merely trying to come up with something that would not only disguise you completely, but not be too common. Then you could put some reddish color on your hair, which would be easier than trying to dye it black. I know how you detest wigs."

"I have procured a pirate and a fox, just in case. The ball is tonight, if you recall."

"So soon?"

Ridley raised his brows and shook his head as the footman served them breakfast.

Arthur spent the afternoon debating which he should like to be: pirate or fox.

He supposed the fox would be better, though he did not quite like dressing as an animal with fur and a tail. It was rather demeaning. However, the whole thought of searching for a wife was not a pleasant task either, but must be done, and at least this would be on his own terms. His natural inclination to keep to himself would have to be repressed for the evening. For how else was he to discover without inhibitions what the ladies were truly like? It would take all of his charm to draw what he wanted to know from them, he suspected.

When it came time to dress, Ridley had outdone himself. The costume was as good as something he would have seen at the theatre.

"Where did you find this, old boy?" Arthur asked appreciatively.

"The parlor maid's sister works as a costumer at Drury Lane. She let us borrow this. And there is no need to color your hair. The headdress covers it completely."

Arthur felt a little silly as his valet dressed him, but he had to confess he would be unrecognizable once the mask was in place.

Ridley was downstairs to see him off.

"Well, what do you think?" Arthur turned around in a circle like a girl wearing her first ball gown. No one in his club would have believed Claremont capable of doing such a thing.

"You'll do," his secretary remarked with a sly grin. "I wish I could see you on the hunt tonight."

"I shall take my costume seriously as though I were playing the part," Arthur assured him.

"A sly fox on the prowl. Mamas and ladies be warned!"

"I consider this armor."

"Indeed. Were you not disguised, it would be like the hounds giving chase to the fox instead of the other way around."

"Pray for success tonight or I shudder to think what will happen if word gets out."

To anyone else, they might think the statement conceited, but Ridley understood how desperate mamas were to marry off their daughters to a wealthy peer. Arthur had become an expert at avoiding them.

Arthur took a hackney cab to make certain even his carriage did not give him away. He arrived fashionably late so that he could blend in with the crowd, so no one knew if he was part of a group or alone. Perhaps he was overdoing the secrecy, but much to his chagrin, he had learned early on that he was considered a prize on the marriage mart.

For a while, it had dampened his enjoyment of socializing, but he had quickly learned which events were safer to attend, though he always had to be on his guard to some degree.

Since it was a masquerade, there was no receiving line, and he found a place within the dim ballroom to allow his eyes to adjust so he could survey the crowd.

The ballroom had been decorated to resemble a forest, and it soon became apparent that Lord and Lady Knighton were Robin Hood and Maid Marian. Arthur always found it a bit ridiculous how elaborate some of these hostesses were to compete with one another, but even he could appreciate how well done this was. The ceiling was a canopy of leaves and pillars were clustered around the room decorated as trees. It even smelled like a forest with pine and moss. Lanterns provided a dimness that lent a feeling of intrigue, and perhaps even a hint of danger that would embolden people. He was surprised debutantes were permitted.

Reluctantly, he knew he'd have to select someone and dance with them—even speak. It was what he wanted, he tried to remind himself.

There were all kinds of characters there. Most debutantes were easy to spot, dressed as shepherdesses or in something equally wholesome. If their costumes did not give them away, then their giggles often did. He moved on. The older generation tended to favor Tudors from Henry VIII to Queen Elizabeth. There were some goddesses and a Cleopatra who caught his attention and he doubted very much that a chit straight from the schoolroom would be wearing such revealing costumes. He continued to scan the room of ballgoers, but no one lady stood out. Had he thought a light from above would shine down upon her indicating with whom he should dance? Absurd. It seemed as though he no longer knew how to go about in Society. He would let his inclination lead him, then. He was almost resigned to go and ask Cleopatra for a dance, when a flash of bright blue caught his eye. The music was beginning for the first dance, and he had yet to select a partner.

A brilliantly costumed peacock walked down the steps into the ballroom, and Arthur's breath caught. The bodice was fitted, with a straight skirt melding to her figure, but the back bustled out into large feathers with eyes made of crystals. A band wrapped around her head with a single, large sapphire hanging over her forehead, the back crowned by a spray of feathers. The mask was bright blue and covered in crystals and formed a peak over her nose. He found himself before her. Likely, many others had noticed as well, but they had already chosen partners. He stepped forward and bowed. "May I have this dance?"

Three

"Is it safe?" Phoebe asked, wondering where the flirtatiousness had come from. Her aunt had warned her not to speak more than absolutely necessary so Fanny may return to herself as soon as possible.

"Alas, there are no guarantees," he answered in a deep baritone that she barely heard over the din of the room. "You do look like a tasty treat for a fox, though."

Dutifully she discreetly looked to her aunt, who gave her a nod. The music was beginning and she would miss out on the first dance if she denied him. Her aunt had scarcely stopped talking to her about all of the rules of proper behavior, along with who the biggest catches of the Season were. If she could just attract the notice of some of the gentlemen, they were sure to think she was Lady Fanny and they would come calling.

He led her to the floor and she was surprised to find that even the simple act of taking his hand caused her insides to churn and her cheeks to heat. Thank goodness the mask hid the reaction. She would have to learn not to blush, if one could control such things. She had danced at her small village assemblies and had never been thus afflicted, so why did one stranger in a costume elicit such? The whole experience was overwhelming, seemingly heightened behind the mask, including his strong scent of bergamot.

She attempted to remain quiet and study her partner, for she knew she would be quizzed about every detail later. Not that she would know who anyone was, but he was very well disguised. Despite being fully covered, she could tell his physique was lean and fit, and his bearing was that of a self-assured man.

"Are you new to Town?" he asked as they joined the dance.

"I suppose I may answer that safely. I arrived but a week ago. And yourself?"

"No, I spend a good deal of the year here."

"To do your duty?" she asked, trying as he was to discover each other's identity.

"Perhaps," he said with an amused smile. She wished she could see his eyes, but she strongly suspected he would be handsome.

"I am fascinated with London. It might be gauche to say, but there are so many things to do, more than in Northu—" She just stopped herself. *My wretched tongue!* She was not even supposed to converse, lest people be able to make the distinction between her and her cousin.

"Alas, north could mean many places, my lady. I do believe your secret is still safe," he said, clearly amused.

"I had not thought to be here, sir. I am neither practiced nor sophisticated in the ways of Society." Her aunt would be mortified that she had said something so un-Fanny-like. Yet, Phoebe did not think her cousin as full of Town bronze as she thought she was.

"I assume your birth is good. Or will the clock chime

twelve and turn the lady back into a maid?" She would swear he was laughing at her behind his mask.

When she did not answer, he spoke again.

"Your manners do not indicate a country bumpkin."

She hesitated and tried to think of what Fanny would say and attempted to mimic her tone. "Society is droll."

"Neither does your costume. It is the most exquisite one here." He eyed her from head to toe, eliciting a sensation that made her have to suppress a shiver.

"That was very handsome of you to say."

He smiled and she thought she caught a gleam in his light eyes. Yes, she was quite certain his eyes were light now that her own had adjusted to the darkness.

"You literally outshine every other person here. Where did you find such a costume?"

"I designed it myself and had help from the modiste, of course."

"Of course." His voice had sounded odd. Was that something she should not have admitted to? Town ways could be so peculiar.

"I am glad you chose to be a male peacock, even though you decidedly do not look male."

She was blushing hotly at his words, though she was pleased her handiwork was admired.

"It is unfair that the male birds are the beautifully colored ones."

"The poor females might have nothing to do with us otherwise," he countered.

"I almost chose a swan, as both are white, but decided to be colorful. And why choose a fox?"

"I wanted to be fully disguised. My other choice was a pirate, but it was not so concealing."

"Are you so important that you do not wish to be

known? Or are you notorious?" she asked, full of curiosity despite her resolve to answer in monosyllables when possible.

He smiled at her and pulled her much closer than propriety dictated in the next turn of their figure. "I shall never tell."

"Are you a rake? Was that something else I should not have asked?"

"You may certainly ask it, but I shall not answer. What would the fun be in that?"

"It is not very sporting to leave me without any clue," she retorted.

"You have only told me a portion of the place where you are from and that you are new to Town. Will you give me more clues?"

"Tit for tat?"

"Very well. I shall tell you something I would never say were my true person known. I do not ever attend balls. People would be shocked by my presence."

"Hence the heavy disguise." She tilted her head in thought. "So you could be either notorious or famous. You did not answer my question."

"I could be both."

Something about him made her want to speak freely despite her aunt's warnings. She was conflicted by the way he warmed her insides yet made her tongue flap as if they were old friends.

"Are all Society balls like this?"

"Not at all. We would normally be conversing about the weather or the theatre, and we would only dance if we had been introduced."

True, that much she did know about propriety. "It sounds like a bore," she said before she thought better of it. She would be much safer were they to stick to such inanities.

He smiled again as though, indeed, she should not have said it. He had a lovely, easy smile.

"I assure you, I know better than to say such things. I will do better the next time we meet."

"If there is a next time. You never know. We may pass each other on Bond Street and be none the wiser."

Somehow, Phoebe thought she would recognize the man anywhere. "Perhaps you are right. What a shame not to know who first danced with me in London."

"Will you at least dangle one little carrot before me?"

It was so very tempting. "Reading is my guilty pleasure, and I intend to see everything there is to see while here—especially the Tower. That was two," she answered in such a way that it was hard to believe it was her speaking.

"May I have the last dance before midnight?"

"If I am still here," she teased, knowing the danger he presented her.

"I shall have to be content with that, I see." The music was drawing to a close and as he led her from the floor, several other men seemed to draw close.

"Are you promised to someone next?"

"No. You were there when I just arrived."

"My advice would be to steer clear of Henry VIII and the pirate. And whatever you do, do not go outside with any of them."

She curtsied and then he was gone, leaving her feeling a sense of loss and distinctly like prey as several gentlemen stepped forward to solicit dances. She resolved to smile and remain quiet with any future partners, or it would threaten Fanny's deception. Her aunt and Sully would both have been appalled at the way she had spoken with him. She would have to hope she never encountered this fox again after this night or she might get ideas above her station.

A DOUBLE MASQUERADE

ARTHUR WAS COMPLETELY CHARMED. HE did not know what to make of this lady peacock, but he was certain he had never met her before. Lady Knighton was a bit of a high stickler, and he did not think her invitations would extend as far as cits and nabobs, but perhaps he was wrong. Certainly, if the costume was any indication, then her family was very well to do, indeed. It probably would not be too difficult to discover who she was, for the mask did not hide her golden locks and porcelain skin below the level of her nose. He did not think she wore a wig. Even her eyes he could see were a pretty blue, though they might have been reflecting the colors of the mask. However, that was not what he was drawn to. It was her refreshing talk and simple scent of orange blossoms. Most young debutantes were schooled only to speak about inanities, and he did not think the masquerade was the only reason she spoke so freely. She also did not seem to be quite so young as most. From a good family with funds, but not high in the instep? Could it mean she had little supervision, or was she from deep in the country where Society's rules had not yet touched her? He suspected it was probably a bit of both. Either way, he wanted to know more.

He did his duty and danced with three shepherdesses, two Aphrodites, and Cleopatra. All of them felt like a filler until the waltz before the unmasking. The other dances only reaffirmed that she was different. Why did Society school their daughters to be so artificial when the opposite was much more charming? Or was it only charming because it was so rare?

It was difficult to pay proper attention to his other partners and not watch the peacock, who stood out like a bright rose amongst the weeds. Perhaps too harsh of a reference, but it was what his mind thought nonetheless. He could carry on the superficial conversations that these young girls were capable of without his full attention on the matter. Cleopatra was a handsome widow; Lady Starling was on the hunt for another husband. Yet he was very careful not to give himself away. She pried and she guessed, but he was able to hold himself aloof—something which he had not done with the peacock. He suspected her identity would be well-known in the clubs later that evening, if she unmasked.

She was the toast of the ball, if the constant crowd around her was anything to go by. Were they all as charmed as he? Or had she been able to hold her true nature at bay for the others? He hoped so. He wanted to keep that charm to himself.

He led Cleopatra towards the edge of the ballroom, then made her a bow and went in search of his final partner, ignoring the pleas and pouts of the woman.

Arthur did not plan on staying for the unmasking, as he was not quite ready to reveal himself as on the marriage mart, but perhaps he would wait in the shadows to see her.

When it came time to claim her hand, the crowd of admirers around her protested as he approached.

"Who are you, anyway?" a young pup named Worthing asked. He was dressed as a knight.

Arthur ignored him and held out his arm for the peacock.

"Haven't you already danced with her tonight? Give the rest of us a chance!" a dandy named Piper complained.

"Let him have her. Perhaps he needs the disguise to have a chance with the ladies," Devon drawled. He was looking roguish as a pirate, though he did not need a costume for that. Arthur did not make eye contact because he feared the duke would recognize him. Devon was one of his closest acquaintances. Even he did not know Arthur was here.

Peacock smiled at them, but went willingly enough as he held out his arm for her.

"Thank goodness," she said, as they moved away from the crowd.

"Poor peacock, have they been harassing you?"

"Mainly trying to discover my identity, but it has been difficult to remain quiet."

He chuckled. "I consider myself honored, then."

"You should. I have scarcely said more than two words to anyone else. If they know my identity, it will not be because of me."

"Your mother should be delighted with your court. You have quite a number of eligible bachelors interested."

As the orchestra signaled they were about to begin, he put his hand on her waist and took her hand and felt instant attraction. "Have you ever waltzed before?"

"No, sir, but I have seen it." He thought she was perhaps a bit breathless. Was she feeling the attraction as well?

"Ah, you are supposed to have permission first, are you not? Would you rather we walk on the terrace?"

"A fox warned me that I should not go outside with a gentleman, no matter what."

"A wise fox."

"But I believe since we are in disguise, the patronesses of Almack's are allowing the dance tonight. I do believe it is safer to risk waltzing than the dark terrace."

He looked around and saw several young ladies being led out. "Very well. I will not be disappointed to have you in my arms."

"You may regret those words on behalf of your feet in a few moments."

He pulled her in a little closer. "I am not concerned. You were very graceful earlier. Just follow my lead and try not to think."

A smile formed on her lips and she looked up at him as they began the steps. They communicated without words, their eyes locked. She seemed to float in his arms and he would be quite willing to carry her away and propose right then, he thought, astonishing himself. The matter was not so urgent, yet, he had a fleeting feeling that the magic of the evening would soon end. "I feel I am going to regret not discovering more about you once this night has ended."

Was he mistaken, or did he detect sadness in her gaze?

"I will cherish it forever. It has been one of the best evenings of my life. There is a bit of magic in the air."

"Do you believe in Fate?" He should check himself and not speak so boldly until he met her by the light of day.

"Perhaps in the sense that God leads us where we should be."

He spun her in a series of circles, leaving both of them breathless as the dance ended and he had to let her go. Servants began to light more candles in time for the unmasking as the clock struck midnight. He looked around for the easiest escape route. Regretfully, he must say his goodbyes and arrange to meet her again. When he looked back, she was gone.

Four

PHOEBE NEVER DID DISCOVER WHO the fox was. Speculation was rampant, of course, and she smiled to herself knowing that most likely they were all wrong.

Her heart was so full of happiness as they rode back to Moreton House that she paid little heed to what her aunt said.

"I am quite pleased with your work tonight, Phoebe. I expect Fanny will be the toast of the Season! Did you see how many gentlemen clung to your side all evening? Lord Worthing, Mr. Piper, even the Duke of Devon! He avoids young misses like the plague!" She clapped her hands together. Her uncle, beside his wife, said nothing and looked as though he were about to fall asleep.

"I hope she recovers quickly," Phoebe said, and meant it. She had enjoyed herself immensely, because of the fox, but she had been rather uncomfortable with all of the other attention. The only one Phoebe cared about was the fox. Fanny could have the others.

"It was quite clever to leave before the unmasking, even though you hardly could have revealed yourself," her aunt continued as though she had not spoken. "It only piques their curiosity even more."

"I have little doubt they already know who she is, Millicent," the earl remarked. "Not with the way you were preening and gabbing."

"It would quite defeat our purposes if I had remained silent. How else would they know who to call on?" she defended. "I do wish I knew who the fox was. Did you hear anything in the cardroom about him?" her aunt asked.

"I heard some speculation, but he was apparently well disguised."

"You should not have danced with him twice without knowing who he was, Phoebe, but I suppose there is no real harm."

"What do you mean to do until Fanny is well again?" Phoebe asked.

"We will have to put all suitors off until the rash fades. I only pray it isn't more than a week! As long as the spots are gone from her face, we can make a few appearances. I believe your success tonight will keep them dangling after her."

When they arrived back at the town house, Phoebe was glad to seek the privacy of her apartment. It was hard to believe the evening had been real. She felt as though she had met her prince, but she knew in her heart she would never be able to have him. In fact, she might never see him again.

She looked at herself in the exquisite costume in the mirror. It truly was a work of art, and she hated to take it off, signaling the night was over, but she could not escape reality forever. Reaching up, she untied the mask and took it off before calling for the maid to help her with the rest.

Would she recognize the fox if she were to meet him in public? She would like to think so, but when would they ever be near enough to discover each other again?

Likely never.

As soon as the maid was finished, Phoebe blew out the candles and sat in the window seat, looking up at the dark evening sky. It was still early by Town standards, and she could hear people still milling about.

She wished she had discovered who her fox was, but perhaps they would not behave the same were they undisguised. Would he know Fanny was not she?

The next morning, she was plain Phoebe again. She dressed herself back in her simple half-mourning gown and pulled her hair into a severe knot, placing a cap on top, so that there could be no possible link between her and Lady Fanny.

Her uncle was reading his paper as she entered the breakfast room.

"Good morning, Uncle."

"Phoebe." He made to stand, surprised that she was there. "I did not expect to see you about so early."

"I am used to the quiet country." In fact, she hadn't slept much. She had been dreaming of a fox and a peacock, only waking to realize it could never be. One day, she hoped she could treasure the evening for what it was, but she was still a bit heartsore knowing it was over. Perhaps she had more in common with Cinderella than she thought.

"Have you seen the drawing room?" he asked.

"I have not," she answered in confusion.

"You should go and look. Your aunt will be beside herself when she comes down, even though it was she who let the cat out of the bag."

Her uncle went back to reading, and she finished her breakfast quickly, wondering what he was talking about, then hurried into the drawing room.

The smells of a garden met her as she entered the room

which, in fact, looked like a garden. Beautiful sprays of blooms, both common and exotic, met her gaze. Was this from the suitors the night before?

Apparently, her identity was known, though she was certain the fox had left as soon as she. Undoubtedly, her aunt had crowed her success, too proud to let the success go unremarked.

Fanny was still indisposed with the rash, and they were not so similar that Phoebe could trade places without the mask, but the work had been done. Phoebe's peacock had been the delight of the masquerade and she was now much sought after. Could Fanny maintain her court?

Her aunt hurried into the room and spun about in delight with a squeal that could sour her breakfast. "Phoebe! Can you believe it?"

Without waiting for an answer, she began to pluck the cards from each bouquet and read them.

Has the mystery been unraveled at last? I await the divinity behind the mask. Worthing.

"Very pretty words!" Her aunt moved on to the next, which was an exquisite arrangement of various blues and greens... like her costume.

My heart belongs to a peacock. I only hope yours belongs to a fox.

"How very forward!" Her aunt made a face but dismissed it for the next card.

I will never look at a peacock the same again. Enchanted, Devon, she read. "The duke! Phoebe, it would be a coup to ensnare him for Fanny!"

"I am glad the charade worked, ma'am," Phoebe said, wanting to take the card from the fox with her, along with the bouquet.

"Phoebe! There will be callers! You must leave!"

"I had planned to go to the Tower with Sully. Will that be acceptable?"

"Yes, yes. No one will mistake you for Fanny dressed as you are with a bonnet, but make certain to use the unmarked carriage and leave by the back." She made a shooing motion and did not notice as Phoebe plucked the card and a bloom from the fox's bouquet before she left the room.

AFTER THE BALL, ARTHUR WENT home and changed out of his costume, then made his way to his club. He knew there would be a buzz about the peacock after she left without being recognized. He wanted to be present before everyone else arrived so there would be no suspicion that he was the fox. Someone would know who she was. He did not have long to wait.

He took a seat and the waiter brought him a glass of brandy before he had to ask.

Devon entered first, looking bored. "May I?"

"Of course." Arthur waved his hand to the seat next to him, and the waiter was already there with the duke's drink.

"Have you been here all night?"

"There was not much to entice me this evening. You?"

"I braved the Knighton masquerade. She is my aunt, you know."

"Is it over already?" Arthur feigned surprise.

"I could not say. I lost interest after the unmasking and left."

"Is that not the opening ball of the Season?" Arthur asked.

"It is. Not many of the new crop are worth looking at, though there was one. Very clever costume—she caused quite the sensation as a peacock."

"Who was she?" Arthur asked as nonchalantly as he could, swirling the liquid in his glass as though bored.

"She left before the unmasking, though I am aware of who she is."

"She told you and no one else?" Arthur raised a brow.

"Much as I would like to say she favored me with such partiality, it was my aunt who told me. Apparently, the mother had been so proud of her daughter's success that she could not keep the identity to herself."

"Matchmaking mamas." He shook his head and they both took a drink. Had it been the peacock's idea or the mother's to play coy? Somehow that did not fit with the girl he had met and danced with, but Lady Knighton would know. "Do you mean to keep me in suspense? Not that I am likely to know someone new to Town."

"Lady Fanny Murdoch, daughter of Lord Moreton."

The name Fanny somehow did not fit the girl he'd become obsessed with in two short dances. He knew Moreton, an amiable, yet spineless Tory. It was difficult to recall the countess, but he thought she was more ambitious than her husband. It was difficult to think her capable of raising such a refreshingly unaffected girl as his peacock. He would not have willingly chosen her for a mama-in-law, and he would certainly use caution.

"Do you intend to throw your hat in the ring?" he asked Devon.

"Doubtful, though she bears further investigation. She was quite promising in her costume."

Arthur felt a strong urge to plant his old friend a facer, but he somehow managed to restrain himself. Perhaps it was worth trying to see her again, but how, without attracting attention or giving himself away?

"You and I are the two biggest prizes yet to be netted,"

the duke said sardonically. "I have no intention of being caught until I am good and ready. I have six heirs at last count, so there is no rush."

"If we could all be so fortunate."

"Hopefully, your cousin will have a son."

Arthur shook his head. "There is no longer an heir." Why had he admitted that aloud? He should stop drinking and go home now.

Devon made a sound of commiseration. "My condolences. Does this change your feelings for yourself?"

"I have not yet decided," Arthur confessed as he set down his glass and stood.

"If you decide you want Lady Fanny, let me know first so I can put my name in the books on you," Devon drawled. He glanced over at where the hallowed book was kept.

Arthur turned to look and, sure enough, many of the young men who had been paying court to his peacock were there, placing bets with great animation.

He cursed inwardly. "Maybe I should see this paragon for myself, but I am not ready to announce anything to the *ton*. If I so much as set foot anywhere near one of these debutantes, my fate is sealed."

Devon looked thoughtful. "Perhaps you could attend the theatre with me. It would not be too threatening if we knew she would be there."

Arthur sighed. "It is probably worth looking. Send me word if you hear she will be attending." He left and walked back to his house, thoughtful. Somehow, something did not seem quite right. But if Lady Fanny and his peacock were one and the same, then she was who he had to have.

The next morning over coffee, Arthur directed Ridley to send an arrangement to Moreton House with very specific instructions about its colors and arrangement.

Ridley raised his brows. "Last night met with success?"

"Let us say potential. I discovered her name, but she has no idea who I am."

"Are you going to call on her?" Ridley's tone was full of disbelief.

"I am not yet ready to make a declaration to the powers that be in the *ton*." Mainly meaning his mother.

"Then how do you plan to woo her?"

"Woo, Ridley?"

"Yes, woo. I have no doubt you could go and sign documents with her father and have his blessing, but you would not be satisfied with such an arrangement."

"Neither would she," Arthur admitted. He did not like the thought of his peacock being bullied into an unwanted marriage, though he thought she was attracted to him, at least.

"The arrangement will send the right message, and I will attach a note to go with it. I have yet to think of what will come next without exposing myself."

When Arthur returned home from his morning ride, Ridley came out of his office to greet him.

"Do you know something, Ridley?"

"I happened to hear something, yes."

Arthur walked into the study, and Ridley followed behind, closing the door.

"It seems Lady Fanny has taken ill."

"Something serious?" Arthur asked.

"I only heard in passing when I went to send her bouquet. It seems some of her suitors were turned away when they went to call."

Arthur frowned. It meant a delay in seeing her again, but at least he hadn't made a fool of himself by calling there.

"Thank you for telling me, Ridley."

He was still trying to decide how to see her again hours later as he wandered through Hookham's Circulating Library. Had she not mentioned enjoying books? What did she enjoy reading? They'd had so little time together. Had she received his flowers? Was she pleased with his note? How much longer until she was well again?

Five

PHOEBE FELT VERY MUCH LIKE Cinderella the next few days. She'd met her prince at the ball and had to leave before midnight, then turned into the common cousin. There'd been no glass slipper to leave behind as a clue to her true identity. And since she'd had the measles before, it made sense for her to help nurse Fanny.

Her cousin was not the easiest of patients, and she wore Phoebe's patience thin. Now the worst of the illness had passed, and Fanny was covered in spots, she began to fret about her appearance.

Her aunt was so concerned that she could not even look at Fanny. Phoebe, on the other hand, was left to console her cousin. It was no simple task, especially while she knew the great city was outside these walls waiting for her to explore.

Day by day, the bouquets from the fox came—each more clever than the last. How long would it continue? Would he recognize that Fanny was not she? And was it horrible to pray that he would know the difference?

It might be vain, but she liked to think he would know her without the mask. He had been completely covered, but still his smile and his scent . . . "Phoebe!" her cousin shouted, interrupting her pointless daydreams. At least her cousin's lungs were working properly.

"Yes, Fanny?"

"Who sent me flowers today?"

Phoebe had already answered this question several times that day and all of the days of her convalescence. "All of the same people as yesterday, Fanny," she answered with admirable forbearance. It was quite remarkable, in fact, that none of the interest in the peacock had died away. Instead, it seemed to have grown with Fanny's being ill. How strange the *beau monde* could be!

There was a knock on the door, and a maid was there. "The doctor is here to see my lady."

"Show him up, please," Phoebe answered.

He was a short, stout gentleman with a large paunch and gray hair, but he had a very kind smile.

"Good, good," he said as he entered the room and was already surveying his patient. "Much better, indeed."

The countess came to listen behind him, but remained in the doorway.

"I am?" Fanny asked, disbelieving. "But I still have this rash. When will it go away?"

"The rash is already fading from your face, my dear. It will soon fade from the rest of you and you will be as good as new."

"So, when may I leave my room?"

"You are out of danger now, and I see no harm in you taking a bit of air and walking about if you feel up to it."

Phoebe felt a rush of relief. Her aunt had been beginning to concoct ways for Phoebe to be disguised as her cousin again before she became known as sickly, but Phoebe did not wish to continue the deceit.

"She is no longer contagious?" Her aunt was still standing in the doorway.

"Not now that the rash is fading."

"How long until the spots fade?"

"That varies from patient to patient, but usually most of the peeling finishes within a few weeks."

"Weeks!" "Peeling?" Fanny and her mother exclaimed at the same time.

He ignored their outrage. "I will be going then. You know where to find me if you have need of me." The doctor wisely hurried away.

"Come, Fanny! Let us take a turn about the garden for some fresh air. Then we can see about covering those spots with some face powder."

"But, Mama," Fanny protested.

"You heard the doctor! Lying abed will not find you a husband, Fanny."

She turned to Phoebe. "Send her maid in to help her dress. Thank you for helping her these past days, Phoebe," her aunt at least had the decency to say.

"If you do not need me for a while, may Sully and I go to the circulating library?"

"Yes, but remember to disguise yourself as best you can, and speak to no one. And see if you can find some Bloom of Ninon for Fanny's face at the apothecary."

"Yes, Aunt." Phoebe curtsied and hurried away before she could be called upon again, certainly not remarking upon the strangeness of the request for her to run a maid's errand. Anything to be out of the house.

She quickly informed Sully of their plans and rushed to change into something plain so no one would mistake her for a fine lady—not that she had anything of the latest fashion, unlike her cousin.

Once they were in the carriage, she let herself relax and smile again. "Freedom, Sully!"

"I do not know how you bear up under it, miss. It isn't right you waiting on her hand and foot."

"It is not quite so bad as that. I did not have to empty the chamber pots," she teased.

"But still, you being a fine lady, yourself. It is shameful, that's what. Your father, bless his soul, would be turning over in his grave."

Phoebe was not so sure about that. He would expect her to make the best of her circumstances, which she was. She was exploring London!

Her aunt had not precisely forbidden her from going anywhere, but she seemed more concerned that Phoebe not be recognized. Garbed in a gray gown and a capote bonnet with a long brim that all but covered her face, it would be something indeed. They rode in the unmarked carriage, which also gave nothing away. To the *ton,* she was quite beneath their notice and if they did, she looked like a young lady out with her chaperone.

Once they had been deposited at Hookham's Circulating Library on Bond Street, Sully found herself in one of the comfortable chairs clustered in the center of the store in which to wait, and Phoebe looked around in astonishment. Her father had frequently purchased books from London shops to be sent to Northumberland, but seeing all the books in one place from floor to ceiling was like having the world at her fingertips. Add to that the smell of leather and paper, and she soon became lost in the realm of Gothic novels, and found herself struggling to choose. She could not regret any story that allowed her to escape into another world for a time.

The bell over the door jingled, startling her from her daze and reminding her to be cautious.

She turned about to see a handsome gentleman

bedecked in a finely embroidered coat, heels, and a wig enter and caught herself staring. Remembering her aunt's warning, she bowed her head and waited for him to pass before she went forward to make her selections. Now, where else could she venture to that day?

~~~~~~

"Were you able to find orange blossoms?" Arthur looked up from his paper.

"Unfortunately, that would require a trip to the country and a very large orangery. However, I was able to procure orange flowers and wrote a lovely note about how they reminded you of her."

"Well done, Ridley. Not too sappy, I presume?"

His secretary wore a look of horror.

Arthur laughed. "Of course not. Now, what shall we send tomorrow?"

"It will be hard to top the last one, my lord."

"We will think of something, but let us hope she recovers soon."

It was a very long wait for Lady Fanny Murdoch to recover. Ten days had passed by the time Devon sent a note requesting his presence at the theatre that night.

He felt his scheme would be grossly conspicuous as he made his way to pick up his friend for the evening. Devon joined him in his carriage.

"You are certain she will be there?" Arthur asked.

"My aunt sent over a pointed note stating that they will be expecting my visit to their box this evening in order that we might be introduced properly to Lady Fanny."

Well then. "We?"

"Indeed. You did not think to require me to face the wolves alone, did you?"

Arthur gave Devon his best annoyed look. "What is on the playbill this evening? Not that we are here to pay it much mind."

"I believe my aunt said Grimaldi is doing his rendition of *Robinson Crusoe*."

There was still a crowd around as the carriage pulled before the theatre's façade on Bridges Street. Most were gawkers come to get a look at the nobs. Despite traveling in an unmarked carriage, they were surrounded the moment they stopped. They were fashionably late as they had intended, and all eyes turned to see the most eligible bachelors arrive together.

Arthur felt exposed, which was ridiculous. He had heard no word that anyone suspected he was the fox. Still, he had been quite bold in his notes to the peacock, so if she discovered his identity, there would be expectations. What if he was wrong about her?

The corridor had mostly emptied and the farce was already being enacted. They had chosen to use Devon's box since it provided the best view of Knighton's. It was quite comical to watch all heads turn almost simultaneously as they entered, but both gentlemen were used to drawing attention wherever they went.

If only he could capture the lorgnettes and quizzing glasses against all eyes in a picture, he mused.

Once seated, it did not take long for him to see her across the theatre and his heart began to race. Was it her at last? Devon had already raised his glasses and was surveying the crowd. Arthur was not yet ready to commit to that. Perhaps after the farce when the lights were dimmed.

He listened for Devon's forthcoming commentary. "It certainly could be her," he remarked.

"Could?"

"I can hardly say with absolute surety from across the theatre, can I? Though, my aunt could be wrong, and there could hardly be another creature so similar, could there?"

"Doubtful," Arthur agreed. He was burning to raise his glasses and look, but thus far he had only been able to see her profile. But she wore a heavily powdered wig with bows in it.

It felt like forever until intermission, and Arthur actually had to remind himself to remain aloof, which was amusing enough itself since he had a reputation for his air of boredom.

There was a crowd surrounding the entrance to the Moreton box, but they parted when he and Devon arrived. "I say, you both mean to cut us out?" Worthing whined.

Devon stopped and looked Worthing up and down with his quizzing glass without bothering to remark.

"He is paying his respects to his aunt," Arthur remarked in passing.

It was true—if he or Devon wanted Lady Fanny, the rest would likely be cut out.

His eyes adjusted once they stepped into the box, then there she was. He observed her as introductions were made, and bowed when it was his turn, but there was no recognition whatsoever in her gaze as their eyes met.

"Charmed, my lady. I trust you will now be able to enjoy the delights of Town." He had tried to give her a clue without giving himself away.

But her look was blank, and her face flushed beneath a great deal of powder, though she pretended ennui—which was nothing at all like how she had behaved at the masquerade. Then she tittered at something Devon said, and Arthur felt his insides clench with a mixture of disappointment and disgust. It felt as though her mask were being ripped from her face right before him. She had been so enchanting! Had he created her into a fictional character that did not exist? But no, he knew he had not imagined their chemistry.

Yet, there were none of the same feelings or aura about her that had been there that night. It was as though she were a different person entirely. A stranger.

He tried to bring himself back to the present, and noticed she was standing. She passed right in front of him, and a whiff of gardenias almost made him ill. She looked very sickly and pale, though it could be attributed to her recent affliction. He made his excuses and waited for Devon in the corridor, angry at himself for trying to spin moonbeams out of cobwebs.

"Not quite what I'd envisioned," Devon remarked when he was able to escape.

"Nor I, though she is hardly an antidote," Arthur said, trying to reconcile his anticipation with the reality. It did not add up.

"Not precisely the way I'd prefer a duchess of mine to be known," he said dryly.

"She seems young and . . . entitled?"

"That is not so rare for an earl's daughter with a hefty dowry."

Except that was not at all the impression the peacock had given him at the masquerade. "Worthing or Piper can have her. They do not seem deterred."

"Care to finish the play?"

"Not I." He felt too disturbed at his feelings and was too annoyed with himself for allowing his hopes to be raised. Which led to the question . . . did his peacock really exist?

"Sorry if your hopes are dashed, Claremont. Stop at the club for a drink?"

The next day, he decided to haunt the places she had mentioned wanting to see. He tried Hookham's again, but when he didn't find her there, he found himself directing his driver to the Tower of London. He had gone completely mad. Perhaps the Tower was where he belonged.

Six

AS SOON AS THEY WERE free of Mayfair, Phoebe shed her cap, knowing no one would recognize her. As they set off across the city, she was grateful for something to distract her from thinking of her fox. When they arrived at the Tower, she dutifully tied a bonnet over her head, and then stepped out of the carriage to feel the cold breeze from the Thames.

"Was there ever anything more wonderful, Sully?"

Her old nurse looked doubtful.

"Come, let us explore!"

"I am not sure if I can keep up with you, Miss Phoebe."

"There is the moat! How I wish we could have entered through the Traitor's Gate."

"Well that would have been something," Sully agreed, already sounding fatigued.

"I am sure there will be plenty of benches for you to sit upon if you grow tired," Phoebe reassured her companion and reminded herself to slow down. She went first to see the Crown Jewels because she thought Sully would like them. Then they went through the torture chamber, because Sully had always had a fascination with that part of history when Phoebe had studied it. However, as they came to the menagerie, Sully turned up her nose.

"The stench, miss!" she complained. "And my feet are tired."

"There are benches nearby. I think there is no harm in you resting for a bit. Besides, no one of the *ton* is about this early, and they would never mistake me for one of them dressed like this."

Sully did not take much convincing; she was used to country ways which were not so stringent. "You stay within my sight," she warned weakly.

Phoebe wandered from cage to cage, feeling more forlorn as she went. These magnificent animals looked sad and lonely in their small cages.

She stood and watched a lion, trying to envision him in his natural habitat. How magnificent that would be. She would be depressed, as well, if she were reduced from roaming the plains of Africa to a cold, stone cage.

For a moment, she felt like she was being watched, so she turned back to Sully to see her sitting there with her head propped back, asleep. Phoebe could not help but smile. But surely the strange sensation did not come from her old companion? Looking a little farther, she saw a stunningly handsome gentleman nearby, dressed in a dove gray coat with a black top hat. Had he been the one to alert her senses? She bobbed a slight curtsy when he noticed her staring, then turned back towards the cage.

Footsteps approached her, and she prayed it was not him. Had he assumed she was unchaperoned and available?

"Do not be silly," she muttered under her breath. He was likely there to see the animals, just as she was. Then he came close, and she was forced to look up at him. She had mistaken his light hair for a wig.

"I beg your pardon," he said, with a slight bow. "I thought you were someone I know."

"There is no harm, sir. I am new to Town, so unlikely."

"Ah. Far from home?"

"The north," she said as though it was the ends of the earth, trying all the while to keep her face hidden.

"Are you here alone?" He looked around.

She smiled fondly as she looked at her old companion napping on the bench. "It seems that I have worn my companion out. It is just that there is so much to see and do here."

"Are you only down for a short visit?"

"A few weeks at least. I am with my aunt and I am at her disposal."

He looked back at the lion. "What do you think so far?"

"I think the animals are magnificent, but I hate to see them caged thus. They look sad to me."

"Indeed. There are many places in London with exotic animals. It is all the rage, you know."

"I did not."

"There are lions and tigers, and even a rhinoceros at the Exeter Exchange. On the Strand, there is a collection of camels. Queen Charlotte has an elephant and zebras in the stables at the palace. She also has kangaroos at Kew Gardens. And that is only naming a few off the top of my head."

"I had no idea," Phoebe said with wonder. She really had been removed from the rest of the world in Northumberland.

"Have you seen the rest of the Tower?"

"All but the armory."

"It is a bit of a bore," he teased. "Have you walked to the top?"

"I do not think Mrs. Sullivan is up to the climb." She could not think why this stranger was still speaking with her, but she felt at ease with him and he was encouraging her sense of exploration.

"Do you think she would mind if I escorted you?"

Phoebe looked up at the handsome stranger with astonishment. His eyes were a bright, brilliant blue, and his smile reminded her a bit of her fox. She knew it was wishful thinking, but he was much as she'd imagined her beguiling prince to be. He even smelled like him. It must be a common fragrance amongst gentlemen. She remembered herself and ducked her head.

"I beg your pardon. I suppose I should introduce myself since there is no one about to do the honors. Arthur Mills, at your service." He made another bow, but this one was almost regal, as if she were of some import.

"Phoebe Cartwright." She curtsied in return, feeling uncomfortably shy, wondering if her aunt would be angry she'd used her real name. She looked longingly up at the battlements around the perimeter. She did so wish to walk along the wall.

"Let us ask permission, then." He offered her his arm, and she only hesitated a moment before placing her hand on it. They were out in the open and there could be no connection to the masquerade or Fanny, she told herself.

"Sully?" Phoebe tapped gently on her shoulder.

"Oh! Dear me. I nodded off a moment. Oh!" she exclaimed when she saw the handsome man with her.

"Mr. Mills, may I present my companion, Mrs. Sullivan?"

Mr. Mills had Sully charmed in mere seconds. He bowed as though she were the Queen herself. "Madam, may I escort your charge along the battlements? We will be within sight the entire time, I assure you. Then you may be able to continue enjoying the sights from here."

Sully looked at Phoebe. "I suppose, as long as I can see you," she said, and Phoebe could see she was relieved she would not have to exert herself.

It was not really much of a climb, just some narrow stairs, but the view was incredible. The wind whipped off the Thames at Phoebe's face, and she stared around in wonder at the city before her. She caught Mr. Mills watching her and looked at him questioningly.

"Forgive me, but your resemblance to my friend is uncanny."

Phoebe turned away, knowing she had forgotten herself. Surely there was no chance that this was he? She had told him of her plans to visit all the places in London, but would he have remembered that and come looking for her? No, it was simply too far-fetched.

"I should be going now. Mrs. Sullivan will be tired."

He glanced casually down at Sully, who was napping again, then back at her sardonically. "May I have the privilege of escorting the two of you to Gunter's for an ice? It is something you must do whilst in Town."

Even Phoebe had heard of Gunter's, and it was certainly on her list of things to do, but it was in Mayfair and too risky. She still wasn't certain why this stranger was being so forward. "I am afraid my aunt would not approve. I do appreciate the invitation, sir."

He hesitated. And she, too, did not want this to be the end, but she could see no way forward. They walked slowly back to where Sully slept, oblivious to the pigeons fluttering all about her.

"Forgive me for being so forward, but I confess a desire to further our acquaintance. Will you be attending any *ton* events?"

Phoebe felt her cheeks warm. She knew nothing about this man and was quite certain her aunt would not approve of her forming an attachment to an unknown gentleman. Yet . . . yet she did not want to be at the mercy of who her aunt chose for her. "I will not. I am still in mourning for my father, you see, and my aunt does not wish for me to be brought out yet." Hopefully, that would satisfy him.

"I see. My condolences. May I recommend the British Museum or Kew Gardens? Astley's Amphitheatre is delightful, but it might be beyond what you wish to do in mourning."

"I appreciate the recommendations. I hope to see everything," she said with a half-smile.

"I will bid you good day, then, and hope that I have the good fortune to run into you again."

She curtsied and he turned to walk away, leaving her feeling as though she had just made the biggest mistake of her life, even though she felt a bit traitorous to her fox. He was just as she'd imagined him to be without the disguise.

~~~

ARTHUR FELT LIKE AN IDIOT as he left the Tower. He had practically accosted the young lady, convinced it was his peacock. Even when she had given him a different name than that of Lady Fanny Murdoch, he had still been drawn to her. The likeness was incredible, though he could not be sure since she had been wearing the mask. He had certainly felt pulled to her in a way he had not with Lady Fanny, then he could not tear himself away.

He had then persisted in trying to draw information from her and even tried to discover her plans! Had he truly invited her to Gunter's? What a spectacle that would have been for the gossips! What was the matter with him? Clearly, it could not be his lady, and yet . . . she was exactly as he'd imagined her to be, though perhaps without the drab gray gown and bonnet of half-mourning. When Miss Cartwright had admitted she was from the north, his pulse had begun to race. She even smelled the same and her voice was similar, or was he just being wishful trying to make her fit?

He had to let go of this fascination. There could be no explanation other than Lady Fanny had been the peacock, and her illness had addled her personality. But somehow, he could just not let it go. Now it seemed he was to transfer his feelings to one Phoebe Cartwright, whose eyes were just the color he'd imagine his peacock's to be, and she bore an equally pleasing disposition. Was it also coincidence she was just down from Northumberland—he assumed? And that she had been at the Tower where she had expressed a desire to visit?

Was there some strange possibility that she had exchanged places with Lady Fanny that night? But how?

He did not care who she was, but he wanted to find her again. Just short of arranging an assignation, he had made his desires to know her better clear, and she had withdrawn from him. There was nothing left for it but to bow away gracefully. He'd never had to do such a thing in his life, and why should he now?

But where could he find her other than looking all over London? She was certainly a lady, if not nobility. Her clothes had been quality and she had a chaperone with her. Maybe Ridley would know how to find her. It was certainly worth a try.

Ridley had no idea.

"Cartwright? Isn't that a rather common name?" Ridley asked as he pulled his spectacles off.

"Not quite the likes of Smith."

"We could start with Debrett's, though that only goes through baronets."

"Perhaps it could be the family name of the countess? If she looks similar, and she was interchangeable with Lady Fanny, it is reasonable to assume there is a connection."

"And if the connection is, er, a natural one?"

Arthur ignored that remark.

Ridley rose from his desk without waiting for an answer and walked through to the library, Arthur hot on his heels. He waited for Ridley to look because he was much more familiar with the tome.

"Let us see . . . Moreton." Ridley ran his finger down the page. "Murdoch married to Millicent Robson. Offspring Lady Francis and Lord Stephen, Viscount Rochdale."

"Not Cartwright."

"No, but it could be her maternal aunt if that is the line of thought we are following here."

"It is. I realize I am looking for a needle in a haystack, but on the other hand, the upper crust is rather small."

"And inbred?" Ridley asked rhetorically. He flipped the pages to Robson.

"Should we not just look for Cartwright? In Northumberland?"

"I am curious now. And I prefer to be thorough. Besides, Cartwright is the family name, not necessarily the title—if there is one."

"True." Arthur had to wait.

"Robson. Millicent and Margaret, daughters of Viscount Farleigh. Born on the same day."

"Twins. So it stands to reason that their daughters might favor one another. Now will you look for Cartwright? How many can there be in Northumberland?"

"Hundreds and hundreds."

It took some searching but, indeed, they found a Sir John Cartwright, who had married Margaret Robson, and bore one child, Phoebe. It appeared her mother had died, bearing her or soon after. And now she was mourning for her father, poor girl. Had she come to live with her aunt, then? And she was not out because of mourning? If Fanny became ill as was reported, a masquerade would've been too much to resist for an ambitious mama like Lady Moreton. But to dangle her niece in front of suitors? It would be a scandal if discovered. No wonder his peacock had been afraid to talk!

"It has to be her," Arthur said.

"It appears so. Well done, my lord."

"Yes, except how does one go about calling on someone who doesn't know who you are? And when that person is not officially out because they are in mourning?"

"That goes beyond my breadth of knowledge, my lord. Perhaps Lady Claremont could be of assistance?"

"At least you have not lost your humor, Ridley."

The last person he wanted in on this scheme was his mama.

Seven

THEY WERE NOT TO HAVE AN at home that day, so Phoebe was allowed to be in the living areas that she was required to avoid when people might be around. She was still hoping to go somewhere for the afternoon, but Sully was tired and wanted a day to rest. Phoebe felt a little guilty, but they were only there for so short a time, and the weather was divine. How often could one say that about England?

Fanny was looking through *La Belle Assemblée* fashion plates, and Phoebe was devouring one of her novels. Thankfully, Aunt Millicent was too busy looking through invitations and answering correspondence to pay her choice of reading material any mind.

Fanny was going on and on about her suitors. "Which one would make an offer first, Mama?"

"Who do you favor, my dear? Piper seems most likely to come up to scratch."

"But he has no title," Fanny whined.

"Worthing is also devoted, but is he indebted from gambling?" her aunt asked.

And so on and so forth they went.

Phoebe had kept mum about the fox, and thankfully

Fanny had not seemed to notice the notes and bouquets had ceased since Fanny's night at the theatre. What did it mean? Had the fox realized it wasn't she? Phoebe was part hope, part agony. No more notes to Fanny meant no more notes for her to treasure, yet she didn't want him to fall for Fanny.

But how was she to find him when she did not know his name?

"What gown do you plan to wear to the Venetian breakfast?" Aunt Millicent asked.

"The jonquil," Fanny answered. "Mama, have you seen the latest styles? The waistlines are changing! All of my gowns will be out of mode!"

"Nonsense! We can have a few of those made, of course, but there is nothing wrong with the ones we just received from Madame Celeste. She would not have made anything out of mode." As Aunt Millicent still favored wide panniers and tall wigs, Phoebe suppressed a snort.

Fanny's lips formed into a pout, but she did not argue. Phoebe glanced at her very simple gray muslin and was so very grateful for not being raised as a spoiled miss. Many of the girls acted very similar to her cousin. Still, she could not think that gentlemen found that attractive.

The equally starched butler, Pugsley, entered the room. Phoebe thought his name fit him to a tee as she looked down at the similar dog resting beside her aunt, snoring. "Your ladyship, there is a caller. She says she knows it is an unseemly hour, but she hopes you will grant her an audience since she is happening by, and the call is of a more personal nature."

"Well, who is it, Pugsley?"

"Lady Claremont."

"Oh! Of course I will see her." She looked around the room frantically at Phoebe.

"I will excuse myself," Phoebe said without any malice. She was quite used to these odd requests by now. She picked up her book, but could not help but overhear her aunt remark to Fanny, "The marchioness and I are not as close as all that. What could it be about?"

Phoebe had never been one to eavesdrop, and frankly, she didn't care much about her aunt's social agenda or who called upon her, but something made her stay near enough to the door that she could hear. She sat in a chair in the small parlor next to the drawing room when she might have otherwise gone out to the garden.

"Lady Claremont," she heard her aunt say. "To what do I owe this pleasure?"

"Lady Moreton, Lady Fanny. Thank you for receiving me at this unusual hour. I particularly wanted to speak to you about something personal, and I did not think it appropriate for a time when we might be overheard."

"Oh?" her aunt remarked. "Let me send for tea and you can tell me all about it."

"Are you recovering well, Lady Fanny? I had heard you were indisposed," the lady asked kindly.

"I am mostly recovered, my lady, thank you."

Phoebe heard the sound of the tea tray being delivered—Pugsley must have ordered it immediately upon Lady Claremont's arrival. Phoebe waited impatiently while the tea was poured and served. Her crossed leg was bouncing up and down as it was. She giggled to herself because her aunt would be appalled at the unladylike behavior.

"Now, what can I help you with?" her aunt asked, sounding much more calm than she was. Phoebe knew she was chomping at the bit with curiosity.

"I know you were already married at the time, but your sister might have mentioned we became good friends during her second Season."

"My sister?" Aunt Millicent paused. "I am afraid I was unaware of the connection."

"Indeed, it was her second Season after you had made such a grand match, and she helped me negotiate my first. We were both fortunate to secure matches, but our marriages took us to opposite sides of England. We were able to maintain a correspondence until her death, the poor soul, but I do know she had a daughter."

"Yes, she had one daughter, our dear Phoebe."

That dear girl snorted in the other room.

"It has come to my attention that she recently lost her father as well, and I was wondering if you knew where I could find her. I would like to send my condolences."

"She did lose her father, poor child, and she is still in mourning. I would have brought her out with Fanny otherwise."

Phoebe looked Heavenward and shook her head at the gross falsehood.

"Very understandable, but she did not remain in Northumberland, did she?"

Phoebe could almost hear the inner battle in her aunt's head. Was it better to reveal Phoebe's presence to the marchioness and thereby have that connection? Or was it better to keep her hidden away until Fanny had made her match? Phoebe was grinning behind the parlor door.

"Why, Phoebe is with me, naturally. She had nowhere else to go, poor soul."

"I am relieved to hear it. Margaret would have wished me to make her acquaintance. May I see her?"

"I do not believe she is home at present. She has been spending her time visiting places that are still appropriate for her current circumstances."

"That is unfortunate. I had so hoped to visit with her,

but I am so pleased to know she is in Town. I will send her a private invitation to call on me. I live in my own place, you know, so we may be quite private. Perhaps tomorrow afternoon? There can be no impropriety in her visiting her mother's friend."

Phoebe debated bursting into the room, but she was quite amused that her aunt had backed herself into a corner. Lady Claremont made it impossible for her to refuse Phoebe to visit, and had extended the invitation privately. Even Phoebe knew there was a Venetian breakfast at Lady Belmont's tomorrow afternoon. She could not take her words back now and admit Phoebe was there, after all, could she?

"I am sure Phoebe would be delighted to make your acquaintance."

"Very good then. Thank you for your time, and I will send her a note with my direction once I am home."

Phoebe could not stop smiling. It was not that her aunt was a bad person and did not care about Phoebe at all, but she was just far more ambitious for her own daughter's position in Society.

―――

It was uncanny. Anytime Arthur so much as mentioned his mother it seemed she would either call or summon him as though she had ears in his house. She probably did. This time, it was the latter.

"Do not say a word." Arthur looked up to see his secretary wearing a knowing smirk. "Is my calendar clear this afternoon at two?"

"There is the Venetian breakfast, my lord, but you did not send in your acceptance."

"Because I had not planned to go, as you well know."

"Then it seems your afternoon is clear to call upon your mother. Please give her my regards."

Arthur gave Ridley his best quelling look, but the secretary was only amused by it.

Whatever could his mother want this time? He wondered about that as he climbed the steps to her house later that day. She had her own dwelling, but it was only one street away from his. Hardly cutting the apron strings, as it were.

Bentley opened the door for him. "Good afternoon, my lord. Your mother is in the drawing room."

"Very good, Bentley. I will show myself up."

He paused at the door of the garden room, as he thought of it. It was a soothing, pale green decorated with vases of bright flowers around the room. It suited his mother, who preferred her gardens to most things—second only in trying to find a suitable mother to her grandchildren.

"Mama. So good to see you."

She extended her cheek to him, and he took the seat across from her and crossed his legs as though he had not been summoned.

"You called on Lady Knighton's box but not your own." She sniffed.

"Ah. So I am here to be scolded. I overlooked your presence that night."

"When was the last time you entered a box with any young misses?"

"You cannot think me enamored of Moreton's daughter, surely."

"No," she confessed. "After calling there yesterday, I would never quite forgive you if you were."

"Are you actually warning me away from an eligible miss?"

"It seems I am. She would be my daughter-in-law, after all, and I found a half-hour near her and her mother was quite enough."

"Well, you may rest easy, Mother. I have no designs on Lady Fanny Murdoch."

"But you do have designs on someone else?" she asked hopefully. "You must admit, I have not tried to foist anyone on you for a few years now."

"And I have appreciated it more than you know."

"However, with dear Leopold's passing, you cannot put it off much longer."

"You know?"

"I know everything, my dear." Her eyes were twinkling dangerously.

Arthur sighed. "Then why bother summoning me here to confirm what you already seem to know?" he asked calmly, wondering who the mole in his house was. She probably had all of them on her side, including Ridley, the traitors.

"What I know is that at Lady Knighton's masquerade, a certain fox was enamored with a certain peacock, but the peacock may not happen to be who she was thought to be."

"Indeed? I had heard about this peacock, but it has become common knowledge that it was Lady Fanny Murdoch." Arthur would not commit to anything at this point.

"Because that is what Lady Moreton wished everyone to think. It is obvious Lady Fanny had the measles. She was without paint when I made my surprise call yesterday, and had not been able to cover her face with powder."

"Are you saying it was not she? The *ton* will not take kindly to being duped."

"If the *ton* were to discover it, but I do not think anyone else remembers that she had a twin sister."

"Lady Fanny has a twin?" Arthur was unaware of that.

"No, Arthur. Try to follow along, please."

Arthur was torn between amusement and irritation, but he was used to his mother's starts.

"Millicent is the twin. Her sister, Margaret, was a dear friend of mine during my first Season. She was very kind to me."

Ah, now Arthur knew where this was going. His mother was very, very good, and very, very sly. How the devil had she discovered he was the fox? He played along. "And how does this pertain to me?"

She waved her hand impatiently. "I was just getting to that. Margaret died giving birth to a daughter, Phoebe. It quite broke my heart to lose her so young."

"I am sorry to hear that," he murmured, trying not to betray himself.

"I have never had the chance to meet Phoebe, but when I heard that her father died recently, I paid a call upon Lady Moreton."

Arthur wondered which came first, the chicken or the egg, but it did not matter. It seemed his mother had discovered a mutual interest and had found his peacock for him.

"And I assume you found her?"

"Well, let us say, I believe I have."

Bentley knocked lightly on the door. "Miss Phoebe Cartwright to see you, my lady."

Arthur's heart began to pound. It was all happening so fast. When he stood and turned, there she was. A vision in lavender muslin, her hair dressed in soft curls with a matching ribbon. She curtsied to his mother, and then she finally looked at him.

"Mr. Mills?"

"The two of you have met?" His mother raised her brows. It seems she did not know quite everything.

"We met at the Tower. We were admiring the lion together," she explained.

"I see. Then permit me to make a proper introduction then. My son Arthur, Lord Claremont, this is Phoebe Cartwright, daughter of Sir John and Margaret Cartwright."

Arthur bowed and prayed Phoebe would not be overly intimidated by the scenario in which she found herself. He was used to his mother's ways, and it was futile to resist them.

He rose, then looked up into her stunned face and smiled at her. She smiled shyly back, and he felt an entirely new sensation of euphoric rightness.

Bentley had brought in the tea tray and his mother had settled to pour.

"My aunt said you knew my mother," Phoebe remarked.

"Oh, yes," his mother said with a beaming smile as she handed Phoebe a cup. "We were quite the pair in our day. I was not as beautiful as your mother, but together we took the *ton* by storm. She could have had anyone she wanted, but she fell in love with the quiet, bookish baronet and he took her far away from me." She pointed to a stack of letters, tied together with a pink ribbon. "I thought you might like to have those, my dear. They are all of our correspondence over the years."

"Thank you. I am honored you would think to give them to me."

His mother reached over and squeezed Phoebe's hand. "I am only sorry I have not met you before. But we have now. Forgive me, for I have not expressed my condolences over the loss of your father."

Arthur looked over at Phoebe, who looked as though she might cry. She took a sip of her tea and composed herself.

Arthur took a sip of his own tea and decided to change the subject for her sake. "Have you been able to visit any of the other items on your list?"

"Not yet. I am afraid I am only permitted to go out when my aunt has company."

"She does not want you to be seen?" his mother asked, appalled.

"Not exactly," Phoebe answered carefully, placing her cup back in its saucer. "She thinks it might confuse people to have me around since I am not yet out."

"Odd considering that she is a twin—or maybe not so odd at all—but I suspect she did not want to detract from Lady Fanny's success," his mother murmured. "How long has it been since your poor father died, Phoebe?"

"Almost ten months now. I know what you must be thinking, but truly, I do not mind waiting."

"Yet you are older than your cousin, are you not?"

"By two years, yes. Father had always thought to send me to my aunt to make my come-out with Fanny, but it was not to be."

"My dear, perhaps I can convince her to allow you to attend a few small gatherings."

"I am not certain. Perhaps once Fanny receives an offer, my aunt might agree."

Arthur was completely certain of the reason Lady Moreton did not want Phoebe anywhere near her daughter in public. She would completely outshine her cousin not only in beauty, but in character. Maybe he could court her right under the aunt's nose, within her restrictions.

"Perhaps you would permit me to escort you to a few places while you must be away from the house? With dear Sully in attendance, of course."

Phoebe smiled. "I would like that very much, my lord."

"As long as you make a point of keeping her away from the *ton* and ensuring proper chaperonage, Arthur."

"You know I am ever mindful, Mama," Arthur replied dutifully, as though he needed reminding.

Eight

PHOEBE ESCAPED THE HOUSE WITH guilty pleasure and walked two streets to meet Lord Claremont's carriage. She had told her aunt they were going to Kew Gardens, just not with whom. A carriage was waiting for them in front of Lady Claremont's house, so there would be no question of propriety should someone happen to see them. Lord Claremont would already be waiting inside, as arranged, so as not to be seen.

He took Sully's hand from inside, who took the backward facing seat, and then he sat Phoebe on the forward one. Phoebe felt her cheeks warm at the contact, and then she laughed as he tried to make them an awkward bow from inside.

"Now, Miss Sully, I was going to be a gentleman and take that seat."

"Oh, no, my lord, it wouldn't be proper. You should sit with Miss Phoebe."

His eyes met Phoebe's and they both suppressed laughter. So much for subtlety, she thought.

He settled into the seat next to her. His long legs almost reached the other side, and his nearness created a warmth in her from head to toe. It was still hard to believe she had befriended a marquess and that he wished to take her anywhere.

As soon as they passed the toll gate, Sully was gently snoring across from them. Phoebe really ought to see if she had adequate sleeping quarters, because she had not seemed to be so tired before they came to London.

When they arrived at Kew Gardens, they began from the Elizabeth Gate along the Broad Walk to admire the orangery first, before wandering along the flowered-lined pathways that were bursting with bright blooms. What she wouldn't give for days to stay there and sketch!

Phoebe thought it was the best day of her life—at least equal to the masquerade ball, but she could hardly say so.

"Do you like it here?" he asked.

"Oh, yes. My favorite thing to do at Thornbury was to walk about nature and admire the flowers and the animals."

"Speaking of animals, would you like to see the kangaroos? I can inquire, if you wish."

Phoebe looked back at Sully, who was beginning to look fatigued. "Perhaps another time, my lord."

"How about we stop for a picnic? I asked my men to set it up near the lake." He turned to Sully. "Are you ready for refreshments? There should be a picnic waiting for us just up ahead."

"That would be lovely, my lord." Sully beamed at him.

Phoebe was surprised that an array of dishes with proper plates and silver had been placed out on a blanket. It was as pretty as a picture and far fancier than anything she had seen at a picnic in Northumberland.

"It was my mother's doing," he remarked, as if reading her mind. "She does not do things by halves."

"It is lovely, thank you." It was always best to be gracious, she'd learned along the way.

There was chicken and cheese and fruit and several delicate little cakes to choose from.

Sully had chosen to sit a little ways away on a bench, and Lord Claremont loaded her a plate with delicacies and took it to her. Phoebe's heart gave a squeeze. He was such a fine gentleman. She could see Sully blushing as he again charmed her into accepting the plate.

"That was very kind of you," Phoebe told him as he returned to the blanket and took a seat beside her.

"It is only what is right. I could not convince her to sit with us."

"She used to be my nurse," Phoebe said. "She has never been quite comfortable in the role of companion. My father educated me, so I never really needed a governess." Phoebe thought Sully was perhaps awed by Lord Claremont's title, but she also wanted Phoebe to find a husband.

"I understand perfectly."

Phoebe ate in silence, unsure of what to say to him.

"You seem a bit more reticent today. Does it happen to be because you heard my title?"

She could deny it, but it was the truth. "I suppose so. I am a bit surprised by the connections—the coincidences. Why did you introduce yourself to me as Mr. Mills?"

"Precisely for the very reason that people treat me differently."

"Guilty as charged, and I apologize. I am not awed by your title, but perhaps I fear you think I will be more interested in you now." She laughed. "My cousin and aunt would be green with envy if they could see me now."

"Precisely why I never attend *ton* events. However, I am interested," he confessed, "but I would prefer we remain incognito."

She was at a loss for words. Had he said he was interested?

"May we simply be Miss Cartwright and Mr. Mills again? I rather liked the simplicity and genuineness of it."

She held out her hand to shake on the agreement, but he took it and kissed the air above it, leaving her quite befuddled.

"What would you like to see next? Do you think we can convince Sully to go farther?" he asked with a twinkle in his eyes.

"I should like to see the pagoda, but I will leave it to you to charm her into it."

He stood smoothly and then held out a hand to bring her to her feet. The footmen gathered around to tidy the picnic as they walked over to Sully. She was putty in his hands.

They walked on towards the Queen's Cottage and the Great Pagoda. It was no surprise when Sully did not wish to climb it. Phoebe could think of nothing she wanted to do more.

They had seen hints of the tall structure through most of the gardens, but when the pathway finally opened up, Phoebe had to keep herself from exclaiming out loud. Sully did it for her.

"What an odd building, to be sure!"

It was a narrow, tower-like structure, with multiple tiers of eaves coming out from each level and a steeple on top. It was made of gray brick, with ten stories or so of layered floors. It was over two hundred steps to climb to the top—She was bursting with energy, even if she was a bit dizzy from going round and round on the way to the top. She grasped on to the railings to steady herself, then felt a warm hand on her back.

"Is it everything you had hoped?" Arthur asked very near her ear. He was standing too close for her sanity.

"Yes. Surrounded by gardens everywhere we look must be something akin to Heaven."

"My mother would agree with you there. One day, you will have to come see her gardens at Eiling. She is what many would call an enthusiast."

"Would it not be something to see London from this high as well?"

"I imagine at the rate buildings are sprouting up, it will not be long."

She walked around the observation deck, admiring the view from all sides.

"Has your aunt agreed to allow you to attend some small gatherings with my mother?" he asked.

"It is hard for her to say no, of course, but your mother knew that would be the case," she answered with a shy smile.

"My mother is quite persistent when she has a bee in her bonnet."

"Am I the bee?" She looked at him with surprise.

"Of sorts. I would venture to say I am also her bee."

Phoebe dared not think he meant anything by that statement. Lord Claremont was the lady's son and she was the daughter of a friend. Certainly not a match for the likes of him. Besides, she had heard her aunt say he was the most determined bachelor ever to grace the *ton*. He smiled at her, but said nothing more about it, leaving her wondering if she was simply having a strange dream.

～•○•～

ARTHUR NEEDED TO REIN HIMSELF in. Phoebe did not know he was the fox and therefore probably wondered at his forwardness. He certainly had been forward, but he had seen the look of confusion in her eyes, and realized that she did not recognize him. It was astonishing how much intimacy had been formed between them at the masquerade. He needed to tell her, he realized, as soon as he left her after the outing at Kew Gardens.

He hated that she had to go back to her aunt's house, where she had to remain hidden. Although, it gave him an advantage in courting Phoebe without the knowledge of the *ton* . . . right under their noses, in fact, which gave him no small amount of satisfaction.

His mother having introduced them formally was a double-edged sword. While he would have found Phoebe eventually on his own, now she seemed wary of his title.

He would have to convince her. Would telling her he was the fox help? That he knew she was his peacock? He had been so close to blurting it out at the top of the pagoda, but he'd been too busy restraining himself from kissing her. He thought it would be too much too soon. But he was impatient. Once he made up his mind to wed and found the perfect person, he saw no sense in delay.

However, Phoebe was new to Town, and had likely not met many eligible gentlemen. For a moment, his conscience made him consider waiting for her to have a proper Season, but then he dismissed it. He was a catch and he knew a proper match when he saw it. He felt it deep inside, and he had years to devote to the purpose of making her happy and giving her no cause for regret.

As he watched Miss Cartwright and Mrs. Sullivan walk away, he decided he should call on his mother, since he was literally at her front door step.

"Good evening, Bentley," he greeted as the butler swung open the door.

"Your mother is in the green room, my lord. She is expecting you."

"Very good, Bentley."

He took the stairs two at a time, then strode into the room.

"There you are, Arthur. I trust the outing was successful?" She held up her cheek, and he dutifully kissed it before taking the seat opposite.

"It was. Miss Cartwright was delighted with the gardens—the pagoda, especially."

"A girl after my own heart," his mama said approvingly.

"I wonder if I was ever so innocent."

"Once upon a time," his mother mused. "Well?"

"Well?" He knew exactly what she wanted, but did not wish to discuss every detail.

"How proceeds the courtship?"

"Slow. She was shy and reticent today. Did you expect me to propose already?"

"I would not be opposed." She waved a hand as though it had just occurred to her and it was a worthy idea.

"I am quite willing to do so, but even you must see that she needs a little time."

"I would think she would be quite ecstatic to be out from under her aunt's roof."

"She is not yet out of mourning, Mama."

"Perhaps her aunt might be persuaded to allow Phoebe to visit me here. I was hoping to host a ball to introduce her and make the announcement. She will be out of mourning shortly."

"A ball?"

"Oh, yes. I have waited long enough for my only son to find his match, and I know her parents would be delighted by this arrangement."

Arthur bit back a groan. However, he would not mind showing his peacock to the world, but that masquerade would forever have to be their secret.

"You need to tell her who you are," his mama said pointedly.

"I rather think you took care of that," he noted dryly.

"You need to tell her you are the fox. Recreate the scenario, if you must. Send her another clever note and a bouquet that only you and she will understand the meaning of. Lure her somewhere with the promise of unmasking her fox."

He really needed to have a talk with his household. Was there nothing sacred to them?

"She likes Arthur Mills, but perhaps she is still enamored with the idea of her masked fox, too. She may be searching for him as you did her," his mother continued.

Arthur scoffed. "Perhaps, but she seemed warm until she heard my title." How ironic that his title seemed to be a mark against him with the only woman he'd ever wanted.

"Then you will have to overcome her aversion to it."

His mind was still on the how of it. Where on earth could he lure her as the peacock to meet the fox? Even if she were able to meet him at Vauxhall, everyone would remember and be on the hunt. It was still talked about in the clubs. No, recreating the disguise was impossible. But he could send her a note . . .

"I must go, Mama." He leapt to his feet and dutifully kissed her cheek again, but he was suddenly impatient to be off to plan. He did not see the knowing smile that followed him from the room.

As he walked home, he thought about the best place to try to meet with Phoebe. There really were not many places he could take her without the risk of being seen together. He was still contemplating his dilemma when he made his way into the study.

"Ridley," he greeted.

"My lord, your afternoon was pleasant, I trust?"

"Yes, yes, but where could I invite Miss Cartwright to meet me in private?" he hurried on to the business at hand.

"I beg your pardon, my lord?" Ridley sounded affronted.

"I do not mean anything clandestine," he clarified. "I merely wish to see if Miss Cartwright would accept an invitation from the fox now that she has made my acquaintance."

"Afraid she is still harboring a *tendre* for the predator?"

"My dearest mama thinks it's prudent to reveal myself to her. Just to be certain."

"Yes. Do you wish to be in disguise?" Ridley asked.

"What if she does not show or she does not want to know who I am?" Arthur paced the carpet in the study.

"They hold masquerades from time to time at Vauxhall, but as you know, she could not go there on her own, and you could hardly invite her to a party and be private."

"Perhaps I should just send a note for her to meet me at Gunter's if she so desires to make my acquaintance."

"It will need to be a time when the *ton* is otherwise engaged," Ridley pointed out.

Arthur rather liked the idea of pulling Miss Cartwright into his arms and kissing her in one of the dark paths at the pleasure gardens, but Ridley was right, curse him. He could hardly envision Sully escorting her charge to such a place as that. While he was considering what words would best convince her to accept his invitation, Ridley was rummaging through the received invitations. He held one up in the air.

"The Richmond garden party. Surely most of the *ton* attends that. It is in two days' time."

"Excellent. I will write an epistle and we can send it with a bouquet in the morning."

Now, what the devil should he say?

Nine

PHOEBE WAS HUMMING AS SHE sat darning some of the household linens. She really thought Mr. Mills—Lord Claremont—might be courting her. He had not spoken to her uncle, of course, but the more she thought about the things he said—including that he was interested—the more she thought he might actually wish to marry her. Was it possible she was misinterpreting his attentions?

She felt a twinge of sadness that she would never know who the fox was, but that night had not been reality, and Lord Claremont was. She would be a fool to pine over someone in disguise that she had only danced with twice, even if it had been the most magical night of her life. However, she had not imagined the connection she'd felt. Lord Claremont was just as handsome and as charming as her fox had been, with an equally pleasing smile. His eyes were positively beautiful and she could stare at them for days.

"Why are you humming?" Fanny whined. "It is too early for such cheerfulness."

Noon was early? Phoebe had been up for hours. "I suppose I am enjoying London. Are you not?"

"Of course I am enjoying Town. But the Season is fatiguing when one is well, and I am still not myself."

"Yes, of course. I will try not to hum in the mornings." Phoebe wondered why her cousin was not still in her chamber if being around others was so taxing, but said nothing.

Phoebe decided to write to her friend, Maria, the vicar's daughter back home, when Pugsley knocked and entered the room holding a bright floral arrangement. It was probably another bouquet from one of Fanny's admirers. Would someone never offer?

"A delivery, Miss Cartwright."

"For me?"

He set a beautiful bouquet of flowers on the writing desk which engulfed the small wooden surface.

"Flowers for Phoebe?" Fanny asked in a scolding, yet disbelieving voice. "Who are they from?"

"It appears to be Lady Claremont's handwriting." Phoebe plucked the card from its holder before her cousin could.

She glanced at it, and the familiar script swam before her eyes. However, she knew there would be no privacy unless she convinced her cousin there was nothing to it.

She tossed the card in the corner of the writing desk behind the bouquet and her ink well. "She thanked me for visiting her the other day," she hastily fibbed.

Fanny raised her brows and muttered it was rather unusual, then shrugged her shoulders and went back to her fashion magazine.

Phoebe calmed herself by inhaling the sweet, musky scent of the bright blue orchid arrangement. It was the first bouquet she had received since the fox had ceased his attentions to Fanny.

Since Phoebe could not run away with the flowers or the note for some time, she finished her letter and waited for Fanny to leave. Then Phoebe hurried up to her own chambers and locked the door before unraveling the note and curling up on the window seat to read it.

There was, in fact, a note on the first fold of the paper: *Miss Cartwright, thank you for a lovely afternoon.*

That was nondescript enough, but her heart sang as she pulled out the note hidden within.

The fox wishes for his peacock to discover if he is a rogue or of great importance.

"However did he discover who I was?" she whispered and kept reading.

If you are able, please stroll past Gunter's Tea Shop with your companion Thursday afternoon near two o'clock while the ton *will be flocking en masse to the Duchess of Richmond's garden party—if you are able to excuse yourself. I will find you.*

Phoebe gasped and held the letter to her chest. How did the fox know to send his missive through Lady Claremont? Had he been watching her? Obviously, Lady Claremont did not object. Had the fox seen her with Lord Claremont and wants to finally show himself to claim her before Lord Claremont does? Or could it be that Lord Claremont is the fox? It was all too much coincidence to fully comprehend.

Gunter's was a place frequented by the *haute ton*, though it seemed he had already considered her potential objections, making it possible for her to meet him. Had she not just rejected the idea of the fox? Lord Claremont was everything she could hope for, but would there always be a lingering regret if she did not at least meet her prince when she had the chance? Besides, Lord Claremont had not offered anything beyond friendship, and there was no guarantee that he would. Perhaps he was only being kind because of their mothers' acquaintance—perhaps Lady Claremont would help bring her into fashion after her mourning had ended. That had not been his reason for greeting her at the Tower, she reasoned, but certainly the trip to Kew Gardens could be accounted for as such. Perhaps all gentlemen behaved thus, but she had no experience to know.

Even as she tormented herself over the risks, including the ruination of her aunt's plans should they be seen, she knew she would go.

ARTHUR WENT BACK AND FORTH at least a hundred times on how best to reveal himself to Phoebe. He could hardly dress as a fox and prance through Berkeley Square. The costume had already been returned to the theatre anyway. However, he sent Ridley out for a peacock feather and knew she would understand the gesture.

He was there early, waiting inside his carriage, and had already arranged for Gunter's to bring a sampling of their most popular flavors to the carriage when his footman signaled.

He thought Phoebe would be delighted to discover he was the fox, but one never knew. She was not a female given to hysterics, but was full of good sense, which was why he was drawn to her. She put on none of the airs or affectations common amongst the daughters of the *ton*.

Impatient at twenty minutes until two, he got down and began to stroll around the square. He had too much anticipation to sit idle. The square was distinctly devoid of the *beau monde*. A few maids and tradesmen crossed on their errands, but the chance of discovery for Phoebe was very low—as he'd hoped.

He checked his gold pocket watch at least five times, so he knew when she arrived a few minutes early.

She was wearing a lavender walking costume with black trim, and was shielding her face with a parasol and wide-brimmed bonnet, but he would know her anywhere, and Sully was less disguised.

His original plan had been to wait inside the carriage, but he strolled forward to greet her.

"Miss Cartwright, Mrs. Sullivan. Lovely day for an ice, is it not?"

A look of surprise mixed with confusion crossed Phoebe's face. He could see she was considering the possibility, but she looked around to see who else was in the square.

"Are you looking for someone, Miss Cartwright? Or are you concerned about your aunt discovering you are here?"

"My aunt and cousin are at the Richmond garden party."

Arthur noticed Mrs. Sullivan had backed away discreetly and sat herself on a bench beneath an old poplar. "Your bonnet and parasol shield you well, so you are unlikely to be discovered."

"But you knew me."

"So I did." He wondered whether or not to keep her in suspense or reveal himself now. Her parasol was twirling rapidly. Likely it was cruel to prolong her discomfort, but somehow he wanted her to make the connection on her own. "May I procure you and Sully an ice?" He lifted his hand to signal the waiter.

"I-I suppose so." She looked around again.

"Are you certain you are not looking for someone?" He looked down into her eyes as she looked up—perhaps there was a flicker of recognition there.

"I had thought I might meet someone I met once, but perhaps I should not have come." Her voice was a little sad, so he decided it was time.

He pulled out the feather and presented it with a flourish.

She paused, staring at the feather, and then gasped as the realization struck her. Still, she said nothing and stared at the feather. He felt a bit foolish holding it out for her inspection. Thankfully, no one was about to see except Sully.

"I do not ever attend balls, you know. People would be shocked by my presence." He hoped that by quoting a line he'd spoken while they had danced would convince her. He then added, "I am glad you chose to be a male peacock, even though you decidedly do not look male."

She looked up and searched his face.

"Is it really you?"

"In the flesh. As opposed to in the fur." He smiled warmly at her, then tucked the feather into the ribbon around her bonnet, before offering her his arm. "I thought you might suspect when the note was delivered inside of my mother's."

"I confess, it did occur to me, but it seemed too fantastical to be true."

He smiled down at her. "Shall we walk? It appears our ices are being delivered to the carriage."

She said nothing as they walked, but when he stopped to hand her in she turned to face him. "How long have you known it was me?"

"Since the night I met your cousin at the opera. Well, that is not quite true. I only knew then that she was not you."

"Then, how did you find me?" After he handed her in, he then signaled for Sully to join them. She held up her hand and shook her head.

Perhaps it was not wise to join Phoebe in an enclosed carriage, but he had chosen this day because they were unlikely to be seen, had he not? The waiter handed him a tray of ices, and with one last glance to make sure they were unobserved, he sent one over to Sully then sat down beside Phoebe and handed her a dish.

"These are quite lovely," she remarked with a sample of the frozen lavender cream in a silver dish.

"To answer your question, I was quite perturbed when I realized that Lady Fanny was not you. I went to the Tower that day I saw you in a fit of pique, wondering if my peacock's brains had been addled from illness or if there was some joke being played on the *ton*."

"What a coincidence that was the day I chose to go there."

"Yes, indeed. However, that was not when I realized." He shook his head when he considered. "I truly never thought I would have so much good fortune. Imagine our mothers were friends."

"Some might call it Fate," she said with a shy smile, clearly remembering that day he asked her if she believed in such a thing.

"I thought I was so clever putting it all together myself—I had discovered who your father was from your clue about Northumberland—and then my mother was one step ahead of me. She delivered you to me in her own drawing room!"

Finally, he drew a laugh from Phoebe.

Her brow wrinkled. "Why not tell me then?"

"I suppose I wanted a chance to know you better, to know if my enchantment with you at the masquerade was real."

A charming blush crept onto her cheeks.

"I also wanted to know if you would like me as Arthur Mills. You seemed to like him better than Lord Claremont."

She bit her lower lip and looked at him with laughter in her eyes.

"Am I mistaken in thinking you return my affections? Now that you know that Arthur, Lord Claremont, and the fox are all the same?"

"I feel a bit foolish," she replied. "I thought I would know my fox anywhere. Of course, I recognized the similarities, but I never imagined that I would have the good fortune to meet not one, but two men that I admired. It certainly makes things easier now that I do not have to choose."

"Minx. You will have to choose," he said with great affection. He leaned over and lightly bussed her lips which were cold from the ice and tasted of lavender. He would have to be content with that because they were still in a public location, after all.

"Choose what?" she asked, looking adorably confused.

"Whether or not to be Mrs. Fox or Mrs. Mills or Lady Claremont."

"There is no choice to make," she replied saucily. "I can be all three."

Arthur quite liked that answer, especially since she leaned over and kissed him again.

"Shall we gather Sully and go tell my mother the good news?"

She began to laugh. "My aunt will be so vexed!"

As soon as they entered his mother's drawing room, she was beaming knowingly. "I gather she did not mind discovering you were the fox?" his mother asked.

"It was a relief to discover the fox was Lord Claremont," Phoebe answered for him.

"And you will be even more pleased to hear that she has

agreed to be my wife," Arthur added, knowing that was what his mother really desired to learn.

"Of course she did! I am ecstatic that you have decided to cast off your professed bachelorhood. I knew eventually you would find the right woman, but it did not keep me from despairing at times!"

Phoebe watched his face with amusement and a twinkle in her eyes as his mother began to plot to have her way with all due speed and efficiency.

"We must contrive to move you out of Moreton House and here with me. We have much planning to do." She rubbed her hands together with glee.

"But how?"

"Right underneath your aunt's nose—with you right alongside, of course. We will plan a ball to present you as soon as your mourning has ended, then your nuptials to take place three weeks beyond that."

"My aunt will be mortified," Phoebe protested weakly.

"I will speak to the earl the morning of the ball. Your uncle may then inform your aunt before they arrive so it will not be a complete shock," Arthur promised.

Ten

One month later...

IT SEEMED A BIT OUTRAGEOUS to be presented at the very last ball of the Season, but she had no wish to delay being married, and she trusted Lady Claremont's judgment. There was bound to be sensation and speculation with her similarities to Lady Fanny and Lord Claremont's sudden marriage, but most of the wonderments would pass by the time the *ton* next convened upon London.

Thankfully, Lord Worthing had made an offer to Lady Fanny, which would hopefully lessen her irritation that Phoebe had made the catch of the Season without being out. It was very hard not to crow about her own good fortune when her cousin would brag while visiting, but Phoebe had kept her own goodwill to herself. When at last the day of the ball arrived, Phoebe was bursting with excitement. Lord Claremont was now at Moreton House speaking with her uncle.

Phoebe and the modiste had made over her peacock costume using the under dress, and Madame Celeste had designed a silver overslip to go on top of it. Even though

Lord Claremont had teased that he wished her to dress in the costume and unmask herself at the ball, she would never so openly insult her aunt or cousin.

She had a light meal in her appointed chamber while Lord Claremont and his mother hosted dinner and the receiving line to the ball. Lady Claremont wanted her to make a grand entrance and dance the opening dance with her son. For someone who had no taste for Society, Phoebe thought it all rather theatrical. After all, she and Lord Claremont had found refuge in their disguises. But the marchioness would not be denied.

Phoebe was at the top of the stairs to the ballroom at the appointed time as the majordomo announced, "Miss Phoebe Cartwright." Lord Claremont was waiting at the bottom to take her hand, looking dashing in cream breeches, a burnt-orange waist coat, and brown jacket, as a secret nod to his fox.

It must be obvious to everyone how in love I am, she mused, for she was smiling at him like the lovesick fool that she was. Had the crowd been able to see his face, they would discover the sentiment was mirrored in his own smile as he watched her descend. By the time he led her to the floor for the opening dance, most people had guessed correctly.

"You look ravishing, my dear," he said as he took her hand and bowed over it.

"You are rather handsome yourself," she said, trying hard not to blush. She could feel a thousand eyes watching her.

"I still think you should have worn the feathers," he teased.

"I am afraid people will guess as it is. I am certain my aunt is livid right now. Do you think anyone else will realize?"

"I hope not, since you did not speak with anyone else that night."

"True. If they recognize the dress, perhaps they will think I borrowed it from my cousin. At least my aunt did not find out tonight. That is, I trust my uncle warned her. Was he cordial to you?"

"Oh yes. He is a very amiable person. He was delighted for your good fortune and gave us his blessing. He even gave me a wink of approval."

Phoebe sighed and decided to enjoy the dance, but she could not help but notice her betrothed was staring at her. "What is it?"

"I am so pleased you do not have to hide anymore."

"I feel the same. To think in just a few weeks, we will be married."

"It would not be so long were it up to me."

She had to wait to respond while they took turns in the measure with other partners.

"You forget no one else was aware of my existence. We must give them time to accustom themselves to the idea of their beloved bachelor being married."

"They can all hang, for I give a fig for their opinions, but I will bow to your wishes."

When the dance ended, he led her over to his mother, who was thankfully standing near her aunt. While Phoebe did not wish to slight her, neither did she wish to discuss the matter with her. Thankfully, her aunt said nothing, and they were interrupted by one of Lord Claremont's friends.

"Ah, Devon. May I introduce this lovely lady to you? His Grace, the Duke of Devon, this is Miss Phoebe Cartwright. Our mothers were great friends."

"Stealing a march on the rest of us, are you?" He raised his brows, which looked a bit arrogant and reprimanding to

Phoebe, but he turned a most handsome, charming smile on her, and bowed before her. "Enchanted, Miss Cartwright." He turned back to Claremont. "You are a sly fox, are you not?"

He knew!

"How the devil?" Claremont asked.

"You didn't think your best friend would recognize you?"

Her betrothed laughed. Then the duke leaned down and whispered to her, "Your secret is safe with me. Will you honor me with the next dance?"

Ton BALLS HAD NEVER BEEN enjoyable to Arthur, as he always felt he had a target on his back. Then there were the ballrooms stuffed with too many bodies in warm spaces full of odiferous sweat, perfume, and flowers. At least wide panniers and tall wigs were mostly out of fashion, except for those reluctant to eschew their glory days. Tonight, he had enjoyed watching Phoebe descend and be appreciated by the *beau monde*, happily knowing he was well and truly caught.

After the opening dance, Arthur waited patiently as every gentleman in all of London danced with Phoebe. At least it felt like every man was fawning over her. He watched her being twirled about the floor, just as mesmerized as he was the first night he'd seen her. It was difficult to give proper attention to his other partners with her anywhere nearby. He wondered if those poor men who were falling over themselves to dance with her thought they had a chance with her. No matter, they would soon know.

Of course, he heard chatter about Phoebe wherever he turned. Everyone was surprised by the sudden emergence of

A DOUBLE MASQUERADE

Miss Cartwright, who was being presented by Lady Claremont, but was the niece of Lady Moreton. Did she not favor Lady Fanny, though prettier?

Pray no one ever made the association from the masquerade. The *ton* did not like to think they'd been duped. However, his mother was a powerful force in Society, and if she was bringing her dearest friend's daughter out because Phoebe had been in mourning, people seemed to accept that. Soon, they would discover she was to be his marchioness—if they had not already realized.

When the time for the supper waltz came, he was able to pull her into his arms again. The music began and he hated the thought of her ever waltzing with anyone else.

"Are you enjoying yourself at your first ball?" he asked more civilly than he felt. "Well, your first ball as yourself," he corrected.

"Oh, yes. Everyone has been so kind."

"Part of me wishes we were making the announcement tonight so none of them gets any ideas."

"It is our second waltz of the night. And somehow, I think when you look at me that way, no one will be surprised to read the words."

"Look at you how?" He pulled her an inch closer and gazed warmly down at her.

"Like you want to devour me," she scolded.

"Like a man in love," he corrected.

"Well if that is all that it is, I suppose I will allow it." Her eyes twinkled back at him.

"I can see you need convincing." He led her through a series of turns and out onto the terrace.

"Arthur, what are you doing? Even I know we should not be out here alone."

It was refreshingly cool and quiet after the crush of the

ballroom. One advantage to entertainments at one's own home was knowing the best hiding places. He pulled her into a little secret garden that would not be so secret by day but would not be easy to find at night. The moon was shining through the ivy-and rose-covered trellis, and with the remainder of the waltz playing in the background, it was the perfect place for their first real kiss.

"If we are caught, we simply announce our betrothal tonight. They will see by morning it was not a compromising situation that brought it about." No one would believe it of him anyway. He had avoided the marriage trap too long to succumb so easily unless he wished to. "But if you would prefer me to kiss you senseless on the dance floor, I will." Before she could answer with more than an indignant little squeak, he pulled her closer and touched his lips to hers.

He pressed his lips softly to hers, reminding himself to go slow, knowing she would soon be his wife, but she was also precious enough to be savored. Once she relaxed and wove her arms around his neck, he deepened the kiss enough to tell her she was his.

He gentled his touches and cradled her face in his hands—he could speak his feelings for her with his touch better than he could say it with words. His thumbs gently rubbed her cheeks, and his lips adored her eyes, her forehead, her nose, her ears, her neck, her mouth.

Even though he did not care much for what the *ton* thought, he did not want his bride to begin with a less than stellar reputation. A fire was burning in his chest, so he pulled his lips away and touched his forehead to hers to look deeply into her eyes and smiled at her. She looked a little dazed and a bit mesmerized, if he did say so himself.

"We should probably return now. The music just ended."

"You were able to listen to the music?"

"Only because it was necessary. Needs must and all that." He took her arm and led her back up the terrace steps to the edge of the ballroom door where people were beginning to look for their supper partners.

Arthur escorted Phoebe to the head dinner table where his mother was already seated with Lord and Lady Moreton, Lady Fanny, and Devon, who raised a knowing brow at his old friend. All eyes were on them as they walked in, whispering words behind their backs as they passed.

Arthur leaned in and spoke softly. "They already know."

Phoebe's cheeks blushed becomingly. "We should have done this better."

"Oh, my peacock, we will!"

Once seated, Arthur resigned himself to tedious conversation with Lord Moreton. As the food was delivered to the head table, Arthur noticed his mother stand, which meant he and the other gentlemen rose to their feet. She waved them back down and began to rap her spoon on her glass, attracting everyone's attention.

"My son, the Marquess of Claremont, has an announcement to make."

She cast him one of her affectionate motherly looks that also doubled as an order, which he returned incredulously while swallowing a groan. "How did you . . . ?"

She cut him off. "I know everything, my boy."

As Arthur began to form his speech in his mind, the Earl of Moreton gave him the same knowing wink from earlier in the day. Arthur turned to Phoebe and said, "It seems it is time to do this better!" He stood, faced the crowd, and began, "My friends, by now you may have guessed, I am in love with this beautiful woman and she has agreed to be my wife!"

USA Today bestselling author Elizabeth Johns was first an avid reader, though she was a reluctant convert. It was Jane Austen's clever wit and unique turn of phrase that hooked Johns when she was "forced" to read *Pride and Prejudice* for a school assignment. She began writing when she ran out of her favorite author's books and decided to try her hand at crafting a Regency romance novel. Her journey into publishing began with the release of *Surrender the Past*, book one of the Loring-Abbott Series. Johns makes no pretensions to Austen's wit but hopes readers will perhaps laugh and find some enjoyment in her writing.

Johns attributes much of her inspiration to her mother, a retired English teacher. During their last summer together, Johns would sit on the porch swing and read her stories to her mother, who encouraged her to continue writing. Busy with multiple careers, including a professional job in the medical field, author and mother, Johns squeezes in time for reading whenever possible.

Follow Elizabeth online at:
www.facebook.com/Elizabethjohnsauthor
or www.Elizabethjohnsauthor.com

THEIR MASKED SECRET

Jen Geigle Johnson

One

LORD JAMES HOLBROOK EYED ALL his friends and lifted a cup of brandy in mock salute. "To fathers." The burning sensation going down his throat did nothing to erase the dread his father's recent mandate had given him.

Everyone in their group each repeated the salute, downing their own cups. Their men's club, White's, had never seen a group of men so despondent.

"Why the sudden interest in your life? All these years spent ignoring his spare and now he wants to interfere." Kit asked the important questions.

Jamie frowned in his friend's direction. "Father wants the coffers replenished."

"Too many nights at the tables?" Monty smirked like he knew more than he did.

"Since one does not remind His Grace of his profundity to spend money, it doesn't matter why the coffers need replenishing. The problem being I am now seen as a source of income to the man, and it's going to be the death of my years of freedom as the spare."

They raised their glasses again to him in sympathy. "We will stand by you, man. We will be sitting right here any night you have free from your new lady." Kit didn't do sympathy well. He snorted into his glass.

"Oh, you can laugh now, but wait, your day will come." Jamie frowned and swirled his brandy. He hadn't drunk much yet. He probably wouldn't. Wits were needed if he was going to find any possible way to escape an early marriage. "He's given me to the end of the Season, naturally." He grimaced.

"The Season hasn't even started yet. You know what that means?" Kit leaned across the table with adventure in his expression.

"What does it mean, ya old bean?" Jamie couldn't help but laugh at the energy his friend exuded any time they did anything.

"It means we need to have the most reckless fun we can possibly have while it's still available to us."

"Hear, hear." Jamie raised his glass. He would drink to that. But he paused. "How reckless?"

"Anything. Whatever. All the things you won't ever do while you're married."

That covered a rather broad grouping of things. Jamie was not of the kind to stray once married. He'd seen the havoc it created in his own home. He'd been witness to his mother's tears. He'd decided long ago that once he was married, he was married. He'd hoped to be able to choose the woman, and perhaps even fall in love, to make things easier. But his father was adamant. So be it. He would do the best he could to find someone who at least seemed reasonable to live with, easy to converse with, and, of course, had plenty of money for the coffers. He'd already talked to the solicitor. Her money would never go to his father. It could be used for Jamie's estate once he inherited the earldom and not before.

"We can be as reckless as you want. You know I'd do anything for you." Kit winked and the others laughed.

"And we all know you don't need an excuse to get into a bit of a scrap, do you?" Monty shook his head.

Monty's brother, Crispin, ran into the room, hardly acknowledging the greetings from others as he passed table after table. He tossed his hat to the center of their group, a servant hastily scooping it up and reaching for his cane and outerlayers. Crispin wiped his brow, out of breath. "It's a disaster." He gripped the table. "A complete, ruddy disaster."

They all stood. Monty came around the table to shake his brother's shoulder. "Crispin. Speak what you have to say. You look as if someone has died."

"They may as well have." He shook his head. "The lot of you are finished. One and all." He waved a hand in Jamie's direction. "It's not just this sap. It's everyone. The lords had a meeting together. Last night, over the tables. We're all in this. Everyone."

"In what? Speak, man." Kit's face had lost a bit of color.

Jamie suspected he knew where this was going. They all did, but they had to hear it for themselves.

"Everyone's fathers agreed. You all have to marry this Season, not just James, every ruddy one of you. To someone with a healthy dowry. Or you're cut off."

Someone's cup crashed on the floor.

A voice in the back of Jamie's awareness called out. "Is that true? The lords of Devonshire have to marry money? This Season?" A laugh carried out.

But Jamie heard no more of it. The men all shared a look and filed out of the public room for the back corner room. Crispin followed.

As soon as the door was closed, Monty punched it. "This cannot be true. Tell us everything you know."

"It's true. Every bit of it. And they weren't drunk, so you can't hope they forgot by morning." He fell into the nearest chair. "Our fathers included me. I haven't even had a Season yet."

The door slammed open. George and Jacob Featherstone entered. "Just heard the news. Our brother's already done this to us. Thought we'd help sabotage."

Jamie raised both eyebrows. "Who said anything about sabotage?"

"Aren't you going to?" George looked at each one in turn. "You're going to just sit back and obey this ridiculousness? Are there even enough women with large dowries in the *ton* for all of us? This Season?"

"Oh, there are enough. But maybe not any we want to marry." Monty ran a hand through his hair.

"That's just it, isn't it? We want to choose." Kit turned to George. "What did you have in mind?"

"Anything. I don't think I'm getting out of my situation." He rested a hand on his brother's shoulder. "Jacob and I just barely pushed past last Season without a wife. Now Charles is serious. But we'll help the lot of you out of principle. And then, perhaps, Brother will see the light."

Jamie wanted nothing to do with that. He wanted to find his own wife, in his own way, plain and simple. He waved away a servant who peeked in. "The real bite to all of this is we're good chaps. We will do our duty."

"When it's time." Monty grunted.

"And we will be good family men. We're going to be earls and marquises, run estates, serve in the House of Lords. We will have children and care for our wives."

"You're right, man, we don't deserve this." Monty put his arm across his brother's back. "But thank you for telling us, Brother."

Jamie fell into a seat. "And there's nothing I can do about it. I don't know about the rest of you, but once my father commands something, there is no changing his mind."

Everyone sat in the nearest chair, one by one, the epitome of defeat. Kit ran a hand over his face. "I don't even have anyone in mind. That's the real problem. Not a single one of these women has caught my attention at all."

"It's unlikely we'll fall in love in such a short amount of time anyway, isn't it? Better make a list of what we want and just hope for some of the list." Monty frowned. "She can't be a harpy, for one."

"Agreed. No nagging, high-pitched voice." Crispin grimaced.

Jamie shook his head. "Misery does not love company. Sorry you're in this with me, gents. I'll do my best not to take the best lady . . ." He stilled. As he looked around the table at some of the most eligible men of that, or any, Season, he realized competition would be something he hadn't been anticipating but should.

"We'll take your castoffs. Your Dukeness."

"Except that I'm not going to be the duke. Spare, remember?"

"But it's the residual glow. Do us a favor and let us know when you've decided against someone." Monty raised an eyebrow. "We should all just sit back and observe you."

"Oh, come off it, man. Every woman would want a piece of you if they knew it was available."

He grunted in response.

"Funny how we've all come to this. A woman would want Monty for his estate. We want them for their dowry. Beautiful family lives we will be creating." George scowled.

That was the crux of it for Jamie. He would be doing his best to create what his parents never had. Even if his father was making it more difficult than ever, he would find the woman who could make him happy, who could help him raise a family of happy people. Or he wouldn't marry at all,

Father's demands or no. He stood. "Well, on that happy note..."

Kit held up a hand. "Wait. We have one more weekend."

"Do we?" Crispin's eyes lit with the tiniest flash of hope.

"The Season won't begin until Saturday next." Kit leaned forward. "And there's the lords' masquerade before then." His eyebrow rose higher on his forehead. "What if we all dress exactly the same, keep our masks on, and do whatever we please, one last night. Is there one lady you've wanted to flirt with, kiss, even, that you won't ever have the chance with again? Is there something you'd like to say that you cannot speak again? Our lives as carefree, unmarried spares or heirs is finished, friends. We have one more ball." His eyes were ice-blue, his face serious, a mask already descending. He didn't even wait for their response. "I'll have my valet contact yours about our costume."

Two

MEREDITH STARKWEATHER (MERRY) HAD A secret. But it would not be a secret for long. As soon as her guardian was unleashed on the *ton*, everyone would know. But until that moment, she happily walked the park across from their townhome in relative anonymity.

She'd somehow managed a few quiet moments absolutely alone, except for her maid who knew what she needed without asking. Her guardian Mrs. Donning would be her chaperone for the Season, and was a dear to do so. Merry told herself over and over how she should be grateful for such a woman, grateful that she could be present at all for the London Season. But everything her guardian did, spoke of, or made Merry wear rubbed all her hairs in the wrong direction. She preferred bold colors while Merry preferred pastels. She preferred a wide and ready smile while Merry was more reserved. She preferred attention, and Merry hoped to hide. Mrs. Donning was indeed everything every male in all of London hoped to avoid, the kind of chaperone that might consider entrapment of a man if she thought no one would know. Merry laughed to herself. Perhaps she would remain single simply by virtue of such a chaperone. She cringed to think what the woman arranged behind closed doors in Merry's behalf. But she was a dear—a wise, savvy, too-conniving dear.

Male voices up ahead had her switching directions to avoid the area, but they all rounded a bend together, deep in some sort of lively conversation.

She yelped to herself and then jumped into a copse of trees, hugging the back of the nearest large trunk. What was she thinking? If caught, she'd have a devil of a time trying to explain herself. If not caught, how long would she have to remain in the copse? And what would her maid do? What was she doing now? She peeked her head around the opposite side of the trunk from the men to see her maid hesitate, pretend to be studying a leaf, peer into the trees, and then put her hands behind her back as if she meant to meander about by herself.

"Oh goodness," Merry breathed.

But the men did not see her, or if they did, they didn't pause to take note. Merry breathed out in relief.

However, instead of moving along, they stopped, right near where Merry stood. She leaned her head back against the bark and silently groaned.

"As far as I can tell, there are ten women with dowries sufficient for our needs." The man had a nice voice, but Merry could not like him, not when discussing women's dowries in relation to men's needs. This mentality was precisely what she dreaded. Not that she had so much money, though she did, and Mrs. Donning was sure to announce this to the world. But that she had also just recently been gifted a title, the kind that opened all the doors and invited every kind of association and introduction. How would she avoid the types of men just feet away who would value her for her monetary worth only? Or for her connections only?

Another man, standing on the other side of her hiding place, closer than the first, said, "Only ten? At least that would be enough to go around, but are any of them worth looking at?"

Merry gasped and then bit her finger. Who was this man? How could he say something like that?

"Kit. Come now. I cannot be happy with the direction of this conversation. This is your future wife you are discussing."

Merry nodded. Not exactly the altruistic reason for being kind she was hoping for, but it was certainly a step in the right direction.

"Not to mention the ladies themselves. Come now. We can be sorry for our situations without showing so little regard for the ladies involved."

Yes. At last, a decent sort of man. She ached to peer around the trunk to see who had spoken sense, but she daren't. If any of them saw her, she'd die of embarrassment and perhaps be found in a compromising situation as well.

Someone grunted in response. And then another man shuffled closer. "I, for one, just wish to find the wealthiest of them all, propose, and be done with it. Our married lives will not be dictated to us by some woman. We can still do as we please even after we are married."

She snorted.

"What was that?" The group went silent. Merry pressed her back into the large trunk, trying to make no sound. Crackling branches and leaves in the dirt behind Merry sounded closer.

She held her breath, hoping they would give up the search before they got any closer.

"It's nothing."

"Are you certain? If word of our conversation got out to any of the ladies, our chances would be nil."

"Look around, Monty. There is no one to hear you. Do you think there's a lady standing behind that tree there, ready to snitch to all of the *ton*? Do you?"

They laughed, and the sounds of feet in the trees faded. Soon their voices were mere murmurs coming from across the park.

Merry breathed out. What a conversation to happen upon. She would give much to know who they were, what they looked like. How would she ever know which men to trust in the coming Season? Everyone could be them, everyone could be looking only to marry money and then to do as they pleased for the rest of their lives. A sick pit of dread crept in and grew in her gut.

But there was the one. He'd defended women, wanted to redirect the conversation, perhaps? If there was a splinter of hope for the men in London, he was it.

Her maid whisper-called into the trees. "Miss?" She sniffed. "Oh, begging your pardon, my lady?"

She would not become used to the title any time soon. "I'm here." She stepped out from behind the tree. When she stepped clear of the copse, she continued on as if nothing untoward had happened. What would it be like to be a maid? What they must think of their employers. She laughed. Her maid had been forced to wait while her lady hid behind a tree.

Merry wondered what the young girl had heard. "Those lords had a very disturbing conversation."

Her maid started, obviously shocked at being conversed with. "Yes, my lady?"

"They were talking of ladies and needing their dowries."

"It's as you say. I was not privy to their words."

"I wish I knew their identities." She turned to her maid. "Did you get a good look at them?"

She fidgeted. "I glanced their way, but I was more concerned with not drawing attention."

"And I thank you for that, Kate. If you saw one again, do you think you would recognize them?"

"Perhaps I could, but I don't know. They all looked the same to me. There was one with brighter clothes, longer hair. I might recognize him. But the others? They had brown hair styled the same, same cravats, jackets, boots. If I stared all day, I might not tell them apart." She dipped her head. "Begging your pardon."

"You may speak freely. Thank you. Did you notice if the brightly colored man spoke much?"

She started to shake her head, then pressed her lips together. "He could have been one of the less vocal ones, yes. But my lady, please. Don't place any kind of importance on what I might have seen. It was fleeting at best. And I wasn't knowing you would be asking."

"I know. Thank you." She turned and continued her walk back in the direction of the townhome.

The modiste was coming, and Mrs. Donning was determined she should be outfitted like the new preference of the Crown she was. She sighed. One of the reasons she agreed to all the extra fanfare was simply a love for her father.

For him she would accept the honor, accept the accolades, accept the visit to the Queen she knew she must make. She would accept it all, including the attention, because her father was a good man, and he deserved her unending gratitude.

But it would be a hard tonic to swallow to stand in front of Her Majesty, knowing that she was alive at the expense of her father's life.

Three

JAMIE LEFT HIS FATHER'S STUDY with barely a polite word. He resisted slamming the door behind him because the servants would have caught it anyway. He did not stomp his feet because he'd been trained out of doing so. But he was irritated, more so than he had ever been. Instead he took himself to Jackson's. He would pound the frustration out into a punching bag. And if some unlucky sap wanted to have a round, then so be it. He donned his hat, allowed a servant to place his jacket precisely across his shoulders, and then exited his home, falling back against the carriage seat and letting the door shut him and his anger in isolation for the short ride to Jackson's boxing club.

The man could not be reasoned with. Jamie had known going into his appointment with his father that nothing would come of it. But he had to try. For his future family, for his own future happiness, he had to try.

He leaned his head back against the soft cushion. But to no avail.

One thing was for certain. He was more determined now than ever that his father would not get one cent of his future wife's dowry. His father had the power to do many things. Force him to marry or cut him off. But to force Jamie to give permission to unconventionally use the dowry for his own gain, Jamie would never allow.

Jackson's was uneventful, except that Jamie won a few and lost a few. He cleaned up and had an equally uneventful afternoon at White's. The betting books were full of different conversations regarding the coming masquerade. People bet that someone would fall. They bet at which costumes some would wear. They bet at people being caught in disreputable situations. But the biggest bet of all, one that made Jamie grind his teeth, challenged that "certain gentlemen would be married by the end of the Season."

If word got round to the ladies that every one of his friends must marry, their efforts would be even more difficult to find authentic connections, love, even.

Jamie had returned home and was dressing for the masquerade. His valet had meticulously pressed his costume. They would all wear black, the same mask, same breeches, even the same boots. They chose a specific hat that hid most of their hair, especially in the dim light, and agreed to slick their locks back, flat against their heads.

What point was there to this evening? Was he, Jamie Holbrook, really going to create a flirtation with a woman simply because he would not be able to do so again? Probably not. But he agreed to participate all the same, simply as a rebellion to the demands of their fathers and as a support to his friends. And who knew but he would find someone to care about at this first event. From what he could tell, everyone would be there. Who knew who he might meet?

With the faintest hope, the smallest acknowledgement that he still wished for a love match, albeit to a wealthy woman, he told his coachman to take him to Vauxhall

Gardens. Someone had rebuilt the place, decorated just for this evening. The outdoors location, the fact that almost anyone in all of London would likely be there, and hiding behind a mask was certainly intriguing.

As he pulled up, the lights from a thousand lanterns twinkled at him. He donned his mask and felt the power of anonymity. Tonight would be remembered.

He stepped out of his carriage and let it pull away completely before he started to make his way to their group's meeting place. All six of them were going to begin together.

Someone had really worked to bring a bit of Vauxhall back to its former glory. Trees were trimmed. Arches were lined with candles and lanterns. The pathways were neat. An orchestra played from a platform raised above a large outdoor ballroom. Despite his frustration, Lord Holbrook smiled. Tonight just might be enjoyable, indeed.

Brightly colored dresses swirled past as he made his way to a group of men already gathering attention. He paused to take them in. They were a sight. Well-built. Their costumes perfectly matched. Everyone would know at least one thing. They were well-bred and likely wealthy. Two things that had come to mean more than they should. He tried to loosen the tightness in his chest and closed his eyes for a moment.

Then a soft form bumped into his chest.

He held out his hands instinctively and ran his thumbs along the soft shoulders of a woman of perfect height.

"Oh." She stepped back.

"Forgive me." He bowed. "I was not paying attention."

"I wasn't either. I'm terribly sorry . . ." She waited, but he did not provide any hint of who he was.

What he could see of her face promised youth and beauty, but her eyes held him captive. They were a nondescript color in the evening light. But they were bright. The kind of light sparkling in them could only be created by goodness. Or happiness. And he desperately craved both at the moment. He lifted her hand to his mouth. "I would love to dance a set... Could we meet for the very next one?"

"I . . ." She hesitated and then dipped her head. "Of course."

"Thank you. I shall find you just under the orchestra there."

She curtseyed and then he moved toward his friends.

They were humming with excitement. Kit bowed to them all. "Come, gents. This is our night. No one knows who we are. And might I remind everyone present. No one will ever know. Is that understood? If you reveal even your own identity tonight, most will connect pieces and know about the rest of us. Whatever happens on this fine evening will be forever anonymous."

"Agreed." Monty seemed bored. But he always seemed less than enthralled with whatever was happening.

Kit continued with his rules. "Don't be obvious."

"We know, Kit. We understand." Crispin rotated his shoulders. "I'll see you tomorrow in exile."

They laughed. But no one corrected him. It felt a little bit like their home had become a form of prison, cast off from their normal social plans.

"Let's enter together." Kit grinned under his mask. "We are already making quite a stir."

Jamie laughed. "It's almost as if you like the attention."

"Of course I do. You sound surprised."

They stepped together onto the ballroom space and a hush grew over the crowd. There was no announcement, no calling out of names. The crowd parted to allow them space. And then the instruments began tuning and warming up.

Jamie dipped his head. "That's my cue. I've already asked for the first set."

"Would you look at that, ol Ja—"

"No names," Kit cut Monty off.

"Right, ol' Bean's beat us to it."

Jamie waved him off, already searching the dresses surrounding them for the one he'd asked to dance.

She stood alone, right under the orchestra as he'd requested. Did she have a chaperone? Friends? Who was this woman?

He held out his hand to take hers and bowed over it. "I am most looking forward to our set."

She curtseyed low. "As am I."

He tucked her hand into the crook of his arm and was pleased that she stood close to him. After a moment he realized she trembled.

"Are you cold?" He paused and began to take off his jacket.

"I am well. Not cold. Quite warm, actually . . . now." A delightful blush filled her face and Jamie admitted only to himself that a part of his heart drifted over to her in that moment. He was a sap, indeed.

"I am embarrassed to say it, but I'm nervous." She lowered her head. "This is my first dance of the Season."

"Your very first?" He stood taller, thrilled with the prospect. "Then we shall make it extra special." He gestured out into the crowd. "Where shall we begin?"

Couples were pairing up and forming groups of four. She nodded toward another from his group. "You make quite a spectacle, the lot of you. Would you like to join your friend?"

Jamie squinted. George. He nodded. "Excellent idea." They joined George and his partner, who was a larger-set woman with a pleasant-sounding voice. Most excellent. They nodded to each other. Then he turned back to his partner. "Are you looking forward to the rest of the Season?"

"I . . . think so?"

He laughed. "Perhaps its terrors have also been shared and you have some trepidation."

She nodded. "And since we don't know each other, I might also share that I'm concerned for the lack of sincerity." She leaned closer. "How shall I know who is a friend or foe?"

He was about to make a quip but then saw in her eyes a seriousness that he decided to respond to in kind. "I ask myself that every morning. The answer?" He shrugged. "I always hope that time will tell. Be watchful. People reveal their true natures if given time."

"And if I don't have the luxury of time?"

His heart pounded as he recognized his own worry spoken with so much purity. "Even then. It doesn't take long. Perhaps attempt to unsettle them. Behave in surprising ways. Test them." He winked, then realized she might not be able to see his eyes, so he smiled. "I don't think you shall have any trouble whatsoever."

"And why is that?"

"In the brief minutes I have known you, you've inspired the most baring honesty from me." He dipped his head. The music for their set started. "And now, let us dance away our worries. This is a night for frivolity only. Tomorrow will take care of itself." He laughed.

And he was rewarded by a musical laugh in return.

George turned to him with a small smile and then they began to dance.

Jamie knew only one thing. He was not willing to give up this woman after only one set. With any luck, she would agree to another . . . and another . . . and then a walk through the park.

Four

MERRY WAS ENCHANTED. THE LIGHTS hung magically all through the gardens. The air was cool enough to freshen every movement. The colors were bright, full of energy, and her partner? He was something out of a storybook. Did such a man exist? In reality? For now she was in a dream. When she awoke, it would fade into the background. And if she did not know who her partner was, would she ever find him again?

She calmed the fluttering in her stomach and determined to enjoy this night. Right then. Without thinking about anything next. If she could not relax and enjoy herself, she would never be able to connect with a single person.

She circled the other man in their group of four. His eyes were the deepest charcoal. He seemed intrigued by her, watching. And he was deferential to his partner. They were good men, these two, and they gave her hope. They all went through the motions of the dance. The mask emboldened Merry, and she decided to show a little emotion. She laughed and moved with intention. Her hips swayed a little extra. Her hands weaved, her feet danced like they skipped along the floor, and she smiled. What did it matter? She may as well enjoy the dance like she had as a young schoolgirl when she first learned it. Who would even know it was her?

And to her delight, her partner joined her. He added an extra skip in his step as they circled and then kicked out his heel a few times. She stepped twice in the beat instead of once so he mirrored her. They laughed at their antics and then the two they were with joined them. The extra steps, the flourishes, all of it felt a bit ridiculous.

Soon they could barely keep time; their laughs were so consuming. As the music ended, Merry's face hurt from smiling. She caught her breath and lowered herself in a deep curtsey. "That was probably the most fun I will ever have in dancing a country set."

Her partner reached for her hand as he rose from his bow. "Until our next." The care which he took in tucking her hand against his side on his arm warmed her to her toes. And with a suddenly parched throat and wavery smile, she asked, "Should we find refreshments?"

"Yes. I'm in great need of a lemonade and an excuse to stay at your side a bit longer. Do you have your next set taken?"

"I have no other sets taken yet, sir." She sighed. "What shall I call you?"

He rested a hand on top of hers. "If we reveal ourselves too soon, it will steal the delicious fun of a masquerade. How about you call me Jamie?"

Something about the way he said Jamie, the hesitant intimacy, the closeness of his mouth as he used hushed tones, made her wonder if it was his real name. A new set of gooseflesh, the most-welcome kind, traveled up and down her arms. Emboldened more, she nodded. "Jamie," she breathed. "How about you call me Merry." She almost sucked back her name as it exited her lips. The boldness in declaring her given name, the secrecy of the evening, heightened her breathing and tightened her chest.

"Merry," he whispered her name, the sound sending a new wave of shivers up her core. She nodded and tried to swallow.

For a few more almost ragged breaths she stared into his eyes through his black mask. Who was this man? Who could have such a profound effect on her? She thought she saw kindness there. She hoped for goodness, maybe even a sparkle of happiness. But she could not tell the difference between a wishful heart and the reality of this stranger.

"Shall we get that lemonade?"

She nodded.

"And walk the gardens?"

She nodded again.

"Perhaps I might have another set after?"

She smiled. "And another."

"Very good." He stood taller, a pleased smile tickling his face.

She wanted to laugh at how similar they seemed. She hadn't had nearly enough of this new stranger and hesitantly hoped he felt the same.

The welcome coolness of the lemonade on her lips, and the refreshing night air circling her arms and cooling her warm face, brought a new lightness to her step as she walked along at his side. "Where shall we go?"

"I'm unfamiliar with the park, but I do know these walking paths circle around and provide a lovely view of the water."

"That sounds just right." She stepped closer, her hand still on his arm. "It's almost the stuff of fairies, isn't it? All these lights?"

"It really is."

They walked together in companionable silence for a moment more and then he turned to her. "Tell me about your home."

"And reveal myself?" She laughed.

"Perhaps I shall guess what I think it true about you."

"That could be frightening." She nodded. "But enlightening too. Tell me where you think I am from."

"The country. You live on an estate that allows you to appreciate the out of doors."

"And how did you know that?" She wondered if she had dirt in her nails before remembering she wore gloves.

"Because you are not shivering from cold. You are embracing the air and the sights and smells. You wanted to walk, as did I, instead of linger in the crush." He leaned closer. "Unless I am misunderstanding and you would secretly wish to be back there?"

They both turned to see the well-lit ballroom area. The sounds of the orchestra tinkling to them even as they walked farther away.

She shook her head. "This is lovely. And you are correct. I live in the country. I was raised on fresh air and long walks."

When he didn't respond for a time, she nudged him. "And I shall guess that you too enjoy the out of doors, but in such a way that shows you don't get enough of it. Perhaps you spend much of your time in London?"

He nodded. "I long for the country like a hound for the hunt." He laughed. "That's not very poetic, is it?"

"But perhaps apt? I understand the longing for country. I feel it even now."

They moved slowly. She did not wish for their walk to end. The path led them along the water. The sound of it swirling and lapping against the riverbank reminded her it was close even when the path swerved away.

"If I could, I'd spend all my days on our estate. Perhaps when I inherit." He paused. "That's too revealing as to my identity."

"I admit to wishing to know as little about those kinds of things as possible. Might we . . ." She paused, uncertain how to continue.

"Get to know one another simply as people?"

A beautiful peace filled her heart. "Exactly. Might we do that?"

"I would love nothing more." He slowed their pace further. "Is it wrong of me to wish this night might never end?"

"Only if I'm wrong too." She brought her other hand to his arm, hugging it to her as they moved through a low, overhanging bough of trees. "Tell me what you want most of all."

"To fall in love." He laughed. "One week ago I would have talked all about a particular stallion for sale at Tattersall's. But now all I want is to love the woman I marry."

She sucked in a breath and held it so long she felt faint. "What are you saying?"

He sighed. "I'm sorry. That was perhaps not the most lighthearted response. What I want is a life of happiness. I want a family. I want to do good with my family name." He kicked a toe in the dirt. "And you?"

"I admit I'm still trying to understand everything you just said, and why you feel so adamant in this moment. But I think that might take a few more conversations. I too long for those things and pray they are possible." She walked a few more steps. "I think, most of all, I want to ride one of those gondola boats." She laughed and pointed to a line of boats hugging the side of the path. An old rickety set of steps led to the water and to the first boat. No one was around. This was obviously a long-forgotten attraction.

He turned to her. "Do you dare?"

"I said it's what I want most in all the world..."

"Then I think we should make at least one of our dreams come true tonight." He led her to the stairs. She stepped down one at a time, all the while wondering if it would crumble into the river, but it held. He helped her into the wobbly boat. Clutching the sides, she prayed it would not leak water.

"It looks as though it might not sink on us." He settled himself in the boat, sitting across from her and took the oars into his hands. "Where to, my fair maiden?"

"Wherever we like; let us float away and come back only when we tire."

"Your wish is my command." He untied the rope, pulled it into the boat, and pushed off from shore.

Five

FOR THE FIRST TIME, JAMIE wondered about this woman's chaperone. Perhaps he'd been a bit premature to send them both out alone in a boat. But she'd said she wanted it most in the world. What was he to do but grant her wish? Something about her, the way she laughed, smiled, carried herself, was capturing pieces of his heart and entwining them so carefully with hers, he didn't know if he'd be able to retrieve them after. He could see himself doing whatever she asked.

Including protect her reputation, if it came to it. But they were in masks. He would not be revealing himself during, or after, this night. She should not either. Perhaps no one would know they carried on alone, and they were free. The thought was so foreign to him, he let it settle for a long time before he really knew what to do about it. Free. No one would know. He repeated the thoughts over and over in his mind. And as far as he could tell, no one was on this side of the park anyway, and the other guests certainly weren't near the water, not at the moment.

"I do believe we have the river to ourselves."

"It's lovely, isn't it?" She situated herself so perfectly on her bench, as if she hadn't a care in the world. Beautiful posture, one hand on the edge of the boat, not to steady herself, but to peer out over the water.

He paddled their boat along the river's edge, winding under hanging branches of trees, around the bend in the water, and out into the open in the middle of the river. The moon had risen and a beautiful path of moonlight welcomed them further out across the river. Her hair shone in the silver light. Her dress sparkled. He wasn't an expert on women's clothing, but this woman was not lacking in wealth at least. Perhaps she would be someone he could pursue this Season. He wished to wipe away the thoughts as they came. Surely monetary considerations would strip any evening of all enjoyment, but in this case, they gave him hope.

What else was she thinking? He'd like to know what she thought about all things. "I would like to see change in England."

Her eyes widened, but she nodded and leaned forward. "Do you? What kind of change?"

"All kinds. My father would heartily disagree. But I feel if we do not do more to support the commoners, to aid them in their poverty and disease, to give them opportunities to choose their fate, we will not survive much longer in our current situation." He waited, wondering what on earth she'd say to those thoughts. He'd shared them with precious few. Most of his friends disagreed. They had little trust in the ability of the uneducated to vote. He understood the sentiment, but he also felt that perhaps they might become more educated if others were to help them. And they were educated enough to know what they wanted and needed to survive.

Merry crinkled her nose for a moment as though deep in thought, and he decided he must get her to do so again, and soon. It was kissably adorable. His mind immediately went to her lips. Would he dare? Was it possible to hope that she might be open to such a thing from him? He shook his head.

"What is it? Are you concerned I'm taking so long to respond?" She eyed him with a hint of insecurity.

"Oh dear no, my Merry. Please take as long as you need. I admit my mind had wandered a moment to thoughts I dare not express, though pleasant." He smiled, hoping to alleviate her concern and hide the ridiculous audacity to dare think of kissing such a woman. "I fear my thoughts are distracted by you." He shrugged. "I shall attempt to think only gentlemanly thoughts from now on."

Her cheeks turned the most lovely pink. He decided that he must always encourage blushes and crinkling noses.

She cleared her throat. "In answer to your thoughts on change . . . I admit that I am not fully aware of the possibilities being discussed for change, but I would welcome anything that narrows the disparity between rich and poor."

"Would you?"

"I would, yes."

He nodded. "You are a rare noble, indeed."

She lifted wide eyes to his. She did not deny noble birth. And she did not confirm it. How intriguing to try and acquaint oneself with a woman without knowing her birth or family.

He paused in his rowing. They were approaching the opposite bank. "What would you change about our world?"

She peeled off her glove and let one finger lazily swirl around in the water a moment. Everything was still, the current slow, the moon lighting everything in a soft glow.

Her bare hand looked soft, white. He wished to cradle hers in between his own, to bring it to his lips. But even more, he wanted to hear what she would say. What would this woman change in their world?

She let the water be and sat up taller, her eyes suddenly intent, almost fierce. "I wish for an end to violence, hunger, cruelty." She sighed and slouched a moment. "Cannot we all just be kind?" Her lips quivered a moment and then lifted in a rather forced smile. "I do believe I've responded too seriously and changed the tone of our outing. Apologies."

"Not at all. And I am so sorry to have upset you." She was visibly affected and he wondered what sort of cruelty and violence she had witnessed in such a young life.

"But what I really must see altered drastically? Bonnets."

He laughed. "Pardon me?"

"Yes, bonnets. They are a ridiculous notion. I'd like a bit of sun on my face. I don't like that I must turn my head in order to see something, and they hide my hair." She laughed.

"You do have rather magnificent hair."

"Oh, well, thank you." She colored brightly again to his great satisfaction.

"I noticed it and your beautiful smile right away. Does anyone tell you enough that you're beautiful?"

"Now you must stop being so kind. I shall quite forget myself and fall in love with a stranger." She sucked in a breath. "I'm in jest, of course . . ." She fanned herself and looked away. "Fall in love. Goodness. Say something before I die of embarrassment."

He leaned forward, careful not to tip the boat. "Do not be embarrassed. You might be in jest, but I am very much in danger of losing my heart to a stranger before this night is out."

Her whole body went still, her eyes captured in his own. "You are?"

"I think so." Their boat bumped against the opposite shore. He sent a rope out and wrapped it around a branch, pulling them into the soft seclusion of overhanging boughs.

He moved closer to her. "I . . . it's incredibly daft, isn't it? And really, I cannot be doing this. My Season . . . It's complicated. I have responsibilities. I'm not permitted to lose my heart, not to . . ." He stopped and took her hand in his own. "But I cannot help myself. You are in possession of some of my heart already, I dare admit. Perhaps we say no more of these kinds of things, and you just tell me more of yourself."

Her hands were indeed the softest he'd ever felt. They were like cream and clouds and the gentlest down. He lifted her palm and placed it at the side of his face. "My dearest Merry. I am not permitted to pursue whom I wish. It is my fondest, most ardent desire that you might be someone I could court. It may not be so. But I wish you to know, no matter what happens in the future, I shall remember our moments together. I shall guard these feelings and your goodness as a fond memory to remind me of the goodness still left in the world."

She swallowed twice before opening her mouth. The pulse at her wrist revealed a pounding and racing heart. But her voice was calm. "Jamie." Her lips wavered. "This is so very sudden. Perhaps we are too bold. Perhaps it is easy to be bold knowing tomorrow brings an escape."

"The only escape tomorrow brings is the most abhorrent kind. Reveal yourself to me."

She gasped. And then began to shake her head. "I cannot. We must meet in real circumstances, and if we fall in love knowing all there is to know, then all the better."

"How shall I find you? How shall I know?"

She lifted a shoulder. "I shall be looking for a man who loves me for who I am, who is not caught in the entrapments of wealth or title, who proves his love by standing at my side . . ." She paused. "What is it?"

He had gone suddenly stiff. He could not help it. Was she without wealth or title? Her comment revealed so much about her situation and station and immediately set a barrier between them. Must he choose between her and his whole inheritance, his title, his family? He swallowed down his alarm. Perhaps she'd not said as much. Perhaps she was simply looking for a love match as he. She could be an heiress, for all he knew. His mind said the words but his heart doubted them. These might be the last moments with her he would ever have.

He turned his head and placed a kiss in the center of her palm. "I shall seek you out every day, at every meeting, every gathering, listen for news from every pair of lips." He faltered, his gaze moving to her mouth.

They were close. He could almost feel her rapid breaths on his face. He leaned closer. "I will find you."

She lifted her chin, her mouth parted, her lips seeking his. "Swear it."

He enveloped her mouth in his. The sweetness was unbelievable. A tightness that began in his core spread across his chest. His arms reached out to pull her close, cradle her, protect her. And then he pressed his mouth to hers once more before reluctantly separating.

Shouts from across the river made them both jump. She peered out through the branches. "They are carrying torches. It looks like they are trying to find someone." Her eyes widened.

"Does your chaperone know where you are?"

She shook her head. "I told her I would meet her every hour or so. She really didn't seem to care what I did. In fact, I thought she'd left." She swallowed. "You don't think..."

"What kind of chaperone situation is this? A family friend?" His mouth went dry. "Your father?"

"Not my father. An aunt. And she is highly motivated to see me married." Her face went white. "She must not see us together. She can't know." She turned in the boat. It dipped precariously on one side. Her hand reached up to a low-lying branch.

"Wait, what are you doing?"

"I'm going to get out and walk home."

His mouth dropped open and then twitched as he tried to hide a smile. It was not an amusing situation by any means, but she was a rare woman, indeed. "We can both walk. I'll get us out safely at least. No need to get wet." He reached up to use a branch to pull them closer to shore.

"You can't walk with me. The problem is you." She shook her head. "Not you. The problem is that I am here with you, alone. And unless you wish to be entrapped . . ."

He shook his head perhaps a little too briskly because she narrowed her eyes and then turned away.

"I do acknowledge that I kissed you. So you probably think me the biggest cad."

She didn't answer but stood up in the boat.

"Wait, you cannot simply leave the boat by yourself."

She stepped out onto a branch, leaving the boat completely. Then she turned back to him. "Looks like I just have. Thank you for a lovely evening." Then she faced forward again, inching along the branch until she leapt from it to soft ground. Without another word, she ran into the darkness.

"Wait!" he called after her. But she was correct. He was the problem. He pondered for only a few breaths and then shook his head. No matter. He could not let her run off into the dark alone. He leapt out onto a closer branch, but his boot slipped, and he landed on his back in the water.

Six

MERRY RAN THROUGH THE BRUSH, feeling her skirts catch on branches as she moved faster. She would use the time to figure out how to explain herself to her aunt. The first thing she must do is return to Vauxhall before the end of the masquerade. And then explain herself. No one must think she was compromised. Her aunt would assist once she saw that Merry was not with another man. She would not want her ruined.

But as she exited the trees out into a more open space, she saw the river stretch for a long time before her with no hope of a crossing. Her shoulders slumped. When was there a bridge? She didn't even know. She turned back the way she came. She would have to use the boat. Alone. Already out of breath, she ran back toward the brush, through the trees and to the overhanging branches where the boat was waiting.

She breathed out in relief that it was empty. Where had Jamie gone? She had a moment of guilt before she climbed in and kicked off from the shore, out into the middle of the river.

He would find his way. Surely he had people who would assist him. She had no idea who or what that could be, but he seemed like the wealthy type of man. She pressed her mouth together. To be kissed by such a man, a man who was hoping to avoid the scandal of entrapment but was free with his kisses, nonetheless? She sighed. She'd wanted to be kissed just as much as he'd wanted to kiss her. Was she so wanton? Apparently, she was. And she could not regret it. At least now she knew what it was like to be near a man who held her esteem, to be attracted to one, to want to know everything about him. She could have sat for hours with him, talking of everything and anything. He was what she'd assumed all good relationships contained. She wasn't even certain of his eye color, but she knew him to be engaging, interesting, careful, genuine . . . and possibly a cad.

As soon as she was clear of the branches and the oars could move freely, she began attempting to use them.

It was at first challenging to find a rhythm. They were heavy. But at last she learned how to get some forward motion. She was paddling against the stream a bit, but after a short enough time, she was close to the other bank and someone saw her.

"I see something!" the voice yelled.

A man holding up a torch ran to the bank. "Are you all right, miss?"

"Yes, I'm fine! I got a bit lost. This is still the masquerade, is it not?"

"It is. You've found it. Did you really go paddling out there by yourself?" He shook his head in half admiration, half incredulity.

"I really did. I've always wanted to, you see, but it's harder to navigate than I supposed. Do you think you can pull me in?"

He chuckled and then stepped into the shallow water, reaching for the edge of her boat. "There you go." His mask was off. His face was handsome. His eyes shone brightly in the moonlight. When he caught her staring, he grinned. "Lord Waverly at your service, Miss . . ."

"Lady Meredith." She dipped her head. "Thank you."

"My pleasure." He held out his hand.

She placed hers inside a large, strong palm and realized her glove had been lost. "Oh! Forgive me. I do believe I've lost my glove."

He turned. "There it is in the boat. And your handkerchief too." He leaned down and snatched them both for her.

She tucked what must be Jamie's handkerchief in her reticule and then tugged on the glove. "Thank you."

A crowd had gathered by then, and when she turned to face them, Mrs. Donning ran forward. "Oh, my dear. You had me so very worried. Where have you been? And with such a fine gentleman?" Her eyes lit.

"Oh no, he assisted in bringing me ashore is all. I was out on the river in this boat by myself. It was difficult to find my way. But all the shouting encouraged me." She lifted her hand to the crowd. "Thank you."

They seemed somewhat disappointed that no one had lost life or limb or reputation and soon dispersed. All except for Lord Waverly and Mrs. Donning. He bowed to her. "Might I have a set?"

"Oh, of course. Thank you." She allowed herself to be led back up from the shore. "Mrs. Donning, would that be all right?"

"Certainly, my dear. But please, do stay in the ballroom area."

"Yes, ma'am. I will."

"I'll tend to her. Don't you worry." Lord Waverly smiled and Mrs. Donning might have swooned on sight.

Merry and Lord Waverly walked together to the

ballroom area, and as they arrived, the music for a waltz began.

"Would you like to remove your mask? At this point in the evening they become tedious, or at least, in my case, very itchy."

She laughed. Everyone around them had taken theirs off except for Jamie's group of friends.

"Except for them." He shrugged.

She removed hers and tied it to her reticule to dangle down at her side.

Lord Waverly smiled. "There. And as I suspected, the most beautiful woman of the evening." He bowed. "Lady Meredith, I'm pleased to make your acquaintance."

"And I yours. Thank you." She curtseyed deep and then stepped closer so that they could dance.

He smelled nice, of sandalwood and cedar. They moved together in the steps with precision.

"You are a wonderful dancer." He smiled.

"Thank you. As are you."

They talked of nothing. She supposed their conversation was similar to all others around them. She wouldn't have been able to recall much. The weather, the costumes, the upcoming Season. At the end, he placed her hand on his arm. "I would like to come calling. Might I?"

"I would enjoy that very much, yes. We have a home off Hyde Park. I believe it is the residence of the Duke of Normandy when he is in town."

The man's eyebrows rose very high. "Then I am in royal company?"

She shook her head. "Not really." She said no more, and he did not ask but eyed her with no small amount of curiosity.

"Then I shall come calling tomorrow." He kissed the

back of her hand as Mrs. Donning approached. "She is all yours." His grin was contagious, and Merry's chaperone actually giggled.

But Merry shook her head. "I think I am quite ready to go home now."

"I would think so." Mrs. Donning fanned herself. "But he is quite handsome. I wonder if he shall come calling."

When Mrs. Donning was informed of his plans, she seemed overly pleased with herself.

"Why did so many seem concerned for my welfare?"

"Well, because you were missing for at least two sets, my dear. I could find you nowhere. No one had seen you." Her face was blank, but Merry sensed a hint of something unspoken. She sighed and let it go. "I should not have gotten in that boat."

"I should think not. You could have capsized. Do you even swim? You would have caught the death of cold, consumption, or something, certainly."

"I do swim, but I should not have liked to get in the water. It felt cold." She shivered. "Thank you for caring for me. It was helpful to be able to return."

She patted Merry's arm. "Let's get you home."

As she was walking out, one of the men dressed exactly like Jamie nodded his head in her direction.

She sucked in a breath. He recognized her.

Did she want to see Jamie again? Yes. But *should* she want to see him again? Perhaps not.

She did not return his greeting but hurried after Mrs. Donning.

Seven

JAMIE ALMOST CURSED WHEN HE returned and saw the boat gone from its spot. Shouts across the river told him she had returned to the party without him. Which he knew he should want her to do. He peered out of the trees and saw her being helped ashore by a man. He couldn't make out who it was from where he stood, but she was surrounded by people, reputation intact, and he should be pleased.

Except that he was now stuck many hours from home and could not reveal himself for quite some time.

But the physical discomfort of his situation was not what weighed on him at the moment. It was her disdain for him.

And she very well should hold him in low regard. He'd panicked. He'd wanted to spare her reputation. He'd hesitated when the idea of entrapment had come up. He had come across as caring more to protect himself from a forced marriage, like she would not be acceptable to him. Of course, he would have done his duty by her and been lucky to do so. She was a woman like no other he had met. But it had all happened so fast and she didn't know that; in fact, she likely thought him a coward or a cad.

Perhaps in the moment her possible lack of dowry had played a role in his reaction, but more than anything he had been hoping to spare her.

But now he might have lost her respect.

She didn't know who he was. He had that going for him at least. He could find her and prove himself anew.

Or perhaps that was not a good thing. She'd wanted to be kissed. She'd sworn him to finding her, bringing them back together. Was such a thing possible? If he revealed himself, he might win her over. Or she might abhor him. He'd promised his friends never to tell. He ran a hand through his hair and ripped off his mask.

He peered out across the water. She took off her mask. He tried to make out even the smallest feature but could see nothing. But so many there would have seen her. That man would soon know her. Jamie could find her. He would. He had promised.

And he didn't know if he could live without her, or at least without knowing if it was possible to have her in his life. He had to finish what he started with this captivating woman.

But first, he had to get home.

He sat down on his haunches and waited for the crowds to clear across the way.

Hours later, when he was certain the music had stopped playing, he made his way to the water's edge, took off his jacket and boots, held them above his head and stepped into the water.

The swim was much longer than he'd anticipated, and much colder, but eventually, he stepped on shore and hurried to his carriage.

His well-trained servants said nothing about their dripping-wet master. One pulled out the warming blocks, unpacked a blanket, and then hurried the horses to his townhome.

When he arrived, the butler took his things without a comment. "His Grace is in the study."

Jamie bit the inside of his cheek and nodded.

He went straight there. What was Father doing in town? He grit his teeth, stopped his shivering, and stood tall.

"Father." He bowed as soon as he entered.

"James. Come in. Sit." He glanced up. "Are you wet?" His frown held the years of too-familiar disapproval.

"I am wet, yes." He moved over by the fire and stood close to it. "I think I'll stand here."

"Have you given much thought to your opportunity?"

"By my opportunity, do you mean your mandate to marry a woman of wealth this Season?"

"Yes, and it is an opportunity. Wealth makes everything easier. And it will help our estate as well." He shifted through the paperwork on his desk to bring out a slip of parchment. "Come now. I have news." He lifted his eyebrows to gaze over the paper at Jamie. "You haven't found her yet, I take it?"

"The Season has not even begun." He felt no need to mention Merry.

"Excellent, for I have just the woman."

Jamie's heart rose to his throat. "Wait, you cannot—"

"Come now, you don't even know who I'm about to mention. You might have chosen her on your own." His expression brooked no further conversation, so James nodded.

"Her name is Meredith Starkweather. She was just awarded a title for her late father and a fat dowry. She's considered a special friend to the Crown. This is your woman." He tapped the paper with every word. Then he shook it in the air. "She's an heiress who holds the gratitude of the Crown. You can fall in love with her as well as anyone else, I'd say."

Jamie eyed his father. He wasn't certain when he'd lost respect for the duke, but he certainly had. As he watched him down a full cup of brandy and then pour another, Jamie knew that he would never be like his father. And he would never inherit the dukedom. He would hopefully manage his earldom quite happily with a wife who was at least not abhorrent. He thought of Merry. If only she too had a large enough dowry.

"Ha! You're smiling. I knew you would see the light."

"Father, to be clear. You are not mandating precisely that particular woman. I'm still free to find my own wife?"

His father cleared his throat.

"My own wealthy wife?"

"Yes, of course. But I've accepted an invitation to a small dinner party tomorrow evening where she will be present. You will be one of the first to meet her. Come, Son, surely you can see how this would be a good move for our family."

"Of course, Father, now, if I might?" He pointed to the door.

"Oh, certainly. Take your bath. I'll be sticking around for this Season. Just to keep tabs on things, so to speak."

"That will not be necessary."

"I'm here to put a fire under your brother as well, you know. So it's quite necessary."

Jamie nodded and then left the room.

Eight

MERRY READIED HERSELF FOR THE dinner. Mrs. Donning had insisted on their attendance, claiming a relation to a duke as well as many other high-standing people in Society. Merry's dress had been chosen for her, her hairstyle as well. She stood before the mirror, looking like a diamond of the first water, sure to attract many a lord's eye.

She sighed. Masquerades were much more her thing. A laugh bubbled up from deep inside as she thought about the previous evening. With boat rides and walks through the dark paths of Vauxhall, it was unique indeed as a first event of any Season. Activities like that were sure to assist in truly knowing a person much easier than a stiff and stilted dinner party.

But Mrs. Donning insisted.

And Merry would just as soon learn to appreciate other gentlemen without the constant memory of Jamie's kiss on her lips. She raised her fingertips to touch her mouth. It had been the most magical part of the whole evening.

Until he'd ruined it by being afraid to be forced to marry her.

She should understand. She did understand. But it was a

bitter pill to see such alarm cross a man's face at the thought of marriage. She'd also learned that the most magical moment of her night had not meant as much to him.

Perhaps he tossed around kisses like his handkerchief.

She dismissed her maid and took the small white bit of fabric out of her drawer. Initials, embroidered in the corner, were her only clue as to his identity. *J.H.* Was James his first name? Had he been honest, as she suspected, as she had been? Jamie and Merry. She smiled and then placed the handkerchief up to her face. It smelled faintly of spices.

Did she want to find him? Or was it better to squelch these new feelings and forget him?

Her stomach tightened. She breathed in deeply the faint smell of him. Could she dim the embers that were heating? She did not want to fall in love with the absolutely wrong kind of man, and she feared she had done so, or nearly had.

Tonight would assist her in forgetting him, surely.

She climbed up into her carriage after Mrs. Donning. The lovely gold and blue ribbons and gems and overlay on her white dress were stunning. She admitted perhaps the slightest bit of vanity. Her new situation had gifted her the most lovely gowns. Her maid had worked wonders on her hair. It rose high above her head, drawing attention to her high cheekbones. The skirts barely fit anywhere, as they billowed out around her in a cloud of fabric, but she admitted to loving it all.

As they pulled up to a fully lit townhome on the most prestigious street in London, she held her breath and then turned to Mrs. Donning. "Do I belong here?"

In a rare moment of sincerity, she placed a hand on Merry's arm. "My dear. Your father was a hero in the war and in saving the Queen herself. You belong anywhere you would like to be in all of England." She clucked. "It might feel uncomfortable, but do this for your father. He deserved all the rewards a man can receive; may he rest in peace and with the knowledge his daughter will be cared for all her days." She wiped a bit of moisture from her eyes.

Merry placed a hand at her heart. She'd not fully appreciated or acknowledged the honor to her father. Merry could live to honor him, accept his gifts to honor him, and even marry to honor him. She sat up taller. She could do this. "I am ready."

"Yes, you are. You're every bit the diamond inside that you appear on the outside."

Merry nodded. "Thank you."

Mrs. Donning waved for a footman, and their door was opened immediately.

Merry's slippered feet stepped onto folds of thick burlap, newly placed over the muddy ground. She walked a lined pathway with footmen on either side, candles and torches lighting the evening air. Delicious smells spilled out onto the path. Sounds of laughter and conversation drifted to her as the door was opened. More light spilled out, spreading a glow on her gown, reflecting on the gems. Blue and white sparkles shone back with each step, pushing her skirts forward in front of her feet. She climbed the steps, Mrs. Donning at her side.

The woman breathed excitement. "This is spectacular." Merry had to agree.

They stepped into the warmth. A stately butler took their outer layers and they were directed to the hosts.

Lord and Lady Smith smiled warmly. "We are so honored you have come. Thank you, Lady Meredith and Mrs. Donning." Lady Smith curtseyed with a welcoming smile.

Lord Smith nodded. "I knew your father. He was a good man. I'm sorry he left us all too soon."

Merry almost choked on her next words. "You knew him?"

"Yes. He was the man who reported to me, so we would have regular meetings. And in the very beginning we served in the same regiment."

Her heart pounded. She wanted to hear anything and everything this man knew of her father's time in the war. He'd said precious little about it, said it wasn't fit for human ears. But it was a part of him and she longed to know.

"He'd not want me singing his praises. But I will tell you this. The Crown has much to thank him for, not just for the life of our Queen."

New guests arrived behind her. She knew she must move on. But she longed for more, for any morsel.

Lord Smith glanced at his next guests and then leaned forward. "I will also mention this. He was responsible for saving his entire team of men during one battle. Quick thinking and bravery. He was one to put everyone else ahead of himself, a real hero." He patted his chest.

"You can see my husband and I are so pleased to have you and to support you in any way this Season. We wish you the very best happiness and a wonderful match." Lady Smith's eyes shone back at Merry.

"Thank you." Merry looked from one to the other. "For everything."

"Certainly, my dear." Lady Smith gave her one last smile and then looked to their next guests. Another had arrived after.

Merry and Mrs. Donning hurried to the sitting room where some were gathered.

Already, four gentlemen were in the corner talking. Two women conversed on chairs. The footman announced, "Lady Meredith and Mrs. Donning."

All eyes turned to them.

Two of the men looked familiar to Merry. But she couldn't place them. Her heart pounded. Perhaps one of them was Jamie! But then they laughed, and one raised an eyebrow very high on his forehead and another looked positively wealthy and bored and so typical of what Merry didn't think she needed in her life, so she looked away.

The women stood and curtseyed. They were pleasant enough. Lady Noelle and Lady Smith, the daughter of their hosts. She was extra kind in her smile and sincere in the light in her eyes. Merry determined to like her straightaway. After they exchanged pleasantries, Lady Smith leaned closer. "Have you yet met Lord Holbrook?" She indicated with her eyes she was discussing one of the men in the corner.

Merry shook her head. "I have not. I'm happy to be meeting all of you. I'm afraid I come to this Season knowing very few."

"We shall certainly take care of that." She smiled in the men's direction who immediately approached.

The room was filling. This was going to be a larger dinner group than she had imagined.

The one looked familiar to her, something about his jaw. But then, all men had a similar jawline, did they not? And then the other, his hair was familiar. How odd to think such things. She surely had met neither of them before. They grinned. "Lady Smith, Lady Noelle, at your service." The bored one bowed and the others smiled. They turned expectantly to Merry.

Lady Smith held out her hand. "I would like you to meet another guest. This is Lady Meredith. She comes to us from Kent. Her father is highly decorated by the Crown."

They looked dutifully impressed. The first one with the recognizable hair dipped his head. "Lord Rappleye, Kit for short."

The ladies gasped. "She would never use your familiar name, and you shouldn't either; come now, Lord Rappleye, you'll create a scandal."

"I am all about creating a scandal."

"Don't say such things. Father will think you are serious."

Lord Rappleye's eyes twinkled with mischief and Merry laughed. "I shall have to wipe your first name from my mind, else I accidentally use it, for you seem much more a Kit than a Lord Rappleye." She held out her hand, which he took and kissed quickly.

"You see, she understands."

She looked to the next who seemed distracted but as he caught her gaze, he stood taller. "I'm pleased to meet you. Welcome to your first Season. Lord Holbrook at your service." He too kissed her hand but then squeezed it. His kind eyes held reassurance. "It can be a bit much, the Season. But this group will help ease the way. The Smiths are some of the kindest."

"That is indeed good to know. I am blessed, I feel."

"As I hear it, we owe your father a great debt. So we too are blessed."

Lady Smith pointed to the next man. "She comes with other gifts from the Crown, so we might need assistance in assuring her of the safe kinds of men."

"The safe kinds?"

"Those who might not be mercenary or perhaps trying to go about things in unconventional ways."

Merry raised a hand to her lips. "Oh, I see, perhaps courting me with hopes for a large dowry?"

Lord Rappleye's eyes gleamed for a moment. "Have you a large dowry?"

She felt her face heat and then she looked away.

Lady Smith shook her head. "Come now, Lord Rappleye, that's hardly a question you ask a lady."

"But it signifies, doesn't it? Isn't that the conversation some people must have?" Lord Holbrook held her gaze. "We may as well just say it, if it's true."

"What's true?"

"That some men are searching the *ton* for ladies of wealth, as they must marry titled women, or women with dowries, their estates demanding such a thing."

The third man shook his head. "But do we need to converse about such things upon first meeting?" He tsked. "Come now. Mr. Featherstone, truly at your service. I'm here to aid in anything you might need and to shield you from such talk if necessary."

"Thank you." She eyed him. "You do look familiar to me."

"It's his brother." Lord Rappleye nodded. "He has a rather famous brother."

She knew it wasn't the brother, but she puzzled over why this group were men she thought she knew.

Lord Holbrook lifted her hand. "We all look the same after a time. I do apologize if my conversation was a bit abrupt. I don't know what came over me."

She studied his sincere expression, watched the true kindness return to his eyes, and then nodded. "All is forgiven."

His smile was tight. He nodded. "Thank you."

The final man reached for her hand. "And I'm of no consequence. I have no title, no famous brothers, and no great wealth. I do believe they keep me around to help them look better." He laughed but then bowed with a flourish. "Mr. Harcourt, also at your service."

She smiled, and then Lady Noelle rested a hand on Lord

Rappleye's arm. "You three are just the most generous. To take in a woman such as this. All of you." She batted her eyelashes and smiled, but Merry knew a slight when she heard one. She just didn't know exactly how to respond.

Lord Holbrook shook his head. "It sounds as though our situations are lifted by association." He offered his arm. When Merry took it, the other men raised their eyebrows as though they were impressed, and then she wondered if she'd made some kind of statement by attaching herself physically to him. Oh, she knew so little.

Mrs. Donning had situated herself in a chair and was conversing with another older lady. Merry had no one to advise her. They were then introduced to the others in the room, and soon they were called in to dinner.

Here, again, she was unsure where she stood in the line or order of things. For a moment she panicked, but Lord Holbrook placed a hand over hers. "Join me?"

"Oh, certainly. Thank you. I wasn't certain where I fit."

"I never know where I fit. Second son of a duke. Where does that leave me?" He waved a hand around.

But then he stood just behind the hosts as they entered the dining room, which meant that Merry too was the second to enter. Their name cards put her near him at the table as well.

She sat across from him. Lady Noelle was at her right and a woman recently from India at her left. He sat in between two men, one of which was Lord Rappleye, and they were immediately engaged in conversation. No matter what she thought of him, it seemed unlikely she would get to know more of him during dinner.

Snippets of their conversation reached her. But she was also looking forward to all that the woman from India might share.

Partway through the first course, Lord Holbrook's voice rose. "But that won't do, will it, as she only has two thousand pounds."

"My other choice has five thousand. Do you think that will be enough? Or are we needing to marry upward of twenty thousand?" He rubbed a hand down his face and their voices lowered so Merry could not make out what they were saying. But Lord Holbrook? Lord Rappleye? Judging women by their dowry? She leaned forward, trying to catch their next words, but she lost most. Then she heard as the two men leaned closer together, "The ladies here all come with a hefty dowry." Lord Holbrook glanced in her direction, but she looked away, pretending not to have noticed.

But she had noticed. The ping of disappointment surprised her. She'd hoped for a moment that the men all around her would not be like those in the park she'd overheard. She'd hoped that they would be more like the masked man at Vauxhall.

Nine

JAMIE KNEW THEIR HOSTS WISHED for him to be entertaining to the ladies present. He knew that his father would also want him to be. His inclination to fight those expectations kept him from engaging Lady Meredith much during the first course. That, and Kit telling him all kinds of things about every woman in the *ton*, and who had money and who did not. He was ill at the thought, and so tired of money by the time the servants brought the second course, that he was ready to marry a pauper just to spite the world.

And therefore, Lady Meredith became all that was wrong in his life. She had a dowry. She was who his father wished he'd pursue, and she was not the masked lady at Vauxhall. His heart hurt thinking of her. As of yet, he had been unable to determine her identity. Without revealing himself, he had been unable to fenagle a manner in which to openly inquire about her to those who saw her without a mask. He hadn't even found the identity of the man who assisted her out of the boat. But it had been a precious few days. He had not given up hope. Even if she would not wish to see him, he had to try.

Lady Meredith laughed. And Jamie started. She sounded so familiar to him. Or he so longed for his Merry that he heard her in every voice. To prove his point, another lady laughed down the table and she carried the same cadence. She could be any of the ladies and all of them at once. He began to doubt his sanity. Perhaps she was but a phantom he'd conjured up.

Young Lady Smith cleared her throat, and when she caught his eye, she glanced at Lady Meredith. Such a pointed urging could not be ignored.

"My lady."

She lifted her lashes so she could look in his direction. He was stunned by the brilliance of her eyes. And for a moment he thought that courting a woman such as her would not be too painful.

But then she looked from him to his friend, and those brilliant eyes filled with disdain. The disapproval stole his breath for a moment. She raised her eyebrows as though waiting for him to say something impressive, but she appeared to doubt he would and then shrugged and looked away.

Kit snorted. He'd apparently watched the whole of it. But Jamie was not about to be put aside so easily. "My lady, I was wondering if you could solve a dilemma for me and my friend here."

For a moment he thought she was going to pretend not to hear, but she at last lifted her lashes again. "A dilemma?"

"Yes, you see, we are of the opinion that the best way to get to know another person is not here in a dinner setting with the whole room listening."

Several people near them paused in their conversations and leaned closer to hear. He nodded at them all and then turned back to her.

"I see what you mean." She watched him with a high level of suspicion. He wasn't certain how he'd come to deserve such from her; why be suspicious of a man she just met? But she was definitely not going to make things easy. She did not take the bait and ask what the best way to get to know a person might be.

Lady Noelle smiled. "And what is the best manner in which to get to know a person?"

He and Kit exchanged looks with a goofy smile. "Whist." He nodded his head. "One must definitely get in a very close game of Whist to see a person's true character."

Lady Meredith's mouth twitched. Perhaps she would be inclined to humor him after all. "Is that so?"

"It is most definitely so."

"And what if I always win? Does that say something about my character?"

"Are you offering a challenge?"

Her eyebrow rose. "I think I am, Lord Holbrook." She turned to Lord Rappleye. "With you as my partner, we shall win every trick against Lord Holbrook."

Kit sputtered beside him and then leaned forward with a wink. "I accept."

"Or?" Jamie eyed her. "What if you don't win?" There was no way she was winning every single trick.

She frowned for a moment, her soft lower lip protruding just enough to catch his eye and hold it. "Are you asking me to place a wager?"

"I am, indeed." He grinned. "In fact, I shall make it easy on you. If you do not win every trick against me, I shall claim the first two dances at the ball on Friday."

Her eyes widened. "Two?"

"Yes, we shall create talk."

"And if I do win every trick?"

He leaned back and crossed his arms. "Then you claim your prize."

She tapped fingers on her lips, which were now a complete distraction to him. And then pressed her teeth gently into the softness of her lower lip. "I think if I do win every trick, you shall have to dance two sets with a lady of my choosing."

He opened his mouth, frowned, and then closed it again. "Very well."

They brought out the next course and she couldn't resist. "Perhaps we should attempt to know one another better, then? We should discuss the most important qualities in a true diamond of the first water."

Jamie raised both eyebrows, in mid-sip of his soup.

"Yes, what is it that you men desire in a woman?" The corner of her mouth wiggled just enough that told him she was having way too much fun.

"Very well." He dabbed his mouth. "I shall reveal men's deepest desires if you reveal a bit of the women's." He gestured around the table. "All of you, naturally."

Lady Smith giggled. "Oh, we shall be so far ahead of all the others this Season, shan't we?"

Lady Meredith smiled in return. "We shall, indeed. So tell us, gentlemen. What is a most desirable trait in a woman?"

Kit lifted a hand. "I should like to go first. I think above all, I would enjoy a cheerful woman."

Someone giggled at the other end of the table and Jamie had to laugh. But Lady Meredith frowned. "Cheerful. Do you agree, Lord Holbrook?"

He knew he was walking into a trap, but he couldn't see how. So he blindly fell. "I do agree. I would love a happy life, indeed."

"And you feel her constantly cheerful state is what will give you that happy life? Are you aware that she might at times carry sorrow? What then? Must she paste on the smile and go about her cheery ways even still?" Her face was flushed and her eyes wide.

Jamie studied her and then cleared his throat. "She could be even-tempered as well, not easily agitated, not tending to overdramatize small things like cheeriness."

"Well, he can be understanding and accepting of a wife who is doing everything she can to be everything for everyone. Caring for the estate, the children, the nursemaids, the servants, caring for herself, the poor, the soirees, and the charities. If her smile seems a little dim, a truly gallant man would help replenish that cheer with a bit of his own and let her know she could rest for a time if she needed."

"Understood. Does anyone else have any ideas?" Kit looked to Lady Smith, who seemed a bit nervous, glancing from Jamie to Lady Meredith and back.

"I think a man should be gallant in his manner of rescue."

"Rescue? Do tell." Kit sat up taller in his seat.

Lady Meredith leaned forward like she was waiting for Jamie to say anything wrong. What had he done to this woman? He held a hand out to Kit and then to Lady Smith. "Yes, please, do tell."

Lady Smith tilted her head in a most engaging manner as though planning that exact pose for months. "I'm not talking about danger, no, more like rescuing the parched throat, providing a much-needed walk on the verandah, escorting a woman through the park, phaeton rides to relieve the boredom, and . . ." She leaned over so that she was looking right at Kit. "Knowing just when to change the subject." She nodded.

"Those are heroic rescues, indeed," Kit agreed.

Jamie was afraid to look at Lady Meredith. "And they require a certain amount of social brilliance." He stretched his neck against his cravat. "Do you think we men are up for the task?"

"One must certainly hope so, for your sakes." Lady Meredith fanned herself.

Before he could ask what she meant by her words, the final course was cleaned off their table, and Lady Smith invited the ladies to separate out while the men had cigars and port.

Ten

MERRY TOLD HERSELF SHE WAS relieved, but as the door closed behind her, leaving the men to themselves, she missed the new tension she felt between herself and Lord Holbrook. As much as she found his goals ridiculous, as clearly as she saw their lives not ever being intertwined, he was quite entertaining and a jovial sort of man that could converse and banter without being too emotional about things. She laughed to herself. She really was putting him through the ringer.

But who openly discussed women as though they were for sale? The question alone heated her blood again.

The women entered the sitting room, which was newly set up with tables for Whist. She laughed to herself again. Was she really going to win every trick? If Lord Rappleye knew at least a tiny bit about the game, she just might. Of course, it all depended on her hand and his hand, but there was a lot they could do to win, no matter which cards they were dealt.

Would she dance two sets with Lord Holbrook? Would that not firmly place her in his sights with regard to other men? She decided she didn't even care. If all men were like him, only seeking out large dowries, London could have them all. She would find love elsewhere. But if there was a diamond here, a unique sort of man who sought love in a marriage match, then perhaps she would find happiness after all. This evening had shown she could also find diversion in tormenting a pair of mercenary lords.

The ladies were shown a cart full of tarts and fruits and desserts with some sherry. The young Lady Smith approached Merry. "You are so bold with Lord Holbrook. I don't know how you dare."

Merry studied her face a moment and decided she had no guile and that Merry could trust her. "I overheard them talking, discussing our dowries like we are chattel to be purchased or bargained over."

"No." She put a hand over her mouth. "Why would they do such a thing?"

"Why would they think such a thing?"

"Well, of course, they think it. That is the way things work. Estates demand dowries to keep them alive. It is why women have them, to help pay for our upkeep and for the future times of widowhood, sometimes for the children, but largely for the estate itself." She shrugged. "It is the way of things."

"But must we be *valued* according to the dowry? Must it be a conversation piece?"

"Well, there you have it. Their conversation was too bold. They should have never discussed such things with you."

"Oh, well, certainly not with me. I overheard them . . ." She paused.

Lady Smith's eyes filled with concern.

"I suppose I was eavesdropping." She sighed. "Which I should not have been."

"And perhaps they would never have spoken so openly with you about such things."

"No, certainly not."

"Which means that perhaps we should not judge too harshly . . ." Lady Smith had the perfect, wide, innocent-looking eyes while she delivered such a careful blow to Merry's sense of well-being.

She looked away. "But I do feel that perhaps I've been given a glimpse into the real thoughts and intent of these lords, have I not?"

"Perhaps. But can you really know? Who's to say if they share such intimate feelings with each other? Perhaps they are discussing the business of their estates and you overheard just the wrong thing." She blinked a couple times with such innocence that Merry at once felt guilty for her rash judgement. She was in no way ready to assume they had good intentions regarding her, or marriage to her, but she also could not assume they were only interested in this woman or that because of her dowry.

"You are so correct. I have been chastened rightly. Thank you."

"I perhaps just don't view it as harshly as you. I've been thinking like they do for most of my life. It's not as if a man would marry me solely for the title or wealth. I am in a pool of women they are allowed to marry, and he must choose amongst those."

Merry nodded, not completely convinced, but seeing things a bit differently, nonetheless. "Thank you. I don't know what to say, really. Should I apologize?"

She laughed. "Absolutely not. I think you've got him half in love with you for being so belligerent."

"No, but certainly he doesn't quite know what to do with me."

At that, the men entered.

"Come, we will sit at the same table." Lady Smith led her to the back corner table.

Merry determined to be a bit more forgiving of Lord Holbrook and to perhaps attempt to see things from his perspective. But as soon as he sat down, she remembered his comments in the same light as before and could not help the rise of irritation because of it. How could they sit there and discuss women as though attached to a price tag?

Lord Holbrook adjusted his seat so that he sat closer to Merry. "I couldn't help but notice the lovely sparkle on your dress. Those gems catch the light exactly so and shine back like little stars."

She narrowed her eyes until Lady Smith's foot hit her shin and then she smiled. "Oh, thank you. How poetic. I do quite like them myself." She tried to distract herself with her cards.

"But?" He leaned closer.

"What do you mean?"

"You do like them yourself, but . . ." He held a hand out as if waiting for her to continue.

"But I do not place value in them. People are worth so much more than what they wear or the gems on their skirts or even, say, their titles or dowries, am I correct in thinking so?"

Lord Holbrook's face lit with such happiness, she was, at a moment, lost for words. How could he be so overly pleased with her thoughts when he himself spoke something so contrary to them?

Lord Rappleye leaned back in his seat. "But it's not practical to talk like that. It sounds lovely until you have to actually live, eat, run an estate, feed tenants, care for the poor in the town. All of that requires blunt, and no matter what we all may say, we are the ones who have to accumulate that blunt."

She nodded. "It is all so very true." She acted as though she would pull a card to play. "And now, Lord Rappleye, we have a wager to win, do we not?"

"Yes, yes, we do." He shook his head at her.

Oh dear. Her cards were not good enough to carry them both. And apparently, his cards were terrible. She chose her highest, most-likely-to-win card and played it. They took the trick. And the next, but then she ran out of definite winners. She laid down her only possible win, hoping Lord Rappleye might have something.

Lord Holbrook laid a higher card right away, with a victorious gleam in his eye.

Then Lord Rappleye laid down a lower card, followed by Lady Smith's lower card.

Lord Holbrook gathered his cards. "And now I will finish out our win."

He and Lady Smith took the remaining sets until the last, when Lord Rappleye threw away a card he could have played earlier to win an additional set. She didn't say anything and he didn't meet her eye. He probably supposed she wouldn't notice.

Lord Holbrook and Lady Smith beat them soundly during the second game as well. But she couldn't care anymore. She'd lost and she would dance two sets with this lord. The servants came to clean up the cards and offer them further refreshment while Lord Holbrook stood and reached for her hand. "Would you like to take a turn?"

She rested a hand in his. "Hoping to gloat over your win, are you?"

"Yes, well, and celebrate it, naturally."

"Very well." She stood. He was much closer than she

expected, and as she looked up into his face, they were close enough she felt the smallest poof of his breath in the hairs on her neck.

They walked to the fireplace. She stood close to the warmth. He joined her as close as he could. "I, um, hoped to mention something."

Her eyes met his and the softness of the blue that looked back into her own warmed her more than the embers. He seemed like everything he should be, didn't he?

"I wanted you to know." He lifted a wisp of her hair out from her eyelashes. "I hoped . . . that is to say . . ." The corner of his mouth wiggled. "I'm having a time of it, aren't I?"

"What is it you would like to say, Lord Holbrook? Come now. As unruly as I may seem, truly, I'm quite harmless most of the time."

"I can hardly believe docile is a word used to describe you ever."

"Oh? And what words would you use?"

"Captivating, if you must know. I have never met a woman like you, I don't think. Very few anyway." His brow furrowed in thought. "Tell me though. Would you like to dance two sets with me at the ball? I would never force a woman to do such a thing. I will admit that I care not for winning or losing at Whist, only that I can dance with you. If you wish." He bowed his head and then glanced up with pleading, hopeful eyes.

She almost melted into the fire at such an expression from him. "I would enjoy it very much, and I'm flattered you would wish such a thing." She adjusted her stance so that she was a bit farther from him. "But tell me this. Would you be so interested in two sets if I had no dowry, if I had no title, and I arrived at the Season with the bare minimum of things?"

He looked away with a concerned expression, and her shoulders dropped. But she recovered. Certainly he would be just as Lady Smith said.

"No. Do not answer. That was unfair of me. I cannot expect any more from you than I would another man." She dipped into a curtsey. "I look forward to our sets."

He did not stop her retreat, and though she couldn't look back up into his face, she knew he watched her.

Eleven

JAMIE REPLAYED HIS CONVERSATION WITH Lady Meredith over and over in his mind on the way to the ball. It helped him to put Merry from his thoughts, as he was attempting to forget her, to stop hoping to see her in every turn of a lovely face. He could not even remember or recall the look of her neck, her mouth, her hair. It was all distant in his memory, so distant he wondered again at her supernatural ability to simply disappear.

He hadn't seen or heard from many of that same group of lords. He supposed they were like him, attempting to make connections and form alliances so that they too could marry. But they would all be at the ball. Everyone who was anyone would attend the ball.

As much as he wanted to move on from Merry and focus on Lady Meredith, or any of the other ladies he must come to know, a part of him longed to see her again, to see if she still had the same effect on him, to wonder if she was someone he could marry. He assumed she'd be there at the ball. But would he recognize her?

Something told him he would not.

And that was the crux of it. His whole problem. Should he allow himself to completely fall for a woman whom he could marry, or should he hold out hope that the woman he thought he could fall for, that he thought he was already half in love with, would somehow reappear in his life and that she would be someone he could marry?

He pulled out the mask he'd worn at the masquerade from his inner jacket pocket and studied it a moment. His life was far too complicated for a second son of a duke. Even though he knew he had very little hope of finding Merry again, he folded the mask up and placed it back in his pocket anyway.

And who knows; perhaps Lady Meredith . . . She was intriguing, as well as beautiful.

The street outside the host's home was packed with carriages. People poured out onto the street, getting dropped off many houses down. The front door had a line dozens of people long to enter. And all Jamie wanted was to ensure he was present for the first two sets so that he could spend the time with Lady Meredith and announce his intention to the others. She was his father's first choice, and ironically, he had been right. She was a delightful gem amongst many of the women he'd already met. Perhaps he could make himself happy while pleasing his father—something rare, indeed.

As he approached, the line parted. And for a moment he wondered if they were parting for him.

But eyes were looking behind him, through him, so he turned.

Prince George approached, dressed in a most ridiculous and elaborate display of gold and red. But his wig was stunning, and his slippers stepped on material thrown down at his feet.

Jamie moved aside and bowed. But the prince stopped and nodded. "Walk with me, Holbrook. Your father and I have been conversing."

"Yes, Your Highness." He stood at the prince's side and walked with him up the steps and into the home.

"I've come as a favor to Mother to dance with a new diamond. She's something special, and it is our wish that she be treated as such."

Jamie had never heard of the family taking such an interest. "Who is the lucky lady?"

"Lady Meredith. Do you know her?"

He started. "Yes, I do. I've asked her to dance this evening."

"Excellent. I'll be taking her first two sets. And then she is all yours." He looked almost bored. But Jamie didn't mention anything about his own two sets.

"Would you like an introduction?"

"Typically, yes, but I'm to make a big scene of it. Shall we have a bit of fun?"

Jamie wasn't entirely sure a scene was what Lady Meredith would welcome, but he was well aware of the prince's distaste at being corrected, and so he followed him into the home, down the hall, and toward the ballroom.

Everyone bowed on either side and moved out of the way. The prince greeted their hosts and then said something to the footman who announced to the room, "His Royal Highness, Prince George."

All sound stopped and the entire party was lowered in bows or curtseys. The footman continued. "Would Lady Meredith please come forward?"

A soft gasp sounded out to the room.

Jamie smiled.

Lady Meredith stood. Her hair towering over her head, her arms gracefully resting on the sides of her skirts, the blue fabric falling in folds down to the floor. She was stunning.

"Well, well. I can see why you have claimed your dances

with her already." He nodded his head in Jamie's direction and then reached a hand out to lift hers as she approached. "Might I have this dance?"

She glanced at Jamie first, to her credit. But he nodded, and she visibly swallowed. "Yes, thank you."

Then the Prince of Wales led his first choice of partner out onto the floor. As she stepped away, he wanted to follow. He suddenly realized that during that very evening, he could lose her.

His friend George came to stand beside him. "She's lovely. You know who she is, don't you?"

"Lady Meredith? A bit, yes."

"No, who *else* she is." He turned to Jamie with a grin. "You don't, do you?"

He started to shake his head and then clapped his friend on the shoulder. "Out with it, man. Say what you mean to say."

"That is your lovely masked liaison."

His heart stopped. "How can you know such a thing?"

"I saw her take off her mask. It's her. She's the one. Now go steal her back from the prince." He laughed, then clapped him on the shoulder in return. "And congratulations. How often does that happen?"

"What?"

"You falling in love with the very person you need in your life?"

"I don't know. Does it ever happen?"

He shrugged. "Not to me. Not yet."

Jamie turned his attention back to Lady Meredith. Merry. And his smile grew.

But then she laughed, and the prince spun her around. And every male eye in the room was on her.

He stepped to the edge of the dance floor, as close to

them as he could. Perhaps they'd all realize a thing or two about his personal interest. But no one gave him any mind. First sons, almost-dukes, viscounts, marquises, all of the men had their eye trained on Lady Meredith. And there wasn't anything Jamie could do about it, not when she was dancing with the prince, who had also expressed a compliment. What if he took a fancy to her?

She laughed again.

What if she took a fancy to the prince?

Twelve

The prince lifted his hand and the music for a waltz started. He moved to the center of the room. "I hope you don't mind, but I requested our sets be waltzes. I have things to discuss with you."

The prince led Merry all over the floor. He was an excellent dancer and a great conversationalist. She did not think he was known for clever conversation, but he was quite funny.

"Thank you for singling me out like this."

"I'm pleased to do it. Your father is a hero in our home and in our lives and now in all of England. Do any of these sorry saps even know what he has done for their monarch?"

"I don't think so." She looked down. "To hear you speak of my father, it makes me happy. Like I honor him."

"You do. And he would be pleased to see you with such acclaim. You are the talk of London already, and after this ball, you shall be the most sought-after hand in all of England."

"But do I want such a thing?"

"Why wouldn't you?"

"How can I know if they truly wish to marry me or my dowry?"

He nodded. "And that is the other thing I wished to discuss."

"What?"

"I'm withdrawing the dowry portion of our gift to you."

"You are?" She felt her face lose a bit of color.

"You seem unhappy. Didn't you just say that the money was confusing things?"

"Well, yes, it was, but to have nothing, that might make it impossible to marry, don't you think?"

"Well, don't tell anyone just yet. Let's see what happens, shall we?" His eyes twinkled with obvious personal amusement.

She frowned. "You're toying with me."

"A bit, but I enjoy the diversion. You wouldn't rob me a bit of my own personal amusement, would you?"

"I might." She stiffened. "Please do not toy with me."

"Oh, I couldn't, not really. My parents would be most displeased. Besides, I do believe I'm doing you a favor. In the moment of a proposal, mention the loss of a dowry and see how they respond. You will know."

She nodded and then smiled. "You are so correct. Thank you, Your Highness."

"I think I'd like two dances, if you would?"

"Yes, I would." She rested a hand on the arm he held up as he spun her again. As they were nearing the end of their second set, he nodded in satisfaction.

"What is it?"

"Everyone in the room is watching."

She gasped, taking in their faces. "They are. Is that a good thing?"

"You look lovely. And yes. Do you have anyone to help you manage all the attention?"

She thought of Mrs. Donning. "I don't . . ."

"Lord Holbrook? He's a good man. He will assist."

"Will he?"

"Of course. He told me he has the next two sets. I'm certain he will linger about like a wolf watching his territory ever after."

She laughed and felt her face heat. "I don't know what I think about that image."

"But it's accurate. I do believe you've won his heart."

"Or his greed."

"Ah, well, this is where you telling him of your new plight as a pauper will assist in reading his heart, won't it?"

She didn't know what was fair or not, or what was good to him or the others. Everything was happening way too fast. She didn't know what she wanted. And suddenly finding air in her tighter-than-usual corset was proving difficult.

"Would you like to rest?" He slowed their pace.

"Yes, thank you. And thank you for everything. I don't know what to say."

"You'll come Thursday next to dine with us, won't you?"

"I would be honored."

"Remember, Mother prefers the traditional court dress. Much as you are now dressed."

"Thank you."

The music ended and he held her close for a second. "Best of luck to our new diamond." He winked and then led her to Lord Holbrook. "Take good care of this flower. She is special, indeed."

Lord Holbrook had a new look in his face, something she couldn't quite place. "I will, thank you."

"Oh, and I've requested two more waltzes. Your father owes me a vote."

"I'll pass that along." He laughed but his eyes were focused only on Merry. He held her close, enclosed her hand in his own, and held the most tender expression she'd ever seen.

She lifted a hand to his face. "What has happened?"

"I've recently learned something that made me the happiest I've been in a long time." His eyes captured hers, drank her in. She was lost in the intensity, so much that she could only whisper, "You have?"

"Yes. And I'll tell you soon. But first I need to ensure that it will also make you the happiest of women."

She tried to swallow past her suddenly parched throat. She could do and say nothing except watch his face, enjoy his arms, participate in this dance that had just become the most intimate experience of her life.

He lifted their hands as though he loved her touch. He stared into her face as though she were the most important person in the world to him. He spun her regretfully and brought her close again as though the separations were a pain. Every touch, every breath, every movement felt as true a love as anything she'd ever known. They moved across the floor, her feet caught in his lead, as though they floated on a cloud. He led her as if reading her mind. They were one.

But as all sets must, their two came to a close.

"Would you like a lemonade?"

"I would, yes."

He turned to lead her from the floor but almost ran into another man. They stopped but the man bowed and looked at Merry.

Lord Holbrook gritted his teeth. "Your Grace."

"I do believe your partner is free. Perhaps I might have an introduction?"

A full moment passed before Lord Holbrook turned to

Merry and said, "Lady Meredith, the Duke of Chatsworth would like an introduction." His eyes held no warmth for the idea. "This, Your Grace, is the finest woman in the room, Lady Meredith. I'm under strict instructions from Prince George to see to her well-being."

"We're at a ball, Holbrook. What could happen?" The duke winked and then he bowed. "Might I have the next set?" He glanced up with bright green eyes. His blond hair fell forward just enough. And she knew right away he was a man who expected to get what he wanted.

"Yes, you may." She lowered in a quick curtsey and then was taken back out onto the floor.

The duke turned out to be a remarkable dancer, a charming person, and highly sought-after, if the seething glares from most women were anything to gauge his eligibility. And when their set was complete, she followed him to the lemonade table and past men who might hope to step in. Few dared to step closer.

Except for Lord Holbrook. He joined them at the table. "How was your set?" he asked her.

She smiled. "It was wonderful. And yours?"

"Wonderful." His voice was flat. "I see you are at last getting your lemonade." He nodded to the duke, who held out her cup.

"Yes, thank you." She smiled at them both and then a new sort of awkwardness descended. "I do believe this is the biggest event of the Season, is it not? Or might I expect others similar to this?"

They both answered at once, or at least that's what she felt was happening. Lord Holbrook clarified. "I don't think there will be anything larger."

"There will be other more intimate settings for greater enjoyment. I'm considering a house party myself. I'll send out invitations in a fortnight."

"Oh, how diverting." She didn't know quite how to respond. Was he inviting her? Not inviting her?

"And, of course, walks and rides in the park. I'd love to come by with my phaeton tomorrow, if you are free." Lord Holbrook took her empty glass and offered her a second lemonade.

Which she took with a smile. "That would be lovely."

"And I, of course, can take you for ices." The duke nodded.

They continued for a moment, thinking of all the activities she could do and attend that Season, presumably at their sides, until she was in desperate need of the retiring room after having two lemonades. "Perhaps . . ." She glanced around in desperation. Lady Smith caught her eye. "Oh, there she is. My lord, Your Grace, would you excuse me a moment? I do believe I have some business with Lady Smith."

"Of course. I'll be right here," Lord Holbrook called after her, and she had to laugh. What on earth?

On the way to greet Lady Smith, two men stepped in her path, but she knew neither and they could do nothing but bow and smile. At last, at the side of her friend, she whispered, "I'm in desperate need for the retiring room."

"I as well, it turns out."

They hurried there. Lady Smith murmured, "Did you know the prince would come?"

"No! I had no idea. What a thing to happen!"

"And the duke! Lady Meredith, he dances with no one. He has rarely been seen in years. It has been said he refuses to marry unless she is truly worth his time."

"Goodness, he has a rather large opinion of himself."

"He can afford to. He needs no money, no title. He simply wishes for a woman worthy to stand at his side. He wants a duchess."

"And he suddenly thinks I am such a woman?"

"You are rather lovely. And gentle and a good person, at least that is what I think you to be."

"Did you tell him these things?"

"Our family might have had a thing or two to do with it. You deserve to be in a duke's family. If Lord Holbrook bothers you so, then certainly the elusive Duke of Chatsworth would be quite the catch."

"No, no. Oh, please do not think me so picky as to think any man not worthy of me."

They entered the retiring room and refreshed themselves. As Merry dabbed a bit of water on her neck and then dried herself, she could only wonder.

Lady Smith was ready to return, but Merry shook her head. "Please, go dance your sets. I'll be but a moment."

Her friend looked one last time in Merry's direction and then exited the room.

Merry left soon after but turned away from the ballroom. Too much was happening at once, and she needed to sort through her feelings, particularly this new intensity in Lord Holbrook.

She slipped out the back and onto a quiet verandah. Somehow she'd found the only place in the house where no one else had yet invaded. She moved to the edge of the balcony, letting the cool air refresh her skin while she looked out over the expansive grounds. The immediate gardens were lit with candles. Couples walked up and down the pathways. It was all rather romantic. And she might have enjoyed it immensely were it not for the confusion in her heart.

Would she ever be able to see a man's sincerity? Why the sudden interest from the elusive duke? Why had Lord Holbrook's manner intensified? Was it simply the pleasure of the Crown? Had the prince that much power over a young woman's life? It seemed he had.

"Well, this is my lucky night." A man slipped out of the darkness and approached her.

"I'm sorry, I'll leave you to this lovely space and some privacy."

"But you are who I've hoped to see."

"We've not yet been introduced."

He lifted his fingers. "We will. I'll bet we'll get real cozy here in just a moment."

"What?" She inched away, but he blocked her retreat.

"Nothing to be running off about. I'm going to take real good care of you." He stepped closer.

"I don't know what you're talking about, but I have to get back." She moved away from the balcony as if to walk past him.

But then another man joined them. "I've been looking for you. We were meant to meet out here an hour ago." He approached and grabbed her arm.

"What are you talking about? I am not meeting anyone." But he pulled her close as if in an embrace.

The other man stepped closer. "What's this? She's out here to meet me."

"I don't understand." She wrenched her arm free, feeling the bruising as she pushed on his chest to give herself more space. "Leave me alone." She dodged another advance and ran from the balcony and turned down a hall, but someone stepped in her path. "Oh, there you are. I've been waiting for you." He pulled her into an embrace just as they stepped out of the hall and into a more lit area of a large library. He leaned down like he would kiss her.

"What are you doing?" She arched her back, narrowly avoiding his thin lips and rather rough-looking face. "Get away from me."

"Go ahead and scream." He laughed. "They'll all come running, find us together, and you'll be hitched."

She gasped. "Is that what this is about? You're trying to marry me?"

"I thought you'd never ask." He dropped to one knee in mockery.

"Leave me alone."

She ran from him, but he caught up to her before she reached the other side of the library and the door. "I think it's time we sealed this new engagement with a kiss."

"Don't you dare." She wiggled free and flung open the door. But he was there beside her, and just as a whole room full of eyes turned to her, he placed a rough kiss right on her mouth.

His breath was hot, his mouth more so. She was pinned within his grasp, and when she tried to break free, he reached for her dress, ripping it at the shoulder.

Several women in the room gasped. Lady Smith's face widened in horror, and she ran from the room.

Merry's heart sank. She was on her own. She tried to free herself.

But a group had gathered and was growing.

Someone from the crowd called out, "Who will speak for her? Who is her guardian?"

The man who still held the fabric of her dress in his hand stood closer. "Call for your chaperone. Don't worry. I won't leave you alone. I'll do my duty by you." He smiled, his whole demeanor changing in front of everyone from a hardened man to a soft cheery one. "We were too caught up in the moment. I cannot wait to be married to my love, you see."

She shook her head.

But he clucked. "Do you really want to refuse? What is

left for you if you don't marry me? You'll be soiled. No one wants this kind of scandal in their life. I'm all you have now." He said those words as if he cared, so others would think he was being tender without hearing the actual words, but she knew they were her new prison sentence.

"How could you do such a thing? To both of us?"

"It's as easy as your dowry will be to spend." He winked and grinned.

The other two men from the verandah arrived. "She has already agreed to marry me." The first one went down on one knee.

The other shook his head. "No, me. You saw it happen and you tried to take matters into your own hands, didn't you?" He scowled. "Come now, Lady Meredith. Tell him how it happened."

And now she had a choice between three men she did not know, all three of which proved to be the type of men to entrap another. And she wanted nothing to do with any of them.

But the crowds were growing.

At last Mrs. Donning approached. "What has happened, child?" She frowned, looking from one man to the other.

Merry ran to her. "Oh, Mrs. Donning. That man kissed me in front of everyone and ripped my dress. The other two are claiming I agreed to marry them as well. It's a nightmare. Let's leave. Posthaste."

But Mrs. Donning hesitated.

"Come, we must." She tugged on the woman's sleeve, but she did not move.

"I'm afraid . . ." Mrs. Donning made a quick look around the room. "I'm afraid if we leave, you might never have another opportunity to marry."

"What are you talking about? Of course I will. We can just go someplace else. Do something . . ."

Mrs. Donning shook her head. "This will spread all over town by tomorrow. You will be untouchable unless one of these men agrees to marry you." Her eyes were serious, sad, and sincere.

"Have I no choice?"

"It looks to me like you have three choices." She sighed. "I'm sorry I wasn't watching out for you. I thought for sure Lord Holbrook would take care of you. Where is that man?"

"I went to the ladies' retiring room. I left him. He and the duke were arguing about who would spend time with me. It grew uncomfortable."

"This is better?" She shook her head. "I think you were in far better company with those two than here." She approached the men.

Merry felt her whole world swirl around her in a gathering storm of disaster. Nothing about this was the way it was supposed to be. Her worst fears were coming true right as she watched.

Thirteen

LADY SMITH GRIPPED JAMIE'S ARM like the world was about to end. Her face was full of panic.

"What is it? What's the matter?"

"It's Lady Meredith. She's been entrapped. Come quickly. It's a nightmare." She ran off, and Jamie followed immediately after, his heart pounding.

What he saw when he arrived in the outer sitting room made his blood boil. A crowd had gathered, and three of the worst gambling-hell cads stood around her, arguing. Mrs. Donning stood by with an arm around Merry, whose face made him the saddest of all. Merry looked as though every good thing had been taken from her life. And probably it had. He'd just never considered how losing her father and her mother would have felt for her. And now this, a forced marriage when it could have been new family.

Sadly.

But now he could do something for her. And he would. "What is this?" He approached gently. "Are you well?"

Merry paused and then ran to him, stopping just short of an embrace. "Oh, Lord Holbrook. You do not want to be here. Leave before you too are caught up in this disaster. I'm to marry. I have to choose one of them." She clutched at his arm. "Before you go, please, which one is the least bad?" Her eyes filled with tears. "Can you believe I'm in such a spot?" She started to tremble.

He could not bear the sight. "No, no, no, come here. No." He pulled her close and wrapped his arms around her. "You will not have to choose any of them. No." He ran a hand up her back.

The crowd began to whisper, but he let them. He could solve this. It was unfortunate timing, but he was going to propose as soon as she let him anyway. "My dear Lady Meredith." He stepped back so that he could look into her eyes.

But she shook her head. "No, no. You cannot. Lord Holbrook, you cannot do this." She whirled around and announced to the room, "The prince informed me this very evening that the dowry is gone. He is going to use it for a new wing at Carlton House. He danced with me to try and make up for the loss." She shrugged. "So, you see, I'm not worth anything now." She stared down the men who had tried to entrap her, and one by one they left.

The crowd stayed put.

And Mrs. Donning wrung her hands. "What have you done, child? You are ruined. No one will have you. Did the prince really say those awful things? We should talk to the Queen, someone should."

<hr />

MERRY SHOOK HER HEAD. "Do not worry yourself, Mrs. Donning. I would rather be single than stuck married to someone of their ilk." She turned back around to find Jamie still standing as close as he had been. "And you. You needn't concern yourself either. I know you must marry for your estate." She waved him away. "I shall not think on you again, I dare say."

He reached for her hand. "Is that true, my lady? You'll not think on me?" His eyes bore into hers and she could not look away. "Because I will think on you every minute of every day for the rest of my life." He started to lower to one knee.

"No, please, no. Don't do this. You cannot."

"I can. I must. I cannot live without you. Dowry or no, I love you."

She tugged on his sleeve. "Please."

He started to rise. "Unless you find me abhorrent like you do those men. Do you not wish for my hand?"

A few of the women closest to them gasped.

"Of course I find in you everything that is good. I will regret this moment all of my life. But I would regret more entrapping you. I refuse you. You're free, my lord." She turned from him.

But he came around to stand in front of her again. "I love you. Marry me. I care not for your dowry, title, or even your newly soiled reputation. I want you at my side forever. If my father casts me aside, if we have nothing, we will have it together."

"Wait, why would your father cast you aside?"

He sighed. "He said if I do not marry money this very Season, he will take my inheritance and my title and disown me."

She felt her eyes blur. "And you would give all that up? To be with me?"

"If you will have me, yes, my Merry."

She gasped. *Merry?* "Why? Why would you do such a thing?" She hugged herself.

He reached in his pocket and pulled out a mask, putting

it on his face. "Because I'm Jamie. And I've loved you since the moment we met."

She felt the tears fall down her face. "What! How could I not see it? How could I not know immediately it was you?"

"I didn't know either. It was George who told me." He lowered to his knee again. "Now, may I?"

She rocked from side to side, her arms tightly wound around her middle. "I don't have the strength to resist. Make me stop. Go."

But he stayed.

She nodded, hiccupping through her tears. "I . . ."

He lifted her hand in his own. "I have nothing more to offer but my love and my hand. Marry me, my dear, sweet Merry. Marry me tomorrow."

She watched his lip quiver, his eyes fill with his own tears, and felt his heart pound through his hand that held hers. He loved her. He was willing to lose it all. For her. She knelt in front of him. "My dear, sweet man. My Jamie. Yes. I will marry you."

He lifted her in his arms and held her as close as he could. "Then we shall be the happiest of any who have ever entered these halls." He spun her and then lowered her feet to the ground so that she stood in his arms.

She searched his eyes, lifted her palms to the sides of his face and pulled him close. "I love you, my dear Jamie."

"I love you too."

When his lips covered hers, the world spun in a happy glow. She clung to him and loved him in return with every softness of his mouth on hers. "My Jamie." She murmured and lifted the mask from his face.

"My Merry."

The prince entered the room clapping. "Bravo, bravo!" he called out. "This is indeed a happy union, made even more so by the sacrifice of both." He chuckled. "Living in poverty for all of your lives?" He shook his head. "Totally unnecessary."

Lord Holbrook held her hand as if he would never let go. "What do you mean?"

"I mean"—Prince George reached for his pocket watch, looked at it, and then repocketed it—"as of this minute, your Merry is a very wealthy woman after all. You see, my parents, the Crown, all of England owe her father a very great debt. Shall I tell you the story?"

All she could do was nod. Jamie seemed to be without the ability to speak.

And so the prince clapped his hands, and the servants brought him a chair. "Much better." He swayed a little as if perhaps in his cups, but his words were clear. "My mother was in her back gardens with fewer than the usual amount of servants. She heard a woman crying for help and slipped out of the back fenced area to see what she could do. A highwayman held a gun to the woman's head and was robbing her of her things when my mother called out, commanding him to desist at once. But he only turned hungry eyes on my mother.

"It was in that moment another who had heard the woman's cries ran forward, engaging the man in fisticuffs. Lady Meredith's father. But he was unarmed. And not too long after was shot by the bandit. But not until he had rendered the villain unable to function. The robber fell to the earth. But Lady Meredith's father had already given his life to save the Queen. He was immediately given title and funds to care for his family and generations after as long as they live on this earth, beginning with Lady Meredith." He dipped his head and then bowed in his seat.

By doing so, every other person in the room in turn bowed in her direction.

THEIR MASKED SECRET

Tears filled her eyes as she thought of her father. "Bless you, Father. I hope you can see this, because I miss you every day."

Jamie pulled her close, wrapping an arm across her shoulders.

"And so, you see," the prince held up a hand, "you both will not live in poverty but in fact have everything your hearts desire, you lucky lovebirds." He frowned. "But I returned having received word of some shenanigans afoot. Is he the man you would choose for yourself? For we will have none of this soiled, ruined nonsense. You are free to choose. I hear even the Duke of Chatsworth has made an appearance. Hmm?"

She turned to Jamie and smiled. "He is all I would ever want if I had every man in England at my feet."

His eyes again filled with tears and he pulled her close. "I will ask you to repeat that again." He kissed her. "And again."

"For as long as we both live?"

"That long and longer. I love you too, my dear Merry."

They kissed once more with the prince and a houseful of people clapping and cheering.

Then the prince stood. "Bring him to the house when you come. We have a wedding to plan."

An award winning author, including the GOLD in Foreword INDIES Book of the Year Awards, **Jen Geigle Johnson** discovered her passion for England while kayaking on the Thames near London as a young teenager. She still finds the great old manors and castles in England fascinating and loves to share bits of history that might otherwise be forgotten. Whether set in Regency England, the French Revolution, or Colonial America, her romance novels are much like life is supposed to be: full of brave heroes, strong heroines, and stirring adventures.

Follow her at https://www.jengeiglejohnson.com.
Facebook: https://www.facebook.com/AuthorJenGeigleJohnson
Instagram: @authorlyjen

MASQUERADE A-LA-MODE

Annette Lyon

One

"Sir, your carriage awaits," the butler said from the door of the drawing room.

"Very good, Topham." Mr. Jacob Amesbury closed the book he'd been reading, *The Diary of Samuel Pepys*, and with a grunt pushed off the padded chair to stand. He consulted the chinoiserie clock on the mantel and nodded toward his daughter, Clarissa, who was embroidering on the chaise lounge. "I will likely not return in time for supper. Cook knows you'll dine without me."

"Shall I have her save something for you?" Clarissa asked.

"I'll have a meal over business at Andrew's." He considered for a moment before patting his expanding belly. "But if she's made her raspberry tart, then absolutely have her save me some."

"Of course." Clarissa turned her cheek to her father.

He kissed it, and then took his leave for Andrew's Coffee House, his favorite location, as was the case with many other gentlemen, for discussing and finalizing business deals. From the corner of her eyes, Clarissa noted her companion, Mary, gazing fixedly as he exited, then waiting expectantly. Clarissa smiled wryly, knowing why Mary was eagerly awaiting Father's absence.

As soon as they heard the front door of Carrington House closing, Mary abandoned her embroidery hoop, then slipped a newspaper from beneath a cushion.

"You could read the daily paper in my father's presence, you know," Clarissa said, pulling the needle through the design of a leaf.

"Oh, but then he'd ask about the *news*," Mary said, and she was correct. She was far more interested in the advertisements, always printed on the right column of the first page. Specifically, she found entertainment in the ones often referred to as "Lonely Hearts" notices. "If your father discovered that I read them and have influenced you to enjoy them as well, you would get a scolding while I would likely be dismissed."

Despite the sober topic, Mary spoke with an airy tone and made a show of tracing the text with her finger.

"Touché." Clarissa chuckled and returned to her needle. She would continue to keep Mary's interests to herself precisely because losing her companion of three years would devastate them both. Mary had become more than a companion; to Clarissa, she felt quite nearly a sister, something Clarissa had never had. In some ways Mary was also a maternal figure, something Clarissa hadn't had since the age of five, when her own mother had passed.

Father *would* be appalled if he knew how avidly she followed the advertisements. He'd declare Clarissa on the verge of scandalous ruin.

"Real news is found beyond the front page," he'd said in disgust more than once.

Not all advertisements were for scandalous attempts at romance, however. Many were rather banal, such as items for sale—a horse, a dress, and sometimes a house or land. Other uses of the advertisements section included individuals seeking a lost possession, such as a family heirloom, or the recent one pleading for someone to find a missing dog.

Answers to the name of Jinks, black with white paws, missing from Covent Garden for a fortnight.

Yet the more mundane announcements had other far more interesting ones sprinkled among them, and it was those that her father would have protested the women's interest in.

Those advertisements were placed anonymously by individuals looking for love or marriage—as indeed, the two were not necessarily the same thing.

Sometimes a widowed gentleman needed an heir, or a man in the trades hoped to improve his standing by finding a wife with the means to expand his business. Therefore, many Lonely Hearts advertisements were unremarkable.

"This first one isn't terribly interesting," Mary said. "*Agreeable gentleman with a significant estate, looking for a wife with good teeth, healthy complexion, a gentle temperament, and a fortune of about 3000 pounds.*" She looked up from the paper. "Typical. He wants a healthy, pretty wife who can make him richer." She shook her head and read on, looking for another to share.

Though advertising for a spouse in any way seemed unrefined at best and vulgar at worst, straightforward texts like that weren't the ones that piqued their interest. Mary typically shared those with unusual details. Ofttimes that meant a surprise. Others, a shock. Whatever she chose to share was always entertaining. After Clarissa had made several more stitches without Mary producing another item worth reading aloud, she looked up. "Nothing else of interest today?"

Mary's mouth had drawn into a flat line. "Perhaps I'm getting irritable in my old age—"

Clarissa snorted at that. "You're scarcely over thirty, my dear."

"An old maid, as we both know," Mary replied. "Regardless, I find the constant requirements of the female respondent's beauty to be tiresome. They're nearly always about physical beauty, paired with a temperament soft as bread dough. Oh, and she must have money." She hmphed. "*Gentle temperament.* Pshaw. A pity there are so few good men left in the world."

Gesturing toward the paper with her needle, Clarissa said, "I don't think those men are necessarily the best representation of their sex."

"The sentiment stands. The authors of these advertisements merely say what virtually all men are already thinking—or rather, demanding to have in a wife. I don't anticipate ever marrying at my age, but I do hope you'll find a husband, and *not* one who merely appreciates your dowry and"—she consulted the paper and quoted another advertisement—"*fair complexion.* But he'd approve of you because you have *very little Brogue.* You're also young, blonde, and wealthy. From a Mr. D.M. I believe you are his ideal match." Mary grunted in annoyance and slapped the paper onto the small table between them.

"That is the lot of most women born into this world, alas," Clarissa admitted.

"Too often the men make demands for a wife that sound too similar to one requesting a specific meal at a tavern."

Clarissa could not dispute that. Despite herself, she picked up the abandoned paper and perused the front page. Her eye caught two words that hinted at her favorite type of ad: "Once Seen." She sat up a bit straighter and read aloud.

"Once Seen: A young woman who attended the Royal Theater on Friday last, wearing a blue dress edged in gold. Sought by a gentleman enraptured by her throughout the final act. He could not avert his gaze until the curtain fell. She noted him, a gentleman in dark blue, with a matching hat that also had gold trim. If the lady is amenable, she will favor him with a letter addressed to Mr. E.S. and delivered to Mrs. Passmore at Needham's Coffee House to inform him whether her situation and fortune might allow him to cultivate an interest in her heart."

Mary gave a sideways look and sighed. "Looking for a pretty woman, of course. I suppose this situation is slightly better—he's seen the meal he wants."

"I think the Once Seen pieces are romantic," Clarissa said. "As you said, they aren't requesting a meal—or a lady with a list of traits. Rather, they've seen the woman they think would be a good match. It's as if fate led them together at the theater but didn't *quite* finish her duty, so they're giving her a little help."

"Spoken like a young woman who believes in love matches," Mary said.

"You do too," Clarissa replied with a smile. "You wouldn't read these if you didn't. We both hope the couples will find love together."

"True," Mary said. "Though the older I get, the more I see, and the less I believe. I think now I merely . . . dream."

"Then I'll keep on believing for both of us." Clarissa set the paper back down on the table and returned to her needlepoint. After a moment she said, "Perhaps *you* could find a love match by placing an advertisement."

Mary leveled a look at her that might have made someone else quake, but Clarissa only laughed. She knew her companion too well to think she was genuinely angry at such a suggestion. Very few women placed advertisements. If replying to one was scandalous, how much worse would it be to pay for one to be printed?

After a moment of contemplation, Mary's face shifted into an expression of mischief. "I will if you will."

Clarissa laughed heartily. What a ridiculous idea. The very mention of undertaking such a thing was so beyond the realm of reality that . . .

Then again, was it?

There was every likelihood that some advertisements weren't truthful about their creators—after all, there had once been an entire paper devoted to such satirical false advertisements, purely for the entertainment of the populace. Any woman placing such an advertisement would need to be extraordinarily careful, not only in secreting her identity but also in verifying the morals and identities of any men replying to them.

Mary leaned slightly forward. "As you've said of the few women's advertisements we've seen, if women of means have placed such advertisements, it's likely men have responded to them, and entirely plausible that they've had success in finding a mate."

"We could never," Clarissa said with a chuckle. Mary laughed as well, and they lapsed into silence as Clarissa pondered the matter.

The proportion of rakes to good men was often weighed in the favor of rakes at balls and social events. Would the odds be any different in a newspaper? One never knew, truly, who a man was until the marriage contract was signed, the wedding bells tolled, and it was too late. A man could play whatever part he needed to woo a woman.

Ladies were no less likely to hide their true selves,

whether with face powder, a beauty patch that might be hiding a blemish, or otherwise hiding one's true self under a metaphorical mask of another kind, pretending to be a good match in every possible way. Indeed, the stakes tended to be much higher for women, for without a marriage that settled her future, she mightn't have a roof over her head, food in her belly, or clothes on her back. An unmarried woman had plenty to worry about as her age advanced.

Clarissa glanced at Mary, who was fortunate in that she could be a lady's companion, but her allowance wasn't enough to enable her to save for the future, and her position here likely wouldn't be permanent. Was it any wonder that women learned to play the part of the proper young lady, complete with an education in French, singing, music, and dancing? None of those things predicted what kind of wife or mother a woman might be, but those were certainly highly sought-after skills during courtship.

How odd the world was.

"Would you . . ." Clarissa said, but her voice trailed off weakly. She wasn't entirely sure she dared make the suggestion.

"Mmm?" Mary said offhandedly. She glanced up from her needlework, caught Clarissa's gaze, and looked back up. "What is it? Are you unwell?"

Goodness, she must look awfully serious—or ill—for Mary to ask such a thing.

"I cannot help but think that perhaps there are some couples who find love this way."

Mary leaned forward, eyes suddenly alive like the flicker of a candle flame. "You want to place an advertisement?"

"Heavens no," Clarissa said, shaking her head. "I thought perhaps we could visit Needham's Coffee House and . . . observe."

The women's eyes locked for a moment as each thought through what she was suggesting.

"Women don't usually frequent coffee houses," Mary said warily.

"Only because so many men go there to talk over matters of business. There's nothing untoward at a coffee house that would put a lady's reputation in danger, is there?"

Mary seemed to be thinking over the question as if her thoughts were swirling water in the side pool within a brook.

"A certain lady might go to Needham's Coffee House to respond to a Once Seen message," Clarissa said. "Or perhaps Mr. E.S. will visit to see if she has replied."

With a slow nod, Mary spoke, but she kept her voice quiet. "Needham's is a common location for many such . . . message exchanges. I've never looked inside Needham's. Do you suppose it's entirely filled with men like Lloyd's Coffee House is? I'd rather we *not* be the only women present."

A smile crept across Clarissa's face. "We're going? I imagine it isn't more than a stroll of twenty minutes from here. Shall we?" She set her needlework aside and stood.

"Now?" Mary stared at her blankly. "You're in earnest."

"Indeed I am," Clarissa said, feeling more emboldened with every tick of the clock on the mantel.

Her companion stood as well, though less confidently. "Your father . . ."

"If he learns of our outing, I'll insist you didn't want to go, but you accompanied me to ensure that my reputation remained untarnished. At least part of that is true." She grinned. "I suspect, however, that your curiosity about the Once Seen gentleman and lady is piqued as well. Can you honestly say that trying to discover what happens isn't as exciting as any of your novels?"

Mary's eyes trailed to the table. Its drawer held a copy of

Joseph Andrews, her most recent acquisition. Not everyone approved of such books; some called them outright lies because the stories were inventions.

"This story could definitely be more exciting," Mary said. "And it would be *real*."

"I certainly hope so," Clarissa said. "I'll be bitterly disappointed if the gentleman turns out to be a snake hiding in a bag that's supposed to be filled with eels."

Two

"I WAS DAFT TO FALL prey to your persuasions in coming here," Charles Ballam said as he stood against the wall of the ballroom beside John Doughty, his closest friend and formerly his battalion commander in the war with the colonies.

"Stuff and nonsense," Doughty said without even looking at Charles. His mischievous grin was ample evidence that he was avidly listening. "It's past time you ventured back into society. Soldiers need things such as balls to re-civilize them."

"Are you implying that military service turns one into an uncivilized beast?"

"Not precisely."

At Charles's raised brow, Doughty laughed and went on.

"I'd argue that bullets, mud, and freezing winters are hardly conducive to fostering a genteel disposition. No matter how refined a man once was, some degree of coarseness will arise through such experiences. Therefore, returning to proper, civilized society, where people speak and behave properly, is prudent." Doughty certainly sounded serious, but Charles recognized the glint in his former superior's eye as containing humor despite speaking some measure of truth.

"I shall endure the night, though I confess I'll miss being able to use the occasional profane term without fear of anyone gasping in horror."

Doughty chuckled quietly and took a sip of his drink. "I'd rather enjoy watching that."

"Assuming you are correct in my need to be re-civilized, couldn't such an endeavor be commenced with something less chaotic and cramped than a ball? An afternoon tea, perhaps? A ride through a park. A visit to the theater."

"The last one would include at least as many people as a ball," Doughty noted.

"Ah, but *not* people I would need to speak or dance with except during intermission," Charles countered.

"And before and after the play."

Charles grunted. "Never mind. The theater is not as good a proposal as I'd first thought." He gestured ahead, where dancers wove formations and women's gowns twirled about. "Virtually anything would be better than . . . this . . . as one's first outing."

War showed things to a man that were darker and deeper than a crush of people flouncing about in an attempt to outdo one another. "I'd argue that this behavior"—Charles tilted his head forward, indicating the dancers—"is not unlike the behavior of some animals. Hardly civilized."

"Such as?"

"The peacock pales compared to this display. Here, both sexes are prancing about in an attempt to woo the other."

Doughty nearly choked on his drink. "Surely you don't yearn for tea with scones and clotted cream, complete with marmalade and a spoonful of local gossip?"

"I don't *yearn* for any posturing and matrimonial

stratagem. Alas, it's a game of chess we all must play." Charles sighed and eyed his glass of punch. "A pity this isn't made of stronger stuff."

He would've happily downed a bottle of port at the moment to numb himself from the discomfort of the ball, with its societal scheming. To think there had been a time when he'd enjoyed social gatherings; even balls felt like a memory belonging to someone else entirely. The years he'd spent abroad with the military had changed him in significant ways. Time alone could change a man, but witnessing disease and suffering, seeing—and inflicting—death... Those left fixed marks on a man's soul.

He'd changed externally as well, of course. His skin had toughened and wrinkled slightly. That week he'd found his first few gray hairs. All visible reminders that the war had aged him prematurely. Those things did not bother him. If his hair went entirely white, he'd never again need to consider whether to powder his hair. The fact that the fashion was starting to slip away was immaterial.

One external change did bother him, however—a remnant of war he was loath to reveal to anyone. His right hand was lame, the result of blocking a flaming piece of metal flying toward Doughty. By some miracle, the field surgeon hadn't amputated his hand—likely because others were bleeding out and would die without attention. The pain had sometimes made him wish for death, but he remained very much alive, largely due to the ministrations of his commander. Doughty had rinsed the wounds morning and night with half of his own daily ration of rum and kept it wrapped in as clean of cloths as they could find. The wound hadn't become foul, and the hand had healed. As much as it ever would, anyway.

He'd forever more have two fingers missing from that

hand, and those that remained didn't function as they should. He couldn't do much with that hand. He'd had to learn to write, eat, and do nearly everything else with his left. That alone raised eyebrows—proper gentlemen used the right hand for those things. He had three options: to never eat in front of another human again, to have a servant feed him as if he were an infant, or to eat with his left hand, his disfigured right one resting in his lap.

As a young man, he'd disliked wearing gloves, but now he praised the skies for the custom. Gloves prevented others from seeing his skin melted in some parts and gnarled in others. The overall appearance was not unlike a sickly crab's claw. He remained eternally grateful that he'd kept his thumb and that gloves were proper attire for all in public.

He simply stuffed his gloves with cotton to disguise the missing fingers. He'd built up the strength in that arm again, which is how Doughty had convinced him that his efforts meant he'd be able to dance at a ball without revealing his disfigurement.

The ballroom air felt thick. Charles's cravat seemed to tighten around his neck. "This was a mistake. How am I to meet a young woman when I cannot take her hand properly as I bow? My arm may be strong enough to hold up my blasted hand, but it cannot properly hold a lady's. They'll see me as a deformed creature, not a marriage prospect."

"Come, my good man," Doughty said, slapping him on the back. "You have two strong legs and feet, a perfectly good left hand, and a handsome face women swoon over."

Charles raised a dubious eyebrow at the latter claim, and Doughty hurried on. "I know. A fellow gentleman can never be a good judge of such things. But I've heard ladies discussing you." Doughty abandoned the amused tone and added, "You might not have the hand you once did, but you have far more than many men can boast of after the war."

His words hung in the air for a moment. Doughty was right. Who was Charles to complain about a hand when he yet had his life? He was otherwise in good health and had a future that likely included a decent sum to live on. All far more than many men had. Yet he did not want a future with the essentials in life if it meant being alone.

"I see guilt is your latest tool," Charles said, trying to retain some levity despite his more somber thoughts. "I cannot say I favor that approach."

"My dear Ballam, if, as you have declared on multiple occasions, you wish to find a wife and create a home, then you'll most likely manage it by meeting young women at an occasion such as this." He gestured toward the floor. "I'm trying to help you find happiness. It's some small repayment of the debt I owe you for saving my life."

The two men gazed flatly at each other for a moment. Charles finally broke the stare, whispering "Blast you" under his breath. "I hate that you're right."

Doughty laughed and slapped him on the back again. "I may be only ten years your senior, but I still feel a bit of a paternal duty toward you. Now come. Let's meet those fine ladies standing by the column there. They're conversing with Mr. Reddenfield, whom I know from the bank. He can introduce us."

One of the ladies in question, wearing pale yellow, Charles had noted earlier. Now he had the opportunity to become acquainted with her. The night might turn in a positive direction after all. He tipped back the rest of his drink and set the glass on the tray of a passing footman.

"Very well. Let's go," he said, knowing his tone sounded comically similar to the one he'd used before battle.

"Glad to see that the manly fortitude I once knew is not entirely dead," Doughty said dryly.

Charles grunted at that, though truly, he was more grateful than annoyed. As he followed Doughty through the crowd, he rehearsed what he might say to the young woman he was about to be introduced to—the first young lady he might dance with in far more years than he cared contemplate.

They made slow progress due to acquaintances stopping Doughty every few steps. Each time, Charles inclined his head and said the requisite pleasantries. More than once the person was an older woman with an eligible daughter whom she was eager to introduce to Charles.

Doughty gave them every attention, lingering in several conversations. Charles grew restless; he'd built up his courage to be introduced to the young lady in yellow, and these interim introductions were slowly draining him. He felt like a solider maintaining a heightened level of readiness in the face of a dozen delays.

Am I truly comparing rituals of courtship to battle?

He'd promised Doughty to give the ball a sincere effort, and that included not only asking a lady to dance but also acting the part of a gentleman who was happy to meet as many eligible young ladies as crossed his path. Doughty was clearly holding him to that part of the agreement, and Charles had to admit that he was gradually losing some of the anxiousness about meeting the woman in yellow. He had yet to take anyone's hand or escort a lady to a position on the floor, but pleasantries were becoming easier to perform.

A woman introducing herself as Mrs. Merrywell stopped them. She stood at least as tall as Doughty and wore a gaudy dress of puce. With hands larger than Doughty's, she held his arm in her ample grasp. Doughty listened to Mrs. Merrywell praise his military bravery, followed by extolling her daughter's beauty. The only notable thing about her speech was the volume, which was loud enough that it would be a wonder if dogs on the other side of London didn't hear.

The Miss Merrywell in question wore a gown only slightly less garish than her mother's, but unlike her mother she spoke in such a quiet voice that, despite leaning in to hear, neither Doughty nor Charles could make out more than a periodic syllable. Her gown, however, was of such an intense shade of pink that it might as well have had a voice of its own, more than making up for her personal lack of volume.

At length, Doughty extracted his arm from Mrs. Merrywell's grip and wished mother and daughter good evening. When they'd moved along, Doughty whispered, "In case there's any question, I don't expect you to consider her daughter as a prospect."

As they rounded the last corner, a glint of green drew Charles's eye. He followed its movement until his gaze lay upon the dancer who wore it. One moment was all it took to banish the yellow-gowned woman from his mind and find himself transfixed by a woman in jade.

She had thick auburn hair, a near-perfect complexion, and she moved with the elegance of a swan. Something more drew him to her, more than her beauty, something in the expressiveness of her face or the spark of humor in her eyes. He could not pull his gaze away.

The music ended, and she curtsied to her partner, her skirts pooling on the floor briefly. She straightened and turned, making the golden slash of her underskirt visible, which seemed to illuminate her face almost as if the sun, long since set, had broken through the roof and spilled its light upon her.

She took her partner's elbow, but before they moved off the floor, she slowed her step as if sensing something or hearing someone call her name. She looked across the crowd, and she saw him—Charles Ballam. In that moment, which felt timeless yet too brief, his heart soared.

If this evening would bring him an introduction to *this* lady, he'd consider the venture a success, no matter where the acquaintance did or did not lead. He simply wished to speak with the haunting beauty in deep green.

"Doughty," he said, reaching for his friend but finding only air. His friend turned back, brows raised in question. "Do you know her?"

"Who?"

"The young lady in green." He turned to find her and point her out more obviously, but the crowd had swallowed her up. The woman was nowhere to be seen.

Three

Clarissa's partner returned her to Mary's side in a corner of the ballroom, thanked her again for the dance, and soon disappeared in the crush.

"I daresay Mr. Denham is one of the handsomest men in attendance," Mary said, still gazing in the direction he'd retreated.

"Yes, he is," Clarissa answered absently. If someone had looked at her then, they might have assumed she was looking in the same direction as Mary, where Mr. Denham had gone. In truth, she was looking for someone else.

Mary stepped before her, blocking her vision and bringing Clarissa back from the lands of gossamer thoughts she'd floated away to. "Are you quite well? You look somewhat flushed." She glanced back over her shoulder in the direction Mr. Denham had gone. "He appeared quite besotted with you. He'd make a good match, I daresay, one your father would be quite happy to arrange."

"Yes, he would," Clarissa said. Even to her own ears, her voice sounded far away.

"Is something amiss with him?" Mary asked, sounding distinctly worried.

"Nothing at all," Clarissa said. "He's handsome, an excellent dancer, an adequate conversationalist."

"He comes from a good family. He attended Oxford," Mary added.

"Yet I don't care." Truly a mystery, as Mr. Denham seemed to possess everything a young woman was supposed to wish for in a husband. Despite all that, she hadn't the slightest interest in him.

Mary asked in a whisper that feigned a scandalous tone, "Perhaps he has an odor that offends?"

That made Clarissa chuckle. Oh, she was grateful for her companion. What would she do without Mary?

"I can happily report to the contrary." Clarissa couldn't prevent her gaze from flitting across the room in hopes of seeing the man who'd caught her eye at the end of the set.

"Come. Tell me what is occupying your mind," Mary said. "I can tell it's busy in some fashion, and I want to know with what."

"It's nothing." Clarissa forced her gaze away from the crowd, though she knew Mary would sense that she wasn't speaking the whole of it. For Clarissa did know, at least in part, the reason Mr. Denham commanded no space in her thoughts: the other man—the one with a name she did not know and a face she would never forget.

"Tell me," Mary said. "It's no use trying to keep a secret from me. You know I'll cajole it out of you eventually."

"I—" Clarissa took a breath for fortitude. "This will sound like a perfectly silly tale, but . . . I saw someone else as the set ended. Perhaps I imagined it, but for a moment I felt certain he was looking right at me, and—" She scoffed. "No. It's daft." She shook her head and turned away, walking toward a corner of the room where she might think more clearly.

"Who?" Mary's voice went up an octave in excitement, and she immediately began looking over the crowd. With countless guests in the room, finding one man would have been difficult even if it had been a relative. She hadn't so much as the slightest description of him, which placed her action quite firmly in the category of vain pursuits. "Where? What does he look like?"

"Doesn't matter," Clarissa said, though his image remained clearly in her mind. He had eyes the color of the sky after a storm and light-brown hair possessing a slight curl, which made taming it a challenge, as evidenced by a lock that had escaped the ribbon at his nape. That bit of hair had hung across his temple, making Clarissa's heart patter strangely.

Silly girl. Getting excited over a glance and a lock of hair. He'd likely been looking at someone behind her, yet even if he had noted her, why would he feel anything but a passing interest? He certainly wouldn't have felt as she did, that fate had brought him there, that he knew her, and that in some inexplicable way, she knew him too.

"The stories about men and women finding love the moment they see each other . . . I wish they were true," Clarissa said to no one in particular.

Mary slipped her arm through Clarissa's and patted her hand. "I do too, my dear."

"Love matches *do* exist," Clarissa said. "My parents had one, and my mother wanted one for me too."

"I know," Mary said quietly. "Let's go for a walk outside. The air is rather hot and thick in here."

"Yes, let's," Clarissa said, and the two of them headed for the doors that led to the terrace and gardens out back. The entire way she couldn't help but look at every man she passed in case it was the striking man with the blue-gray eyes, but no such luck.

The cool night air was a relief as it reached her, and with the breeze, something else came over her as well: thoughts of the day her mother, in bed with consumption and only weeks from her passing, gave Clarissa some prints and told her the story they portrayed.

The tale showed the folly of marrying for social or financial gain, and while Clarissa enjoyed looking at the images, the thing she treasured most from that day was her mother's yearning for Clarissa to be truly loved by a man.

"Don't marry for money or title," Mother had said, then coughed for several long seconds, bringing up bright-red blood.

Clarissa had heard the physician telling her father that such blood was an omen, that there was nothing he could do now. Her fate was sealed. That day, Clarissa had stared at the handkerchief and its scarlet stain. Had Mother heard what the physician had said?

"Promise me you'll marry for love," her mother had said after catching her breath.

"I promise, Mother."

Now a grown woman, Clarissa stood outside the ball and sniffed. Her vision blurred.

"What is it?" Mary asked softly.

Clarissa glanced around to ensure that they had a modicum of privacy. She took a few steps closer to a columnar tree before speaking, and Mary followed. "As a girl, I believed I'd find a love match easily enough."

"Oh." Mary sighed. "It's not so easy after all, is it?" She, too, came from a good family, had a proper dowry, yet she'd never married, and, seeing as she was past thirty, likely never would.

Clarissa dabbed a handkerchief to her eyes and then worried the cloth between her fingers. "Mary, we've never discussed such matters in relation to *you.*" She glanced up, and for a moment her companion looked stunned, her eyes widening so much Clarissa didn't know whether she was shocked or merely surprised.

"We've certainly discussed matters of matrimony," Mary said, clearly trying to sound lighthearted, but her voice had thickened with emotion. "After all, we've spent hours reading and commenting on Once Seen and Lonely Hearts advertisements, and we've had loads of conversations about such things on our walks."

"Yes, we have," Clarissa said quietly. That wasn't what Clarissa meant, and she felt sure they both knew so. Mary suddenly coughed to clear her throat and turned slightly away. Clarissa wondered if her friend had tears of her own welling.

Suddenly she had to know Mary's heart—what she'd done with her hopes and dreams when she'd become a companion after several failed Seasons. How she envisioned her future. How she'd felt about it then and had prepared herself for it. How she felt now. For everything Mary had experienced and felt then and now were things that might be in Clarissa's future.

"Did . . . did you ever come close to marrying?"

For a moment Mary didn't move. Then she lowered her chin and stared at a nearby shrub. A tear, silver in the moonlight, slid down her cheek. "No," she said, her tone pinched, close to crying. "Oh, I had gentlemen who caught *my* eye, but I did not attract anyone's attention, not in *four* Seasons."

Clarissa hadn't realized it had been so many.

Mary sniffed and glanced at Clarissa with a shrug. "I suppose my adequate-but-not-impressive dowry wasn't enough to tempt anyone without beauty attached to it. I have never been a beauty or a girl with a silver tongue, flirtatious looks, or whatever it is young women do to make men swoon. I refused to behave as if I had wool in my head, though friends warned me that men do not like intelligent women. When that was proved true, I thought perhaps I should pretend to be silly and empty-minded, but apparently, I lack the capacity for feigning stupidity." She laughed ruefully. "Which perhaps is itself a kind of stupidity." After a sigh, she straightened her shoulders as if steeling herself against the future—an adversary to every unmarried woman in society.

"Do you wish you'd have managed it?" Clarissa asked. "Catching a man with flirtations?"

Silence stretched between them as Mary pondered. Clarissa didn't interject, waiting as her friend formed an answer. She must know that this conversation was about her own future as much as Mary's past.

"No," Mary finally said. "I don't. I believe that entering such a union without a clear idea of who you've chosen to be paired with seems like the best way to ensure you'll have a miserable marriage." She took a deep breath and let it out. "Sometimes I wish that someone might have wanted me as I was—and as I am. Yet I cannot complain. I am more fortunate than many. When I am too old to be a lady's companion, I will have the means to live—simply, but well enough, if alone."

Clarissa hadn't given much thought to a spinster's later years. Having food and shelter would be a blessing, but the prospect of living her later years in solitude sounded dreadful. How much better to have a man at her side whom she loved, with children, and later grandchildren, to warm her soul.

Understanding her friend in a way she never had before,

Clarissa rested her head on Mary's shoulder, and the two shed tears as they looked over the gardens. Few stars were visible due to smog, but the moon broke through with a faint glow that seemed to echo their dreams from younger years.

I might not ever find a love match, Clarissa thought. *My future could be lonely.*

Yet even as she acknowledged the realities before her, she couldn't keep away the memory of the man with the piercing blue-gray eyes.

Four

CHARLES AND DOUGHTY REACHED THE small group at the column. "Mr. Rathmull," Doughty said to the man with a powdered wig and a thin mustache, an unusual but not unheard-of combination.

"A pleasure to see you again." Doughty bowed.

The elderly gentleman, round enough in the middle to assure any bystander that he certainly did not lack for appetite, nodded. "Delighted to see you again."

Doughty gestured toward Charles. "I'm pleased to introduce Mr. Charles Ballam, who served in my battalion. Mr. Ballam, this is Mr. Rathmull, a banker of high esteem, in whom I entrust my business needs."

The two exchanged pleasantries, but when the older man didn't introduce his daughter, Doughty asked—surely to imply the desire for a further introduction—"How is your family faring? You have at least one daughter yet unmarried, I recall?"

Charles briefly caught the eye of the young lady in question, dressed in a lovely pale yellow gown, who stood beside a couple who were likely her parents. She returned his smile with her own shy one, complete with opening her fan with a flick and modestly shielding the lower portion of her face.

"Goodness," Mr. Rathmull said. "Apologies for my lack of manners." He opened one arm to the side, a gesture that invited his wife and daughter closer. "Mr. Doughty, Mr. Ballam, this is my wife, Mrs. Rathmull, and our daughter, Miss Edith Rathmull. She is my youngest and, if I may so, the apple of my eye."

Her mother held out a gloved hand to the men, and, blushing, Miss Rathmull did the same. Doughty took Mrs. Rathmull by the fingertips, bowed and brushed the glove with his lips. "A pleasure, Mrs. Rathmull," he said, then did the same for the daughter.

Miss Rathmull curtsied at that and then held out her hand to Charles, who now stood as still as the frozen Hudson River, staring at two feminine hands extended to him. He'd intended to use his left hand in greeting them, but now that the moment was here, he felt as if he must use his right hand. Yet that hand lacked the ability to grasp anything. If he were to attempt anything like it, they'd likely feel the odd weight of a hand that lacked muscle and coordination. They might also note his missing fingers.

Doughty cleared his throat, a gentle way to encourage Charles to act. He did what he should have done initially—he took both women's fingertips with his *left* hand. Better to have a successful action, even if it wasn't precisely in line with expectations, than to have none at all. He bowed first to the mother and then the daughter.

When he straightened, Miss Rathmull withdrew her hand and exchanged a look of mutual confusion with her mother, but she was discussing a new speculation venture with Doughty and noticed nothing. Miss Rathmull dismissed the reaction almost as soon as it had appeared, so quickly that Charles contemplated whether he'd imagined it. Then he chased away worry altogether. Confusion, if that's what he saw, was far preferable to several other possibilities.

"Would you do me the honor of being my partner in the quadrille?"

Miss Rathmull bobbed a curtsy. "I'd be delighted."

"I believe it won't begin for a spell," Doughty said. "Perhaps you could take a turn about the room, get some refreshment, and become better acquainted first?"

Charles flashed him a look. He'd only ventured to *speak* with a woman he didn't know. Must Doughty shove him entirely into the pool by demanding a long conversation, as well?

"That would be lovely," Miss Rathmull said. And that decided it. She crossed the distance and slipped her hand through his left elbow—a good omen, he hoped—and they took a turn about the room.

"Tell me, where are you from?" Charles asked, an attempt at conversation. Goodness, loading a flintlock musket felt more natural than socializing with a woman he'd just met.

"Born and reared in London, in Belgravia," she said. "But that's hopelessly dull. I hope to travel the Continent and spend time in Paris." She flashed a flirtatious smile and cocked her head in a way that seemed to emphasize the little star-shaped beauty patch above her lip. "Have you been to the Continent?"

"Several times," Charles said. Goodness, this was awkward.

They reached the refreshment table, where Miss Rathmull took it upon herself to fetch herself some punch. As she returned, someone called his name, and Charles turned to look for Doughty. At the same moment, Miss Rathmull pressed one of the glasses into Charles's right hand.

He'd scarcely realized what was happening until it was too late. He tried to grasp it with his left, but the glass fell and shattered, sending shards in all directions, past the widening pool of punch at their feet.

"Oh!" Miss Rathmull said, hopping backward as if that would undo the splattered mess of her gown. She bumped into the table and could withdraw no farther.

His neck hot with embarrassment, Charles said, "Forgive me. I'm so clumsy," then looked about for a solution. Instead, his boot caught a particularly slippery spot of the mess, and he fell to his knees. Humiliation flared through him.

Before he could scramble to his feet, a servant came to clean the mess—but did not see him. With the heel of his boot, the man stepped squarely on Charles's fingers—the remaining ones. The sudden jolt made Charles yank his hand back and suck air between his teeth, shaking his hand against the pain.

When the stars in his vision had cleared, he became keenly aware that a sudden, eerie quiet had descended over that portion of the ballroom. He looked up to see a circle of witnesses gaping at him.

Rather not at *him*.

Or at the spilled punch or the splinters of glass.

They were instead gaping at his warped, misshapen right hand, pulled free from the glove when he'd yanked it from under the servant's boot.

He snatched the glove from the floor, got to his feet, and attempted to shove his hand back into it. The wet leather made it difficult, and as his right hand was no use in aiding the endeavor, he failed, so he shoved the glove into his waistcoat pocket.

Only then did he note Miss Rathmull. She stared, pale

with fear as if she beheld a monster. She gripped the edge of the table as if for strength, then took a few steps along its perimeter, holding it the entire way as she increased the distance between them. When she reached the end of the table, she turned away and fled out of the ballroom altogether.

Charles stood there alone, covered in punch, splinters of glass, and humiliation.

Five

CLARISSA AND MARY SET OUT for a stroll through neighboring businesses and the nearby park, or so they told her father. They'd been going on such outings almost daily for nearly a fortnight now, ever since their first visit to Needham's Coffee House. This was their first stroll since the ball in Mayfair, and Clarissa had more than Lonely Hearts advertisements on her mind—the man with the steely eyes.

Father and Topham stood at the door of Carrington House as the ladies left, tying on their bonnets and stepping down to the street.

"If you happen to pass Morton's," Mr. Amesbury said, "would you ask when he anticipates my hat being ready?"

"I most certainly will," Clarissa said.

"Enjoy the exercise," her father said, lifting a hand in a wave. "I do believe it's doing you good. You have a new spring to your step and a color in your cheeks."

Mary, who faced the street and therefore whose back was to Mr. Amesbury, silently chuckled. She grinned like a hyena. No doubt if a single giggle escaped, she'd sound like one too. In the wake of Mary's amusement, schooling her own face took all of Clarissa's effort.

"I'm glad you think so," she replied to her father. "These afternoon walks have been most enjoyable."

After he returned to the house and Topham had closed the door, Clarissa took her companion's arm and hurried her down the lane, not daring to so much as speak a word until they'd turned a corner, where not even a window into the house could betray them.

"You nearly ruined everything," Clarissa finally said. Her jovial tone belied the scolding words. "Truly, we must be careful. Father will suspect something is awry and possibly put a stop to our visits to . . . places."

In addition to Needham's, they'd taken to stopping at a nearby circulating library, a milliner, and a few other businesses mentioned in advertisements as messaging locations.

"That would be a pity," Mary agreed.

For Clarissa, it would be a particular disappointment, as the advertisements and their efforts to find any of the individuals behind them had provided a distraction from her constant thoughts of the man at the ball.

Every time she thought of him, her cheeks pinked and her heart increased its pace. Seeing as she knew nothing about him, and that her reaction to merely his glance was foolish, she fought to cast him out of her mind. Discussing the latest advertisements helped. If they did not keep him entirely out of her mind, they nudged him to the periphery.

"Your father cannot protest his daughter and her companion going to local shops, can he?" Mary said. "There's nothing untoward about that."

"He may think otherwise about coffee houses, seeing as the only women we've seen in them thus far are servers and a proprietor," Clarissa countered. "But he wouldn't look upon our activities with favor, no matter how proper they are, if he learns we haven't been entirely honest."

"We *do* stroll about businesses," Mary said. "And we always finish our exploration with a walk about Hyde Park or a small one nearby. We aren't telling any falsehoods." They always made sure to return with reports about a delightful ribbon at the milliner's, flowers for sale, or, as today, news on when his hat would be ready.

"Yet we aren't telling him that the advertisements he disapproves of are the reason for our outings."

Mary gave her a sidelong look with one eyebrow lifted into a high arch. "Forgive me. I thought I was the companion of a grown lady, not the nursemaid of a child."

Clarissa returned the look with an arched brow of her own but then laughed. "I suppose my conscience is a bit overly sensitive. We've not done anything nefarious. And we haven't even had success in our innocent ventures."

"Alas," Mary added with a wistful sigh.

Indeed, despite avidly following the Lonely Heart advertisements, they had yet to see anyone responding to such a message. They'd not witnessed one person, male or female, consulting with Mrs. Passmore at Needham's, or any other of the contact people mentioned in any of the advertisements, whether someone replying to an advertisement or looking for replies to their own.

Their first visit was particularly disappointing, as both Clarissa and Mary had created a castle-in-a-cloud fantasy. In it, they sat at a table, and the moment after they'd received their coffee, a woman would enter. *The* woman in the Once Seen advertisement. They knew because she wore the same blue gown from the theater.

Their dream had included the man who'd placed the advertisement. He'd be at Needham's as well, waiting in hopeful expectation, also adorned in the ensemble he'd worn to the theater. He'd stand at the counter, counseling with

Mrs. Passmore about how long to wait for a reply from the woman he'd fallen in love with. A few steps would sound on the wooden floorboards, and the murmur of conversations would still. All would turn to watch as the woman practically floated toward the man who was destined to be her husband.

He'd sense a shift in the room as if a cloud had moved away from the sun. He'd turn around. His gaze would land on her, and in an instant, the couple would know they'd found each other.

Of course, none of that had happened.

After walking a block or two in their own thoughts, Clarissa asked, "Where are we going first today?"

Mary usually made those decisions, as the outings were mostly due to her interest in the stories. "Needham's," Mary said.

"And who do you think we might chance to come upon today?"

"Hmm," Mary replied. "Much easier to say whom I *hope* to come upon."

The London Mercury, the daily paper to which the Amesbury household subscribed, had published half a dozen more Lonely Hearts advertisements referring interested parties to various establishments.

Both Clarissa and Mary had favorites about the individuals who hid behind the notices, as well as about those who might respond to them—though many lacked the potential for romantic ideas, such as advertisements using terms and phrases that seemed an attempt to hint at darker truths. Perhaps that the man was old, infirm, ugly to look upon, destitute, or desperate to fulfill gambling debts—or perhaps three sheets to the wind every day by teatime.

"Who do you hope to happen upon?" Clarissa asked, though she suspected she knew.

"E.S.," Mary said.

"I would have thought S.P."

That gentleman's advertisement had appeared that very day and had a tragic tone. *Widowed gentleman with darling child of two years in search of a wife to love and who will love his child as her own.*

His situation nearly made Mary swoon that morning. The advertisement went on to describe the man as having a moderate-size fortune, good health, and a respectful business. Then it listed the preferred age range and other details for the lady.

"I suspect S.P. won't look for a reply so soon as the same day. He probably has business to attend to, and, of course, his child to see after, and we don't know how far he lives from Covent Garden. He might be able to visit Mrs. Passmore but once a fortnight."

"Excellent points," Clarissa said.

They reached the door to Needham's. An exiting gentleman held it open for the ladies and nodded a greeting, which they returned. They found a table in the back, where they'd be less noticeable. Two newspapers sat atop the table. Mrs. Passmore subscribed to several, which encouraged patrons to read and linger.

Since the advertisements began on the first page, one had no need to read surreptitiously. Besides, many weren't for love at all but for things as mundane as renting a cottage or selling a peach tree. One could feign interest in the most pressing news of the day—in the left column— whether that be scandal in the aristocracy or a military victory abroad.

Mary immediately began perusing the right column of the *Leicester Gazette*. "I wonder if E.S. has heard the woman from the theater." She was quickly consumed by reading the advertisements in the *Gazette*, so much so that Clarissa requested coffee and scones for them both.

Clarissa took it upon herself not to read at the same time, for one of them should remain alert so they wouldn't miss the clandestine meetings they hoped to witness. She glanced about the coffee house, taking care not to stare at anyone.

"This one," Mary said, sliding the *Gazette* across the wooden table. "It's terribly sad."

"You'll watch?"

"For E.S., S.P., and anyone else," Mary said with a knowing nod, and Clarissa tucked in to read.

A lady of about four and twenty, in possession of an independent fortune, solicits the attention of a gentleman of birth and education. Due to the ill usage of her relations, who have the intent of robbing her of her fortune and leaving her destitute, she seeks a gentleman who can stand forth as her protector. He will be rewarded with her affections and her fortune. Address letters to Persephone at Horn Tavern, where the utmost discretion is ensured.

"Poor girl," Clarissa said. "She's somewhat educated, seeing as she chose Persephone for her nom de plume. Likely sees herself as living a hellish existence to be saved from."

"A rather apropos name," Mary agreed. "Yet she directs letters to a *tavern.*"

"That's not so disreputable," Clarissa countered. "It may be the best she can do in a dire situation. Perhaps she lets a room above it."

They imagined the woman who'd placed the advertisement, what her relations were like, and who, precisely, among them was out for revenge against her—a stepmother? A jealous cousin? Sister?

"My dear Miss Amesbury, what are you doing here, of all places?"

Clarissa startled to the sound of her brother's voice. She

glanced up to see Ethan's jovial smirk and blushed hotly. "Enjoying an outing with my companion, as you can see." She slid the cup and saucer closer to her but didn't partake, unwilling to reveal her trembling hands.

With flair, Ethan flicked the tails of his coat backward and sat beside Clarissa. For her part, Mary did poorly in her attempt to hide a smile; her mouth definitely twitched. Clarissa shot her a look, which only made the twitching worse.

"What would Father say if he saw you here?"

"Nothing whatsoever," Clarissa declared. "We are doing nothing wrong."

Ethan eyed the newspapers, then tapped one with his finger. "One wonders what Father would think of discussions about scandalous advertisements." He opened his mouth in comic shock.

"Are you here to shame me? Or threaten to tell Father?" Oh, goodness. What if he did?

Ethan must have sensed her dismay. "Forgive me. Abandoning the brotherly instinct to torment one's elder sister is far more difficult than one might imagine."

Elder sister. He wasn't yet married, but he had no worries on that count. Age mattered little to a man with a good fortune. He could marry a young woman of beauty and means no matter how the years marched on. The unjustness of life sometimes felt like a thorn in one's slipper—a constant, inevitable pain one could ignore for only so long.

"You *won't* tell him?" she asked quietly.

Ethan, bless him, shook his head. "I won't. You have my word. But *I've* had my suspicions, so I followed you. If I suspected something was afoot, Father might just as easily discover your visits and put a stop to them. I wanted to warn you."

"In that case, thank you, dear brother," Clarissa said. He'd once been little more than a pest to her, and though that mischievous nature hadn't gone anywhere, he'd grown into a good man with a kind, if impish, heart. "We'll be more discreet."

Ethan stood and chuckled. "Just don't get entangled with any of those," he said, gesturing toward the *Gazette*. "Reading them and hoping to find the authors is one thing; responding to one would be a scandal of another size entirely." He gave her a quick peck on the cheek and headed out the door.

Only when it thudded behind him did his words settle into Clarissa's heart, though certainly not as the warning he'd intended.

What if she *did* reply to an advertisement? What if she placed one herself?

She had no idea how much they cost, but she probably had enough pin money saved up for such a thing. She didn't spend much, always thinking she'd want to have money for a future need.

Poor Ethan had no idea that his visit to Needham's had only lit up a potentially improper idea in her mind. And with those ideas, thoughts of the Mayfair ball returned.

What if she placed her own Once Seen advertisement in search of her mystery gentleman?

Six

"INDEED I WILL NOT," CHARLES declared with finality. "Placing an advertisement would do nothing but open myself to further public embarrassment."

The humiliation from the Mayfair ball had yet to abate, burning his stomach whenever he thought of it. Almost a week had passed, but the acrid memory would remain far longer.

"Come now, my good chap," Doughty said from across the table at The Black Horse. "It's a certain way to find a wife."

"*Certain*?" Charles scoffed. "Hardly the word I'd use to describe such a puerile venture." He poured some coffee onto his saucer so it could cool. Then he lifted it to his lips to drink, resting the saucer upon his bad right hand and guiding it with his left. Perhaps one day, people would drink from the cup as they did with tea, but until then, he'd eat and drink as closely to customs as he could. Doing so drew less attention.

As he lowered the saucer back to the table, he looked at Doughty. Charles's lips curved dubiously on one side. "I went to the ball as you asked me to. Look what came of that."

"Fair point," Doughty said with a sigh. "I merely wish to see you settled with a good wife and a passel of children."

Deciding to ignore the comment about the number of offspring, Charles addressed the more pointed topic. He leaned forward slightly to increase the odds that their discourse would not be overheard. "You cannot sincerely believe that any respectable woman would respond to such a vulgar thing as an advertisement."

Doughty opened his mouth to reply, but Charles held up a hand to cut off his words before he could speak a single syllable. "Which tells me you are not, in fact, genuine in your attempts to eliminate my bachelorhood."

"Then what, pray tell, *is* my intention?" Doughty asked.

"To make a mockery of me, I suppose."

His friend looked profoundly wounded. "Do you truly think so little of me?"

A stab of guilt pricked Charles in the chest. "Forgive me, John. I've trusted you with my life on the battlefield—you *saved* my life after my injury—and I'd do the same for you."

"You *did* do the same for me," Doughty said.

"Since our return . . . I don't know what to think or do anymore." Charles stared at the basket of scones between them on the table.

Doughty's gaze darted about the room as if he was searching for something, and then he leaned forward as Charles had. "I know a man who found a wife in just such a manner—both highly respectable individuals. He's an MP, and she's from a family you've certainly heard of."

"Who?" he asked, intrigued.

"Ah, can't tell you, can I? Not when such a method of finding a wife is *vulgar*. I would never let the confidence pass my lips of *your* finding a wife in such a way, either."

Charles leaned back in his chair again and pondered.

"I've heard tell that most of the purported advertisements are satiric inventions written by the paper to sell more copies."

"Some may be," Doughty acknowledged. "There was once a publication devoted to such fictions. Today, however, most appear to be authentic."

"I suppose one success story proves that such ventures are, for the most part, fantastic failures." Charles almost—only almost—hoped this might be a way to find a wife, but the idea still seemed preposterous. "Who, besides a public disgrace or a physical monster"—he gestured to himself, meaning both descriptions applied—"would engage in such a preposterous scheme?"

"People who loathe balls," Doughty said flatly.

Charles attempted to maintain an irritated glare, but a smile broke through despite his efforts. He even laughed—and far louder than he had in ages. "Touché. At times, I think no one will have me. I'm not a full man; I'm a maimed one."

"You underestimate yourself," Doughty said.

"For someone in my situation, perhaps . . ." Charles spoke slowly, carefully. "And I say this without any hint of intention, only pondering possibilities—perhaps an advertisement *could* be a way to find a wife."

"*Your situation*," Doughty repeated, and rolled his eyes.

"I'm hardly in a position to make grand demands. I should be grateful if *any* woman would have me."

"No matter how much you belittle yourself, my aim will remain finding you a love match. Seeing as you are pondering the possibility, let me say that I've heard that many types of men place such advertisements."

Charles narrowed his eyes, half challenging, half curious. "What types?"

"Gentlemen unable to attend other social gatherings

due to time constraints, business matters, or distance from them." Doughty tipped his head back to finish his coffee straight from the cup instead of cooling it in the saucer first. He clapped the cup onto the table. "I'd venture some are much like you—men who do not wish to play to society's games that expect us to dance, preen, and otherwise look like fools to find a match. When you can state clearly who you are and describe the type of person you are looking for"— Doughty tapped a newspaper on the table—"you obviate the need for the usual sport of courtship. In fact, when I placed—" Doughty's voice cut off sharply, and his face reddened. He coughed to clear his throat, and he tried to drink from the cup again, though he'd already drained it.

Charles grinned. "You've dabbled in this method yourself."

"You must swear to never tell a soul." It wasn't a direct admission but only a hair short of one.

"The secret will never pass my lips; you have my word." Charles raised his right hand in a promise, then grimaced at the habit of using his bad hand and quickly returned it to his lap. "But how can you be certain of others' propriety? How can you be sure others won't reveal your identity and communications?"

"That's the brilliance of how it works," Doughty said. "The advertisements always include a person who acts as the intermediary—often an owner of a business. The person gives that person a fee for their time *and* for their discretion, as well as a fee for coordinating communications, such as how to tell you about any replies. They can make a good sum carrying out these services, so it remains in their best interest to keep confidences. If word gets out, their reputation as trustworthy intermediaries will crumble."

The whole concept was starting to sound far less daft

than at first hearing. "Can the intermediary place the advertisement for you, or must you do it at the printing office yourself?" Any additional layer of protection from gossips or scandal would be welcome.

"I sent mine with a messenger." Doughty thought so much like Charles that they really could have been brothers.

Charles tilted his head toward the wooden bar, where the owner of The Black Horse, Timothy Pingree, arranged dishes on a shelf. "Is he one such agent?"

His friend glanced over his shoulder at the man in question. "He is, but he knows me, as I frequent The Black Horse. It's here I got the idea when I met a few men who'd come to discuss arrangements with him."

Unable to believe he was considering such a mad proposition, Charles licked his lips and asked, "Who did you hire as your agent?"

Doughty's smile widened as if he'd just won a steeplechase. "Mrs. Passmore at Needham's Coffee House in Covent Garden. She works closely with two papers. I chose the *Leicester Gazette*."

For several minutes, Charles argued with himself over various angles of his friend's proposal. "I'll think on it." He'd convinced himself to do it, but he couldn't say the words yet.

"Good." Doughty took a scone from the basket and grinned. "Because no matter the result of this experiment for me, I insist you try it." He took a bite of the scone, which he'd topped with preserves, then added, "Nothing short of a pack of wolves will alter my ultimate objective: seeing to it that my brother-in-arms finds a wife."

Seven

"This," Clarissa said. "This is the man." She tapped the page several times, seemingly unable to say anything else. Indeed, she couldn't find the clarity of thought to voice how this particular advertisement had affected her. All she knew was that her pulse had quickened, and she felt drawn to the man behind the words in a manner she could not quite understand.

Mary set aside the hat on which she'd been stitching a new ribbon and came over to see the advertisement in question. "You're assuming that whatever the honey-tongued man wrote—or had someone write for him—is truthful."

"Oh, I certainly hope he's real," Clarissa said, holding out the paper and pointing to the spot.

Her companion peered over her shoulder and read the small text aloud. "*Gentleman of almost thirty seeking matrimony with a lady of proper education and a keen mind. Desires a quiet, simple life. His fortune of 6,000 pounds will provide a comfortable living. Has no use for anyone who approves of or mimics Mr. Silvertongue's antics. Address letters to W.H. and deliver to Mrs. Passmore at Needham's Coffee House.*" Mary straightened. "A 'quiet, simple life'?

Perhaps he's embarrassed to be seen or speak in public. He could have a speech impediment or could be terribly old—or ugly." She continued speculating with, "Or he could be lame or disfigured—"

"He's none of those things," Clarissa said, flustered, knowing full well there was no way to know such a thing. "That is, he may be any or all of those things, but none of that matters."

Mary's voice rose at that claim. "None of it?"

"A lie would matter," Clarissa said, "so if he's elderly, then that would bother me, but only because of the falsehood. *This* part is what caught my eye." And, perhaps, a tiny portion of her heart. At least, it had awoken her dreams of finding a love match.

Mary read it again but shrugged in confusion.

"He doesn't approve of Mr. Silvertongue's antics," Clarissa said, as if that made everything as clear as a new windowpane.

"Silvertongue cannot be a real name." Mary made her way back to the settee and spoke her musings as she went.

"It isn't. But this man—W.H.—knows of Silvertongue the character," Clarissa said. "*And* disapproves of him."

"What does that mean?" Mary sounded truly bewildered.

The explanation came from Clarissa in a torrent. "Silvertongue is known for a few things. Among them, as his name implies, for excessive, untrue compliments and general falsehoods. He's also the one arranging the marriage contract. And he later becomes the wife's lover."

"Ah," Mary said, beginning to understand.

"There's more. This means that W.H. wants a love match." An unexpected thrill coursed through Clarissa, as if she'd found a hidden key to her own happiness. "He despises the fakery of many modern marriages and values loyalty, modest living, and honesty. He wants a love match, not a marriage that is little more than a business contract."

"You inferred all of this from his use of the name Silvertongue?" Mary clucked and returned to her stitching. "Don't let your hopes get too close to the sun, my dear. Remember Icarus."

"Icarus was doomed by hubris," Clarissa said, "not hope." She would not surrender her hope, certain as she was that she'd deduced W.H.'s character correctly. "I'll explain." She stood and lifted her skirts to hurry across the room. She selected a book from a shelf, a volume she hadn't opened in years. She opened it not to a page but to six prints that had been tucked between the pages—those given to her by her mother.

"The world is a dangerous and difficult one for a girl to grow up in," Mother had said as she lay on her sickbed, propped by pillows. "The dangers increase as a girl reaches womanhood, when she must survive in a world where a woman's wellbeing largely rests upon the fancies of the men around her. I pray you will not be forced to wed an old cuckold because he needs money and wants a pretty plaything."

Clarissa hadn't known what a *cuckold* was, but it sounded terrible, and she imagined an evil man with horns.

"Your father has set aside enough to provide you with some manner of living so you will not be destitute, and you should have enough of a dowry to attract respectable suitors."

Clarissa had nodded, swallowing against a knot made of worry in her throat for both her mother and herself.

"You shan't go hungry or unsure whether you'll have a place to lay your head. You have an opportunity many girls will never enjoy: the ability to choose a marriage based on love."

Her cold fingers had squeezed Clarissa's warm ones. "Fetch the green book from my dressing table."

Clarissa did as she was told. She climbed back up to the bed and handed the book to her mother, who let it fall open to several pieces of thick paper, each with an illustrated print. "Come sit closer, and I'll tell you the story in these pictures."

She climbed up and nestled herself beside her mother against the mountain of pillows. Then her mother had told the story depicted in the prints known as *Marriage A-la-Mode*. The story showed the progression of a marriage, beginning, as so many did, with a contract.

The circumstance was clearly little more than an arrangement that benefited both families, as the bride-to-be looked none too happy about her impending marriage, and the groom-to-be was interested in nothing but a large mirror and his own reflection in it.

The second print was a scene shortly after they'd wed, with evidence that both parties had squandered money, had unpaid debts, and lived disloyal, lascivious lives.

The third image was of the husband bringing a girl to a doctor. The child's identity wasn't clear, likely either his own or a too-young mistress. Either way, the patch on the husband's neck hinted that he had infected the girl with a disease that Clarissa's mother explained was a sign that he'd been unfaithful and immoral.

The story continued with more debauchery and unraveling of their lives. The fifth panel depicted the tragic end of their marriage. The husband had discovered the wife's adultery and was furious, despite having committed the same offense. The wife's lover had run the husband through with a sword and was escaping through a window. The broken blade lay on the floor near the dying husband beside remnants of masks from the evening's revelry at a masquerade.

The final panel showed the wife, now a countess, moments before death after drinking poison. Her lover was visible through the window—hanged—and an elderly woman held her child with hints that disease has been passed on from the parents.

"Marriage sounds awfully dangerous," Clarissa had said.

"Most—even unhappy ones—do not end in bloodshed," Mother assured her. "But the artist's message is important: If you have the ability, marry for love. Happiness is much more easily attained when your husband loves you, and you love him."

"As you and Father love each other?" Clarissa had asked.

"Precisely." Mother had leaned over and kissed the crown of her head.

Clarissa had never shown the prints to anyone, but now she showed them to Mary and told the story. She didn't mention that she'd heard the tale on Mother's deathbed. Some moments were sacred and not to be shared, even with one's closest friends.

"Remarkable story," Mary said, "but what does it have to do with the advertisement?"

"One of the fathers is a merchant who is eager to marry his child into the aristocracy." Clarissa picked up the first and fifth panels to show Mary. "Look. The lawyer who arranges the contract in the first print is the wife's lover in this one. Note his name." Clarissa pointed to some small text.

"Silvertongue. Ah . . ." Mary nodded with understanding.

"There's more. The artist of these prints was one William Hogarth. Look at the initials in the advertisement."

"W.H. If you're correct in supposing that he's referring to this story . . ." Mary shook her head with a look of ennui. "Would that you could find him."

"You speak as if he cannot be found," Clarissa said as hope brimmed in her chest. "But he's told us how to find him."

If ever there were a man who understood what she wanted in a marriage, it was a man like W.H. If he was this familiar with Hogarth's *Marriage A-la-Mode*, that meant he was educated, likely a gentleman. He clearly had intelligence and wit, not to mention an appreciation for art made for the masses and not only for royalty and the aristocracy.

"If he'd ended the advertisement with a quotation from a Sarah Fyge Egerton poem, I'd consider replying with a proposal of marriage."

"Don't mention *her* again or your father will become apoplectic," Mary said only half joking.

Egerton was known for her poetry arguing for the strengths of women, and many men, especially of Father's generation, had a harsh dislike for Sarah Fyge Egerton, her writings, and anyone who felt kinship with them.

The ladies laughed, and Clarissa dabbed a finger along the lashes of one eye to prevent a tear from falling. "This is all silly, of course. I'd never have the courage to even reply . . . even if he would essentially be, well, perfect."

"He could still be hideous to look upon, with a foul odor and manners not befitting society," Mary said. When Clarissa gave her a look of dismay, she raised a hand in surrender. "Merely stating the truth. Despite the delightful tales we've woven, we don't have the luxury of living in a fairy world. We, alas, are mere mortals, remember."

"How could I forget?" Clarissa stacked the prints in order, slipped them back into the book, and returned the volume to its rightful spot on the shelf. "It's encouraging to think that somewhere in England is a man who views matrimony as I do—and who knows Hogarth's work. Truly, such a thing is most improbable."

Mary tilted her head to one side. "Shall we answer him?"

"I—goodness, no. I—That is—" Playful talk of replying to an advertisement was one thing. Implementing such a thing, quite another. "I don't know that I could bear meeting him and being rejected."

"The masquerade," Mary said, as if the word held all the answers in the world.

"The what?"

"The Kennington masquerade," Mary said. "The invitation arrived a week ago."

"Oh, yes. I'd forgotten." The invitation had fallen out of her mind because her general dislike of balls looked like ecstasy compared to the sheer agony a masquerade promised.

"We could still go. I'm sure Mr. Amesbury would be happy to see you attend another ball."

She knew her father wouldn't insist on another so soon. But perhaps a masquerade would provide her with the courage to meet W.H.

Her silence must have encouraged Mary. "If you could meet W.H. at a masquerade, perhaps that might feel less . . ." She sought the word she was looking for.

"Exposed?" Clarissa said, finishing Mary's thought. "I never thought I'd want to attend a masquerade—they seem silly and childish—but this *would* be a good way to meet W.H. without revealing too much about myself."

Mary scooted forward on her chair. "So, you'll compose a reply?"

Clarissa bit her lip for a moment and then nodded. "Yes."

Eight

"I MUST BE MAD TO have even considered this," Clarissa said. She whirled about and crossed the street, narrowly missing a carriage. Mary followed behind, gathering her skirts and marching over the cobblestones in pursuit. The nerves in Clarissa's stomach had prevented her from eating anything that morning but dry toast and tea, and now she felt faint as she clutched a wax-sealed note.

"You are not mad," Mary soothed. "But you *will* regret it forever if you do not deliver that note."

Clarissa gave Needham's a quick glance before turning around and striding in the opposite direction. Keeping up took effort on Mary's part, though Clarissa spoke as if her companion were at her side. "What if someone finds out? What if he doesn't respond? What if, as you warned me, he's vile in some way? Oh, goodness. What if he's a criminal or a miscreant?"

Mary took hold of her arm with a firm hand; Clarissa's step came up short. Noting Mary's hand on her arm, she realized that her emotions were overtaking her reason. "Breathe," Mary said.

MASQUERADE A-LA-MODE

Clarissa closed her eyes, grateful for her dear companion, who could always return her feet to solid earth. After several deep breaths, Clarissa opened her eyes.

Mary raised her brows in question. "Better?" Clarissa gave an affirmative nod. "Good. Now, I insist on nothing, but I must remind you that replying to W.H. was *your* idea, and that when you read his words, you were certain he was the perfect man for you."

"Yes, but—"

Mary lifted her other hand to cut off the objection. "He may not be, or he *may* be. You'll never know which without investigating the matter."

"Remaining in ignorance would, at least, be a safe course of action."

Mary's expression turned tender. "Safe, perhaps. Not happy. In your lonely safety, you'd always wonder whether you'd lost your chance to find the man your mother hoped would be yours. Talking is all well and good, but *acting* is what determines one's future..."

"You're right." Clarissa sniffed and looked up to hold back building tears. She shrugged. "Yet if I don't reply, I can't know."

"Or be disappointed," Mary added. "I know, love."

Could she bear learning that W.H. was not the man she'd imagined? Worse, how could she bear learning that he was indeed the man who belonged in her imagined castles in the sky, but he didn't want *her*?

Still with a hand on Clarissa's arm, as if to ensure she wouldn't flee, Mary called over a small boy on the street. He scampered to them, his white eyes surrounded by a dirty face that was thin with hunger. "What is your name?"

"I'm Arthur," the boy said.

"Well, Arthur, I'm Miss Redcliff."

"Pleased to make your acquaintance," the boy said, doffing his cap briefly.

"Would you like to earn a farthing?" Mary asked.

The boy's entire body lit up. "A whole farthing? Yes'm."

Mary took the sealed note from Clarissa's hand. "Do you know Needham's Coffee House?"

The little boy shook his head. "Can't read, neither."

Mary took his hand and walked him back to the corner. Clarissa followed a few steps behind. Best not to draw attention even at this stage of the venture and invite wagging tongues.

Mary nodded at the establishment across the street. "See the sign with the white cup?"

"Aye."

"That's the place. To earn your farthing, you must deliver this note to the proprietress." She held up the sealed paper.

"I can do that," Arthur said.

"Ask for Mrs. Passmore. Can you remember her name?"

"Mrs. Passmore," the boy repeated. He sounded much older than he looked.

With dismay, Clarissa realized that he might be quite a bit older than he looked, so small due to poor nutrition and living on the street.

Compassion for the child usurped her earlier misgivings over the possibility of being noticed. She stepped forward and interjected, "Arthur, if you deliver the note to Mrs. Passmore, and then bring us word of what she said in response, I'll give you a whole penny." She pointedly did not introduce herself. Best to stay anonymous.

Mary gaped at her. Yes, a penny would double the boy's reward. It was still a small sum compared to the three shillings she'd considered paying for an advertisement of her own. If some of her pin money could help this boy eat comfortably for a few more meals than usual—and if such a promise would motivate him to fulfill his duty quickly and honorably—it would be well worth the cost.

"Yes, miss," the boy said. "Thank you."

He moved to take the note, but Mary held it out of reach. "You must go directly there and speak to no one save Mrs. Passmore. She is the only person who may know of this message—the only person who may touch it after you. It is most important."

The boy nodded solemnly. "You have my word."

"Good." Mary gave him the note, and the ladies watched him run across the street to deliver it.

Clarissa felt she ought to turn away to avoid gossip or scandal, yet her gaze remained fixed on Needham's as Arthur scurried across the street and through the door. They waited with bated breath until little Arthur returned with an affirmative report.

"She says she'll give the letter to W.H. and to check for a reply tomorrow afternoon."

Clarissa gave him a penny from her reticule, then watched him scamper away with renewed energy.

She headed toward home with Mary. "Have I truly just invited a strange man to a masquerade?" she whispered. "I *am* mad."

Mary slipped her arm through Clarissa's elbow as they walked. "You're nothing of the sort. You're a brave woman, and quite modern, too. The masquerade will be a night to remember."

"Yes, it will," Clarissa said, feeling even more light-headed, and not only from hunger.

For better or worse, the masquerade *would* be memorable.

She'd signed her note *SFE*, a reference to Sarah Fyge Egerton. If W.H. responded favorably to those initials, it would be a sign that she'd interpreted his letter correctly.

"Wait," she said and stopped suddenly.

"What is it?" Mary asked with concern.

"I've already forgotten what I said I'd wear so he'd know me."

"A silver mask tied with a blue ribbon."

"Oh yes. Of course." Clarissa continued their walk. "What would I do without you, Mary?"

"You'd be lost," her companion said.

They chuckled at that, yet Clarissa had to wonder what Mary's influence had done. She'd set into motion a series of events as inevitable as a log heading toward a waterfall. She was atop the log, and heaven only knew what the trip over the edge would hold.

Nine

CHARLES ENTERED THE MASQUERADE WITH Doughty at his side, and for the first time in ages, he anticipated enjoying the evening.

Amazing what a disguise can do, he marveled, striding forward with his chin up and shoulders back. No one, save Doughty, knew who he was, and therefore, no one would note him. Rather refreshing. His mask covered most of his face, and he wore a tall powdered wig—most unlike him—tied with a red ribbon of the same shade as his waistcoat—more burgundy than the crimson of his former uniform.

Though SFE, the lady who'd responded to his advertisement, would be looking for a man with a gold mask to complement her silver one, Charles wore a black mask.

He had every intention of learning about the lady—but with certain precautions. After the debacle that was the Mayfair ball, he would not again allow himself to be in a position to be discarded and humiliated over his deformity.

Therefore, he'd enlisted Doughty to take on the role of intermediary, much as Mrs. Passmore had been intermediary in the first step of this undertaking. Wearing the gold mask, Doughty would meet the lady. He was hopeful that the initials she'd used referred to poetess Sarah Fyge Egerton and that she'd used them to convey her recognition of his use of W.H. as a reference to William Hogarth.

So far, it appeared that this was indeed a woman with his view of the world, one who knew literature, had a liberal view of society, and would likely be a pleasant late-night companion for conversations by a fire and a cup of tea as they discussed all manner of topics.

Yet he had to ensure that she was indeed the kind of lady he'd described as desiring to meet. He'd received two others, clearly from women who did not know or recognize the name of Silvertongue. Worse, their letters had been filled with flattery and foolishness. At fifteen, one of the two was far too young. He wondered at how she'd managed to send a reply without a chaperone learning of it.

Charles made his way through the crowd, back straight with an old confidence that felt comfortable. Doughty hung back, seemingly nervous to play his part. Charles found the situation amusing; their usual dispositions entirely reversed for the evening, though few people, if anyone, would have been able to detect Doughty's discomfort.

As a longtime friend, however, he could read Doughty like a well-worn magazine. He slowed in his step and looked over at a distinctly uncomfortable Doughty, whose neck was splotched with pink, a sure indication of his nerves.

"Are you quite well, my dear man?" Charles asked, grinning.

"I cannot believe you connived me into doing this," Doughty said under his breath.

Charles tsked. "Oh, but *you* dragged me to balls and other nonsense against my will. This is merely returning the favor. You can hardly complain at such a clear example of fair play." He raised his elbow slightly, drawing his friend's

MASQUERADE A-LA-MODE

gaze to his arm. "Besides, didn't you say it was your sole aim in life to see me married? You are merely helping that happy event come to pass. And there is the small matter of how I wounded myself while protecting you in battle."

"Remind me to never let you risk your life for me again. The price to pay is far too high." Doughty's amused tone belied his strong words. He touched his gold mask, possibly to adjust it so he could see better, though just as likely because he wanted to tear it off but couldn't.

"Do you see any sign of her?" Charles asked, trying to survey the room with a casual air rather than study every face as he wished to. Before Doughty had the chance to reply, however, Charles spotted two women, one of whom wore a silver mask—the only such mask he'd seen so far. She might be SFE.

"There," he whispered, elbowing Doughty slightly. He indicated the direction, forward and slightly to the right, with the slightest nod. She stood not twenty steps away. She wore a white powdered wig, obscuring her true hair color, which was a pity, though hiding one's true appearance was indeed the point of a masquerade. Indeed, Charles had concocted this mad plan and had managed to convince Doughty to follow it because they could attend without anyone knowing who they were. He and Doughty wore their own tall wigs as well, in addition to their masks, as did many others in attendance. They were clearly not the only guests to enjoy ensembles that reflected fading fashions.

Doughty glanced in the indicated direction and then away. "I see her," he said under his breath. He ran a finger at the back of his head beneath the ribbon that secured his mask to loosen it a tad. "As God is my witness, I'll never attend a masquerade again. This blasted thing is suffocating."

"Play the part well and you will never have a need. Now

go introduce yourself. See if she is SFE. And remember that you are W.H."

Doughty nodded at the reminder. "As if I could forget." With that, he moved forward toward the woman in the silver mask and lavender gown.

Under usual circumstances, of course, one could not simply appear before a lady and introduce oneself, but at a masquerade, many rules of standard etiquette fell to the wayside. Charles remained close enough to Doughty to observe his introduction to SFE while remaining unnoticed. He watched dancers weaving in and out of formations. He purposely stood close to the woman who had to be SFE, but his back was to her.

"Milady," Doughty said behind him, followed by a pause and swish of fabric, indicating his bow and her curtsy, which shifted her skirts.

Alas, Doughty spoke too quietly for Charles to hear much more than a few words over the music and conversational din. He very nearly turned to see what was happening—to come to Doughty's aid if needed, or perhaps to nudge him to take the requisite step—when the couple appeared, the lady walking on Doughty's arm toward the dance floor in preparation for the next set.

Charles let out a breath. The first stage of their singular plan had successfully commenced. Doughty and the lady took their positions. Charles knew he'd be unable to leave this spot until the dance was over and Doughty have given his report on the lady.

If the lady seemed respectable, intelligent, and personable, Charles would set up a meeting where they could be properly introduced. She'd never need know that he wasn't the man she'd danced with. Even without masks, he and Doughty looked similar enough to have been mistaken as brothers more than once. Their voices weren't terribly dissimilar, either. All good fortune for him, and reasons this outlandish plan of his might be fruitful.

The dance began, and despite the regular meeting and parting of couples as they moved through the formations, Doughty and SFE were clearly engaged in conversation. A very good sign.

Charles felt, more than heard, a rustle of silk beside him. He turned to see a woman who had stepped beside him. Her attention was on the couple as his was, easily visible from their vantage, with the floor slanting upward and candles lit brightly above them in many chandeliers. He did note, however, that her face, or at least as much as was visible beneath her mask, was somewhat pale, and her lips were pressed into a thin line.

"Are you well, milady?" Charles asked.

She didn't appear ill, exactly, but he could sense worry. He couldn't see much of it, save for the pressed lips and tight jaw. Her mask was black, much like his, only decorated with red accents.

She glanced at him, then looked again in surprise, clearly not expecting a strange man to address her in such a manner, even at a masquerade. She managed a smile. "I am quite well, thank you. It's just . . . rather warm in here. And my . . ." Her voice trailed off, and Charles very nearly asked her to complete her thought, but he suddenly felt as if doing so might feel too intrusive for a stranger, so he held his piece.

"Do you need some air? I believe the gardens are pleasant here, and yesterday's rain is gone, so the paths should be dry."

"Perhaps later," she said, staring ahead again. "I'll take a turn after this set, when my friend is free."

He'd had a similar thought—that a stroll through the

gardens with Doughty would be an excellent opportunity to hear everything about SFE before they left the ball.

"I'm not accustomed to so many people," the lady said. "It is a little intimidating."

"I am of the same mind," Charles said. "I'd much prefer a quiet evening with a handful of people I know well and care about rather than a crush of a ball with dozens of people I know nothing about and have no desire to learn of."

"Precisely," she said with a nod and a laugh. "My brother thinks I must be entirely uncivilized because I don't adore balls."

"And yet here we are," Charles said, "attending a masquerade because we must abide by the rules of modern society."

"It *is* what is expected of us," she said. "Alas."

After a mutual chuckle, they lapsed into an easy silence punctuated by the occasional comment as if they'd known each other for years. Strange how conversing with a lady felt effortless when there was no possibility of her learning of his disfigurement and being shocked by it.

In a most unexpected twist, hiding parts of himself allowed him to be at ease and speak as his true self. Indeed, in that moment, speaking to a woman he did not know, he felt more like the Charles he'd been before the war. He felt as comfortable with this woman in the pale-blue gown as he did at the gentleman's club or with Doughty.

He gazed on her profile as she watched the dancing, seeming entranced. What if she wished to dance? He would have to say no or risk exposing his misshapen hand.

Any ease within him drained away, and he felt the need to escape. He was about to take his leave when she turned to him with her head tilted as if in question—a small act that stopped his speech from exiting his lips. He swallowed, praying to the gods above that she wouldn't suggest a dance. How could he say *no* to this lady with the laugh of a friend and the heart of an angel?

"Do you know the gentleman in the gold mask?"

The question hung between them as Charles repeated the last few seconds in his mind, needing to gather his wits.

She gestured toward the dancers. Doughty, in his gold mask, stepped around his partner, the mysterious SFE in the silver mask. "I ask because you seem to have noted them these several minutes."

"I—well . . ." Blast, how could a ballroom be so stifling? Were the chandeliers lit with torches rather than candles?

"I ask," the lady said, "because my friend . . . in lavender . . . is his partner."

"Yes, I see her now," Charles said, as if he hadn't had his eyes all but tied to her the last several minutes. The room didn't feel quite so suffocating. "Do you know her well?" Ever the soldier, he played the strategist: he'd use this happenstance meeting with SFE's friend to learn about her. Perhaps this daft idea of finding a wife through a newspaper would prove fruitful after all.

"I know her very well," she said with a nod and a smile that lit up what little of her face he could see. The edges of her smile vanished beneath the mask, and a temptation briefly flitted in his mind to lift her mask so he could see the whole of it. He quietly wondered if she might, in some small way, resemble the lady in the green gown from the last ball. *She'd* been nothing short of stunning.

He would certainly like to have a wife who looked like her. But that was pure stuff and nonsense. Who was he, a man with a hideous defect, to entertain, even for a moment, the desire for a wife so beautiful? That was indeed the height of pretension.

"Tell me about your friend," Charles said as casually as he could muster. He'd have made a terrible prisoner if the Rebels had captured him. They'd have been able to merely look at him to read his mind. Good thing this was a masquerade, making such a thing impossible. He reminded himself to speak as if he were John Doughty. Anything he told her about SFE's dance partner must be true about *him*, Charles, not the man she was walking beside. The entire situation was somewhat addling in his attempts to keep everything clear in his own mind.

I shouldn't reveal too much about myself as I ask about SFE. I must tread lightly, or I'll speak out of turn as myself instead of as Doughty.

The music drew to a close. The couples bowed to one another. Charles cursed silently. He'd lost his opportunity. He'd have to rely entirely on Doughty's observations.

As Doughty and SFE left the formation, they did not move in Charles's direction as he expected. Instead, they headed for the large glass doors leading to the gardens.

At his side, her friend made a noise of surprise, which fit his sense of the moment exactly. How to extricate himself? He needed to follow and hopefully listen to their conversation.

"It's rather warm in here," the friend said to him. "Would you care to escort me outside for a turn about the garden?" She held out her hand, now flashing a crooked, mischievous smile. She'd had similar thoughts to his—she wanted to hear what her friend was saying to her dance partner; he was sure of it.

"Sounds delightful," Charles said. He pretended to bump into a passing server, which allowed him to turn about and stand on the lady's right side instead of her left. He hoped the ruse wasn't obvious, but he would not endanger the entire evening's ruse if he could avoid it. Best to have her on his left arm.

"Shall we?" he said, holding out his arm to her.

"I'd be obliged," she said with a small dip of a curtsy.

They hurried toward the doors, their progress hampered by the sheer number of people in the room. Yet when they passed into the cool night, where torches lit the descending stairs to the pathways below, they spotted the couple in question.

In unison, they slowed their step as if the change had been planned. They walked in slow, easy movements, though their breathing was slightly labored from the rush.

She leaned in and whispered, "Would it be terrible if we tried to hear their conversation?"

Charles leaned in as well and murmured, "I was pondering the very same question . . . Miss . . . I don't know what to call you." He looked at her, only to realize that he was still leaning in, making their faces only inches apart. He inhaled a divine aroma—vanilla, perhaps, with a hint of peaches and something else, floral, he thought. Magnolia?

She looked at him, and through their masks they locked gazes, though the shadows made determining anything about her eyes—shape or color—impossible. He noted she made a single distinct swallow, perhaps feeling this same . . . something.

What was this he felt? He wasn't sure, and for the moment, he was happy not to think too long on it; he was enjoying himself at a ball, with a woman on his arm. *Not* to feel a flutter in his middle and a buzz in his chest would have been odd.

Surely he'd feel the same, only more strongly, when he met the mysterious SFE.

Without pulling away from him the slightest bit, she

said, "You may call me Miss . . ." She swallowed again, then licked her lips—and perhaps flushed? He couldn't be certain—before finishing, "You may call me Miss Redcliff. And you?"

Options raced through Charles's mind like a shuffling deck of cards. He couldn't bear to lie directly, though why, he could not entirely say, seeing as everything about this evening was arguably a falsehood. Besides, his true name would likely mean nothing to her. "Ballam," he said. "Mr. Ballam."

"A pleasure to officially meet you, Mr. Ballam." She curtsied.

"Likewise, Miss Redcliff," he said with a half bow. "Now, shall we see if we can listen to our friends without being noticed?"

She chuckled, and her defined brows rose with it. Oh, if only he could see her full face. "Most definitely, Mr. Ballam." She took his arm again, and they set off along a garden path.

Ten

OH, WHAT HAVE I DONE? What am I doing? Clarissa thought as she walked a garden path with Mr. Ballam.

"The fresh air is a relief," she said, then inhaled deeply of the cool evening air. "I suppose it's shocking to admit that I don't enjoy balls and even worse to say so while in attendance at a masquerade." She laughed, and he did as well, a genuine, warm sound that put her at ease.

"Then it is your good fortune to have confessed it to someone of the same mind. My concept of a pleasant evening is *not* one in which I am surrounded by strangers, with music played too loudly to comfortably converse, and everyone is playing a part rather than being themselves." He chuckled. "And, as you noted yourself, I say that while attending a masquerade."

Clarissa placed her free hand over the one looped through his arm. "I am glad we are in agreement. I've always had the sense that the *ton* wears masks of a sort at every event. It's only at a masquerade where the masks are tangible and self-evident. What a strange world we live in."

"Oh, how I wish my friend agreed."

"Your friend?" she said, hoping she sounded airy. "You

mean *him*?" She gestured ahead of them where Mary walked with W.H., becoming acquainted with him in her stead.

One more level of masks and deceit, she thought guiltily, though it was all in the name of seeing through the masks and learning who someone truly was.

"Well, yes, I do mean that friend."

She was attuned to his vague reply, not giving a name or expanding on how he and his friend differed. Did W.H. enjoy balls and the social games, then? She hadn't expected that, and the idea was somewhat disappointing. That might not be what Mr. Ballam meant at all. She'd need to learn more for herself.

"They are definitely too far away for us to hear any conversation," Clarissa said of the couple.

"They'll remain so unless . . ." Mr. Ballam looked around and considered. "We could wind about the side paths until we are parallel to them but hidden behind other shrubbery."

"Excellent idea," she replied. "Are you familiar with these gardens, then?"

He sighed. "No. We'll have to explore, I suppose, and hope for the best."

As they did so, they spoke on other topics. "Are you new to London?" she asked. His answer might give her insight into W.H. If either or both resided in the City, that would provide ample opportunity to become better acquainted in the future if they chose to.

"I'm not entirely new to London, but I am relatively newly returned."

"And your friend?"

"The same."

She eyed him, though doing so wasn't a surreptitious act, as her mask prevented her from looking on him without turning her head slightly in his direction. "You spent some time away?"

"We both did," he said. "Some years in the former colonies."

"During the war?" she asked, and he nodded, murmuring in the affirmative but offering nothing else. The easy flow of words was becoming dammed. She should have asked his opinion of the weather instead. For some, the glories of war were a fruitful source for conversation. Clearly not with Mr. Ballam.

They walked along in silence, save for the crunch of gravel under their feet. Clarissa wondered if they were drawing any closer to Mary and W.H., and if Mr. Ballam regretted coming outside with her.

Then he spoke suddenly. "We fought together. I was in his battalion." He said it plainly, without airs. Something about the simple statement made a quiet respect settle over Clarissa.

"You must have become intimately acquainted."

"We are very much like brothers." He smiled and shook his head. "Sometimes he seems more paternal. He enjoys telling me what to do as if we're still on the battlefield. After a bit of time in the country, we've returned to London, and apparently, we've both taken to trying to get the other to the altar. Though if anyone needs a wife, between him and me, I would argue he is the one who is more in need of ending his bachelorhood. After all, he's closer to forty than thirty."

"I wouldn't have guessed," Clarissa said. W.H. had said he was "near thirty." She'd inferred that he was approaching that age, not past it. W.H. was likely more than ten years her senior. Older than she'd imagined for herself, but not terribly so. She knew plenty of women who'd found themselves with a husband old enough to be their grandfather. W.H. wasn't *that* old. If he had the manner she'd guessed, then it could still be a good match.

"Tell me more about yourself. And about your friend."

They took a few more steps, and then Mr. Ballam stopped and looked at Clarissa. "You surprise me. I'm used to being asked about the war."

"Do you *wish* to be asked about it?" Clarissa wondered if she'd muffed the situation entirely.

"No, actually."

They resumed walking, and Clarissa breathed a sigh of relief. She decided to explain herself, as she was certainly not behaving as a typical woman did around a soldier. "My brother's experience returning from the war showed me elements I hadn't known or considered. I've seen his pain, though he tries to hide it. He has scars and nightmares that might never go away. I have no desire to dredge up difficult memories such as those for anyone."

"Thank you," Mr. Ballam said. "That is most considerate of you, Miss Redcliff. Plenty of women, when they hear one's seen battle, ask for tales of heroic deeds worthy of a Greek god. Truly, it's my pleasure to avoid such things that are part of the games I do not wish to play or expect anyone else to."

He viewed the common method of courtship as a game, much as she did. His words warmed her—all but the name he used, of course, for Mary, not she, was Miss Redcliff. Clarissa yearned to tell him her true name.

I am Miss Clarissa Amesbury, she thought, imagining herself speaking the words to him. But she was there for W.H., not Mr. Ballam, even though the most enjoyable parts of the evening had been in conversation with him. She ventured to address the topic neither of them had mentioned. Perhaps that would stop her from thinking about how wonderful Mr. Ballam was and how she'd have been happy to remain in the gardens all night, talking about all manner of things until dawn.

"Your friend . . ." she said, taking a moment to muster the courage to mention what Mr. Ballam must know. "He called himself W.H. in his . . . advertisement."

Her words clearly took Mr. Ballam by surprise. "Yeeees." He said the word slowly.

"You can trust me. She does," Clarissa said, gesturing ahead. She looked up at Mr. Ballam and asked, "What is his real name?"

Mr. Ballam made a noise that sounded like surprise. He cleared his throat—twice—and shifted his weight, making his boots scratch against the path. He took a deep breath. Would he ever answer?

"I presume he has a name," she said. "More than initials, I mean." She added a chuckle and waited, hoping that the tension in his jaw would release. She raised her free hand in the air to emphasize her next words. "I withdraw the question. After all, this is a masquerade, where identities are allowed to be secret, are they not?"

"Indeed." He nodded, then sighed, and, to her relief, his jaw relaxed.

Good. The sight affected her far more than it should have. She didn't know this man at all—was Mr. Ballam his name any more than Miss Redcliff was hers?—yet she found she did care about his feelings. She cared a great deal.

A breeze kicked up for a moment. His scent, a mixture of bergamot, cedar, and a hint of cloves, brushed against her nose. Her middle seemed to be excitedly moving like a burbling brook with a secret to tell.

His step slowed and then stopped, and he began looking around them. "Did you see where they went?"

Clarissa looked around. "They must have taken a turn onto a side path." But where? They looked one direction, and then another, without success.

When they both concluded that there was likely no way to find the couple without drawing attention to themselves, they stood facing each other. Neither spoke for a moment, though Clarissa suddenly felt the absence of his nearness and wanted to draw near, slip her hand through his arm, and walk these paths with him as the moon rose and arced across the night sky.

Would it be terrible of her to abandon her designs on W.H., as perfect as he'd seemed in writing, for Mr. Ballam? She didn't know if she could marry a man who enjoyed balls and socializing as much as W.H. appeared to. And Mr. Ballam was, well . . . so far, he was everything she'd hoped W.H. to be.

"Shall we continue on our own?" he suddenly asked, holding out his left arm to her as before.

"I'd be delighted." She slipped her hand through the crook in his elbow, and they continued.

Mary's prior warning echoed in her mind, words that seemed entirely foolish now. *What if he's deformed or terribly ugly?*

Clarissa made an amused sound at the memory.

"Do share what has you so entertained."

She licked her lips and pondered. She'd already mentioned W.H.'s advertisement and had implied, by association, her own—or rather SFE's—reply to it. Would discussing advertisements in the manner she and Mary did be terribly poor form? For most people, the answer was clearly yes, but Mr. Ballam knew his brother-in-arms was here in hopes of finding a wife because of one.

"My friend once warned that one shouldn't put too

much stock into how a stranger describes himself, such as in an advertisement looking for a wife." She looked over to see his reaction to the words, but he merely walked on with a slight smile.

Encouraged, she went on. "We often read them together, you see. Many are quite diverting, though some of the demands gentlemen list as requirements for a wife are telling. They include a required age, a certain temperament, a fortune of a certain size, and, of course, they *must* be attractive. No deformities or ugliness. Yet my friend once suggested that the very men making such demands might themselves be unattractive or deformed or—"

Mr. Ballam's step slowed to a stop. As before, his jaw had tightened, though now even more so. He fairly clenched it, and he swallowed a few times. In the dimness of the torchlight lining the path, she couldn't be sure, but she thought his neck and face were flushing, and not with laughter. She wished she could see the whole of his face, but at the same time his displeasure was plenty clear.

"I must take my leave, Miss Redcliff. I apologize." He released her arm, stepped back and bowed, then whirled around and strode—nay, stalked—back toward the estate.

The change in him was so abrupt that it left Clarissa breathless and confused. She didn't call out to him; she instinctively knew that doing so would be futile.

She watched him walk away, followed behind for a short spell, then hung back as his dark figure withdrew. His strides grew longer and faster until, shortly before he reached the doors, he wrenched his mask off and tossed it to his left, discarding it at the base of a bush.

What she would have given to have been able to see his uncovered face. But that was not to be.

She'd likely never lay eyes on Mr. Ballam again, with or

without a mask. She might never be able to apologize for angering him. She'd never know precisely why he'd left in such a manner.

She did the only thing she could think to do: she ran to the spot where he'd discarded his mask and plucked it from beneath a rosebush. Holding his mask, she sat upon a bench and stroked its edges, its black ribbon still tied in the back, and she waited for Mary to return.

Eleven

CHARLES MARCHED THROUGH THE KENNINGTON mansion until he exited the front doors, stopping only for the briefest moment to order his carriage to be brought about and to instruct a footman to fetch Doughty at once. "He has a gold mask and was last seen in the gardens with a lady in lavender. He may answer to the initials W.H. Tell him C.B. must see him at once. It's urgent."

"I'll find him, sir," the footman said and headed off.

He knew not how much time had passed as he paced back and forth on the drive, all the while cursing his impulsiveness in discarding his mask. He simply hoped that no one, especially Miss Redcliff, would see him. He didn't think she'd follow him, but he still kept an eye trained on the doors for anyone's arrival, whether the footman, Doughty, or someone else.

His bad hand throbbed, something not uncommon when it was forced for too long into a glove that his hand no longer fit into. He yanked the glove off and shoved it into a pocket, then flexed and shook out his misshapen fingers to give them some relief. If the pain didn't lessen soon, it would likely increase with swelling, and that meant imbibing port just to get to sleep.

Miss Redcliff had been refreshing and delightsome . . . right until the end. Her words echoed in his mind like a haunting specter.

What if he's deformed?

He'd been foolish to think that a woman like SFE or Miss Redcliff might bear to look upon a man physically scarred by war. It was time he accepted that no woman that he'd desire would have him. Not SFE, not Miss Redcliff. Not anyone.

He was finished pursuing women. Never again would he attempt to find someone to share his life with. Would that Doughty *hadn't* taken such care of Charles's wound on the battlefield; that it had taken him. Then he'd have had a heroic death to be praised for, not the pathetic life of a monster stuck in a society that saw him as nothing other than hideous.

What a calamitous night this had turned into.

The sound of quickly approaching heavy steps, likely men's boots, sounded. Charles, protected further from any light from the windows or the moon above by a tree canopy, turned to see who it was.

A gold mask glinted in the moonlight. John Doughty. He was alone.

Charles felt like a rag doll, ready to drop to the ground in relief. He might as well have been a doll—he certainly felt as if he were scarcely a man any longer.

Doughty looked about, not seeing him, and at first, not calling out to him, either.

At least I can trust him to keep a secret.

Charles raised a hand in a wave to catch Doughty's attention as he strode in that direction. "Here," he called. He realized only after that he'd raised his bad hand. At least no one was about to see it bare—unmasked, as it were.

MASQUERADE A-LA-MODE

"My dear man, what is the trouble? Are you injured?"

Only my pride.

"This charade was madness. I must go. I'm waiting for the carriage to be brought about."

"You must forgive my confusion." Doughty's forehead wrinkled, and he drew near. "I haven't given you any report of the lady. Who, I might add, likely thinks *I* have gone mad due to the way I ran from her. I suppose I should say she thinks *you* are, seeing as she believed me to be the man who placed the advertisement signed W.H."

"Lovely," Charles said with a snort. "One more woman on the list of those who would never have me."

"Ballam," Doughty chastised. "Come now. Don't wallow like a—"

When Doughty's voice cut off, and he didn't continue, Charles folded his arms in challenge. "Like what?"

"Nothing," Doughty said. "Replace your mask, and let's go back inside. The ball has hours left yet."

"Not for all the gold in the world," Charles said. "Even if it were possible, which it is not, seeing as I tossed my mask somewhere in the gardens."

The carriage rolled into view. "Come," he told Doughty, heading that way. "You can give me your report, such as it is, as we ride."

When Charles reached the carriage, Doughty was not behind him. Charles turned around to see the cause of the delay, praying it wasn't one of the ladies coming in search of either of them.

It wasn't. Rather, Doughty was gazing back over his shoulder at the grand stone building with what looked almost like—could it be?—yes, indeed, it appeared to be *yearning.*

"I didn't know you yearned to dance and stroll through

gardens, pretending to be someone else," Charles said. He'd never seen Doughty afflicted by affection toward a woman. This behavior was highly unusual, and Charles assured himself that he was interpreting it incorrectly.

Doughty sighed and closed the distance. As he stepped into the carriage and sat across from Charles, he took off his gold mask as well as his wig and discarded both on the bench beside him.

The carriage shook to a start, the wheels creaking behind the clop of hooves. As they pulled away from the estate, Charles watched his friend gaze out the small window until the road curved and the estate was no longer in view. Then Doughty leaned back against the seat and sighed deeply.

Unsure what to make of the behavior, which Doughty himself didn't seem to realize he was displaying, Charles asked, "So, what is your report?"

Doughty sighed again, even more deeply. "I played my part well. Miss SFE, I believe, is quite smitten with you."

"Smitten with *me*?" Charles inquired. "Or with *you*, John?"

Doughty leveled a look at his friend. "With W.H., and that is *you*. I would never have tried to woo her for myself. Anything I told her about myself was about *you*."

"What is your assessment of her? Is she a viable candidate for a wife?"

"She's nothing short of . . . wonderful." Doughty stared at the passing scenery as if he were no longer in the carriage with Charles but back on the Kennington estate, dancing with Miss SFE.

"You say that as if she's your first and only love and you'll never again see her due to a fatal case of consumption." The words were an attempt at lifting both his spirits and Doughty's. The only response Charles received was the shrug of one shoulder. This mood of his was something entirely unlike the former commander.

Understanding suddenly struck Charles as if the clouds of a storm had parted, sending a bright, unwelcome ray of sunlight upon his mind. "You like her. For yourself."

Doughty didn't deny it, but his throat made a strangled sound as if he was trying to hold the truth inside. He lowered his head and shook it side to side. "I'm sorry, Ballam. I never imaged that perhaps I'd find Miss SFE suitable to myself, and yet I admit that I cannot stop thinking of her. I am certain that, for years hence, she will frequent my thoughts and dreams in ways I didn't know were possible." He lifted his face to Charles's. "But I will *not* stand in your way. Your words were intended to find a woman befitting *you*, and I am most certainly *not* W.H. I know nothing of the real William Hogarth and his prints. I practically forced you into this situation, so the painful result is a folly of my own making."

To hear that Doughty would be loyal to him, even at great personal cost, was no surprise at all. But as Doughty refused to hurt Charles, so Charles would not allow him to hurt for his own sake.

"If she was drawn to you—and I have no doubt she was drawn to *you*, John Doughty, not the part you played—"

Doughty cut him off. "Fortunately, I was able to maintain the ruse of being W.H. because we didn't talk of the prints at all. If she had, I don't know what I would have done."

She hadn't mentioned *Marriage A-la-Mode*? That was odd, considering his mention of Silvertongue was the thing that had convinced her to respond to his advertisement. He'd included that name specifically to find a woman of a similar mind.

"I'm glad you didn't have to remember the details," Charles said, mentally unwinding the logical knot Doughty had presented to him. "But you could have spoken about the prints with aplomb, I'm sure. We went over the details plenty of times beforehand."

"The moment she was in my presence, all sense fled entirely. Somehow, I remembered how to dance and to use the name W.H., both of which are nothing short of a miracle. At times, I believed she was drawn to me, but that is surely a folly."

What if she was besotted with Doughty as he clearly was with her? Charles stroked his chin with his good hand and stretched his bad one, which still ached from the evening's confinement. Perhaps Miss SFE wasn't the woman he'd imagined. He'd thought that referring to Hogarth's work, and her reply mentioning it—as well as her use of the SFE initials—were all proof that they were of a similar mind. No matter her mind; her heart seemed to be attracted to John Doughty.

It was Charles's turn to sigh. "If you find her again, and discover her to be the kind of woman you could love and share your life with, you have my blessing. Assuming, of course, that she'll forgive the deception."

The men exchanged a look that held volumes, made from the bond created by struggling, enduring, and triumphing together in the worst of situations. "I am and always will be loyal first to you, Charles. I always will be."

"I know," Charles said. "That is, until you wed, at which point your loyalties will lie with your wife." He let his smile drop slightly into a more somber expression. "And if this lady might take on that role, who am I to stop you from finding your happiness? So tell me. Might this lady be that woman for you?"

MASQUERADE A-LA-MODE

Doughty replied in measured words. "After such a brief encounter, I cannot say with any certainty, but . . . I believe yes, she could. Even so, I will not pursue her unless you are utterly certain—"

"I am," Charles said.

If this lady were to love him, and he her, that would be a happy outcome. Perhaps his advertisement was Providence's way of finding John Doughty a wife. "You will always be my brother-in-arms. Closer than blood. I will not stand in the way of your happiness."

Doughty's eyes were rimmed with red, something barely visible in the glow of the city's oil streetlamps.

Charles held out his left—good—hand, and Doughty took it in his. They held each other tightly, wordlessly.

The carriage stopped before Charles's townhouse and the driver opened the door. Doughty lived one block away and would walk the short distance. As he moved to alight, Charles put a hand on his friend's shoulder. Doughty looked back, his brows raised in question.

"Truly," Charles said. "If you think she is the woman for you, or that she may be, find her and pursue her. Promise me."

After a moment, Doughty swallowed hard and nodded. "I will. Thank you." He ducked through the exit and stepped out.

Charles followed and waved, and his friend headed down the street toward his home, but as he went inside his townhouse and climbed the wooden stairs, Charles wondered if he'd ever experience what Doughty might soon have: a marriage that was a true love match.

Miss Redcliff had seemed like the perfect woman for him, right up until the end.

Charles stopped on the landing and held up his bad

hand to the window. Moonlight streamed through. He gave his hand a hard look. It wasn't so terrible to him, but then, he'd had years to get used to it. The silver moon was visible through some spindly branches lifting their arms to the skies as if in prayer. In that moment, he uttered his own.

"May John Doughty find the love he is looking for."

Twelve

SEVERAL DAYS AFTER THE KENNINGTON masquerade, Clarissa brought Mary to the theater in an effort to improve her melancholy mood. What was supposed to be a diverting evening proved to be nothing of the sort. The evening had felt interminable from the moment she'd begun her toilette to the moment the carriage lurched to a start on their way home.

Mary, usually effervescent to a fault, had been listless ever since the masquerade, which hadn't gone well for either of them. Apparently, W.H. had run off, abandoning Mary on the dance floor. And Clarissa had thought they were in the gardens the whole time. Both women were left confused and disappointed, especially after Mary had confirmed that W.H. was indeed everything a woman could possibly desire in a man.

Truthfully, Clarissa hadn't decided what to do about W.H. Should she send him another message through Mrs. Passmore? Forget all about him?

And what of the mysterious Mr. Ballam? She'd entirely enjoyed her time with him, yet she'd offended him, and he'd fled as if his life depended upon his escape.

She had difficulty thinking of Mr. Ballam, indeed because she'd *more* than enjoyed speaking with him. He'd been exciting, funny, stimulating, and more. He seemed to admire her intelligence—highly unusual. He'd almost proved himself kind and loyal, as evidenced by his eagerness to ensure his friend's well-being. In short, he'd presented her with qualities she hadn't realized she wanted or would admire in a man. Every conversation since then, whether with her father, brother, or even Mary, had seemed lacking. Lusterless.

Due to his wig and mask, she couldn't say if Mr. Ballam had a handsome face, but he was certainly broad shouldered and tall. She'd lived long enough to know that one's features had precious little to do with whether a person would be a suitable match.

As the carriage rattled along, Clarissa shifted in her seat beside Mary and smoothed out her skirts. The green silk seemed to glisten in the light of the streetlamps, reminding her of the last time she'd worn this dress—the Mayfair ball.

A pity she hadn't gotten his name and would likely never see him again. She could still remember the weight of his gaze and how his steely eyes had seemed to pierce straight through to her heart.

She still had no inkling of anything about him but the way he'd sent her heart to flight. She'd imagined his voice, though she didn't even know what he sounded like.

Perhaps instead of answering W.H.'s advertisement, she should have placed her own Once Seen notice in hopes of finding the man from Mayfair. Neither Clarissa nor Mary broke the thick silence that had hung between them ever since the masquerade.

"I . . . I have a confession to make," Mary said, her head lowered, hands wringing a handkerchief in her lap.

Clarissa turned from watching the street pass by. "What is it? You can tell me anything, dear Mary. I hope you know that."

Mary's eyes were downturned, and the corners of her lips matched. Her brow furrowed, and if she didn't stop twisting the handkerchief, she'd work a hole through it.

How selfish of me to be thinking of myself all evening when my dearest friend is suffering, Clarissa thought with no small portion of shame.

"Are you ill?" she asked.

Mary shook her head side to side, then sniffed, clearly holding back tears. "My heart has betrayed me, but I promise that it will not affect my loyalty to you."

Clarissa shifted to face her friend better. "Whatever do you mean?" She took Mary's trembling hands between her own. "You are the dearest, most loyal companion and *friend* a woman could hope for."

With a quick glance up at Clarissa as if Mary were a small child about to confess a sin, she said, "I'm afraid I've found myself falling in love with W.H." She pulled her hands back and covered her face with them, shaking her head. "I cannot stop thinking of him. I know he is the man *you* wish to court. I assure you, I said and did nothing at the masquerade to smirch your name or reputation." Her companion's words were stunning, though they explained so much about Mary's subdued behavior since the masquerade.

"You never would hurt my name," Clarissa said. "You needn't tell me so. I know your heart." She placed a hand on Mary's arm to communicate her affection.

"Can you ever forgive me?" Mary asked.

"How can I, when there is nothing to forgive?"

Mary sighed with relief, though the breath came out ragged. "I will banish all feelings for him. He is yours to pursue. I have no right to him. I will honor that. I merely . . . I had to speak the truth of it to you so the weight on my shoulders would no longer be so unbearably heavy."

Clarissa opened her mouth to speak, but Mary raised a hand and stopped her words. "I say none of this for pity or with any intention of your somehow *giving* him to me. Not at all. You were right to answer that advertisement. He *is* . . . perfect."

The carriage stopped before Carrington House, and the handkerchief fell to the carriage floor. In the sudden quiet, Clarissa picked it up and pressed the linen into her friend's hand. "I am not entirely certain that he is the man for me, especially if he is perfect for *you.* Is he? *That* is the question. If the answer is yes, seek him with my full blessing."

"You would do that for me?"

"Yes. How could you think otherwise?" Clarissa said. "You are as dear to me as a sister. I want your happiness as much as my own."

They embraced, wiped a few tears, and alighted from the carriage. As they climbed the steps to the door, Topham opened it, clearly expecting them.

As he closed the door behind them, the butler cleared his throat. "Two gentlemen are waiting for you in the drawing room."

Clarissa had nearly reached the staircase but turned around in befuddlement. Who could possibly be calling on her so late in the evening? She looked at Mary, who'd hardly seemed to note the butler's words as she was dabbing at her eyes.

"Where's Father?" Thoughts of putting on her nightdress and climbing into her warm bed were awfully tempting to succumb to. Surely these visitors were not her responsibility.

"Mr. Amesbury and your brother are at the gentlemen's club, and I was told not to expect them home until one or two o'clock." Topham tilted his head in the direction of the drawing room. "The gentlemen seemed most insistent on seeing you tonight." He eyes flitted to Mary and back. "Miss Redcliff, too."

"Mary will accompany me, of course. I wouldn't presume to meet strange men alone. Topham, will you accompany us? It might be best to have a male in attendance as well."

"Miss," he said with a nod, then held out an arm toward the drawing room.

Clarissa stepped that way and gestured for Mary to follow. Inside the drawing room, she indeed found two men sitting on wingback chairs, facing the crackling fire.

On hearing her footfalls, they stood and turned to greet her, each holding a glass of port, no doubt poured by Topham.

There, in the flesh, she gazed at the blue-gray eyes from the Mayfair ball. If there had been any doubt about whether this was indeed the same man, it vanished the moment he looked on her and his mouth hung open ever so slightly in surprise.

A cord of energy seemed to spring to life between them, much like the night at Mayfair, only stronger.

Yet his expression of shock told her that he had *not* expected to see her.

Who was he, and what had brought him to Carrington House?

Thirteen

CHARLES QUITE NEARLY DROPPED HIS port. There she was, standing before him—the very same woman from at the Mayfair ball. The lady in green who had seemed to see right to his soul. Was *she* the secret Miss SFE, whom he'd promised to step aside for, so Doughty could court her?

The thought sent a pang through him. He'd never go back on his word, least of all to John Doughty. If his friend, brother in all but blood, loved this woman, then Charles would never say a word about how he'd thought of her every day since the ball.

The room was tense with silence. Doughty glanced from Ballam to one lady and the next, as unsure of what was happening as Charles was. Fortunately for them all, Doughty found his voice.

"I am Mr. John Doughty, and this is Mr. Charles Ballam. We are in search of a certain lady who attended the Kennington masquerade last week. A messenger said that she might reside at this address."

The woman in green seemed to catch her breath. She reached for the hand of her companion, who'd gone white. They both looked ready to faint to the floor, and for good reason. The identity of anyone involved with advertisements was supposed to remain an utmost secret. He'd loosened Mrs. Passmore's tongue with a promised sum she could not refuse and by swearing he'd use the information in a gentleman-like manner that would not put her reputation as an intermediary at risk.

"Oh goodness," the woman in green said quietly, surely words intended only for her friend, but the room was not large, nor the distance between them far, so her words carried easily enough.

The other woman—somewhat older, wearing a gown the color of toffee—was the first to speak directly to the men. "We attended the masquerade." She gestured to her friend, whose cheeks had flushed a delicious pink and seemed unable to look Charles in the eye.

"I danced at the masquerade," the elder woman said, then gestured to her friend and added, "though Miss Amesbury here did not."

Amesbury. Charles didn't know that name, but the woman who possessed the name addressed them at last.

"Forgive my rudeness for not introducing ourselves. I am Miss Clarissa Amesbury, and this is my companion, Miss Mary Redcliff."

Charles could not quite grasp what was being laid out. The woman in green was Miss Amesbury. The woman in brown was . . . the very lady he'd spoken to and had believed might be a complement to him, a woman he might truly love.

And yet Miss Amesbury, in her green silk, seemed to have reacted to hearing his name—and he'd given his true name to his mysterious partner on the night of the masquerade.

He could not resolve the confusion.

"I danced at the masquerade," Doughty said. "Twice

with the same lady." He took a step toward Miss Redcliff. "She wore a lavender dress . . ."

Miss Redcliff stepped forward as well. "I wore a lavender gown, and I danced twice with the same gentleman. I admit your voice is familiar."

A green dress swished across the carpet as its wearer took a step toward Charles. "Some clarifications and explanations are due."

"That would be most welcome," Charles said, which might as well have been the most understated comment of his life, for he could scarcely bear the wait.

Miss Amesbury's voice grew solemn. "I must have your assurance as gentlemen that anything spoken in this room tonight remains here."

"You have my word," Charles said with a bow.

"Yes, of course," Doughty said with an eager nod and bow.

"Very well." Miss Amesbury bit her lower lip in thought and then lifted her chin to the men as one bearding a lion. "To be clear, Mr. Doughty, you placed a newspaper advertisement under the name of W.H., and you communicated with a Miss SFE, arranging to meet at the Kennington masquerade?"

Doughty glanced at Charles. "Not precisely. That is, parts of your information are accurate, but—"

Charles interceded. He clapped a hand onto Doughty's shoulder and said, "I created this mess. Therefore, it is my duty to correct it."

"Pray tell, correct what, sir?" Miss Amesbury asked.

It was time to reveal all. "I placed the advertisement, calling myself W.H., and it was answered by one Miss SFE." He nodded at Miss Redcliff. "You, I presume."

"*You* placed the advertisement?" Miss Amesbury said to Charles. "Did you dance with Miss Redcliff?"

MASQUERADE A-LA-MODE

Charles himself was still muddling through the whole of it. "Let me explain our actions, and perhaps all will be clear." He hesitated, unsure of how much to say. "Mr. Doughty stood in my place when meeting Miss SFE, and he did so under my assumed name of W.H."

"*You* wrote the advertisement," Miss Amesbury said slowly, as if the information was settling in her mind like settling sand. "So you are W.H. . . ." She turned to Mr. Doughty. "But at the masquerade, *you* were W.H."

"Correct," Charles said.

"We intended no malice with our deception," Doughty said. "It was conducted for a good reason." Fortunately, he did not elaborate; Charles was not yet ready to explain in full.

"The truth is that Mr. Doughty, known at the masquerade as W.H., found the lady he danced with exceedingly becoming, and he has been unable to stop thinking of her these past days. In short, *I* am the man who identified himself with the moniker of W.H., but it is my dear friend Mr. Doughty who danced with you and now hopes to become better acquainted, if you would be amenable despite our charade."

"I am very amenable," Miss Redcliff said, answering Charles but gazing straight at Doughty. "But I must confess an untruth of our own."

Miss Amesbury spoke up suddenly with a voice that trembled, and the words came out in a flood. "*I* am Miss SFE. I sent the message to W.H. through Mrs. Passmore, and it was I who asked Miss Redcliff to meet W.H. in my place at the masquerade."

Charles furrowed his brow. He couldn't have heard correctly. "You are SFE? We both had another act in our place?"

"It appears so," Miss Amesbury said, her worried

expression softening into a slight smile. "I asked her to judge the merits of W.H., whose advertisement I found intriguing and . . . hopeful." If she were to flush any more than she already had, she'd be entirely red. "You see, I recognized your reference to Hogarth's story, and I hardly dared hope that there was a man who might feel as I do toward matters of . . . well, people with characters like the Earl of Squander and . . . such." Her voice grew quiet, but her eyes held hope, a light that Charles wanted to see grow. Wanted to cause to grow.

"And what is your opinion of the doctor in the third print?" he asked.

"An evil quack," she said with a wider smile. This *was* Miss SFE.

Doughty broke in. "Miss Redcliff, do I understand that you and I spent the evening together?"

She nodded happily, silently. They gazed into each other's eyes as if they'd been caught in a spell and had been transported to a fairy world.

"It appears our friends may be a good pair," Miss Amesbury said. "A happy accident."

The more she spoke, the clearer it was that Miss Amesbury was indeed the woman he'd spent most of the evening of the masquerade with. First they watched Doughty and the actual Miss Redcliff dance. He'd so enjoyed conversation with Miss Amesbury and their turn about the gardens . . . right until she'd spoken of men with deformities.

He suddenly felt bitter in his stomach. Avoiding the eyes of either woman, he said, "We came tonight so Mr. Doughty could find the woman he'd found so compelling at the masquerade, and we have done so. We shall retire now."

Miss Amesbury looked at Charles with concern, clearly sensing his mood shift. "I—"

"Your butler has Mr. Doughty's card. Miss Redcliff may call upon him at her leisure if she so desires. Forgive us for usurping your evening. We shall be off." He bowed, then moved to place the port on a side table at the same moment that Miss Amesbury called to him.

"Mr. Ballam."

Hearing her say his name brought something in his chest to life, but he could not bear to consider what she'd think if she knew of his deformity.

"Mr. Ballam," she said again. "Please don't go quite yet."

He looked about for his walking stick. Where had he placed it? He was briefly so taken by his search that he failed to notice Miss Amesbury trying to get his attention. She reached for him as he walked by her, and she took hold of him . . . by his right hand. In the time it took for her to grasp his hand, he'd taken another step. For the second time in a month, his glove came off before a lady.

He whirled about and gaped at the black leather glove in her hand. Some of the padding had fallen to the floor at her feet, which she did not note. Instead, her eyes had widened, and her mouth opened.

Embarrassment washed over Charles. Well, she now knew. Let her laugh about a hideous man placing an advertisement as she'd predicted. He would not wait to have the glove returned; he would not stay a moment longer to be gawked at. Let the servants at Carrington House find his walking stick. He would send a man to fetch it.

He walked to the door without looking back but stopped at the threshold. He spoke over his shoulder. "I remind you of our mutual agreement that anything in this room this evening is to remain here." He believed she would keep his secret even if she cringed at it.

"Forgive me," Miss Amesbury said. "I did not know, and I never thought—"

"Good night, Miss Amesbury." Charles dipped his head and left the room. He marched out of the house, down the steps, and continued along the street, hoping to find a hackney carriage for hire. He shoved his bare right hand into a coat pocket. Despite the dark night and the shadows cast by oil lamps, he could not bear to have his ugliness exposed.

Behind him, he heard a quick tatt-tatt-tatt—footsteps, perhaps, but a higher pitch. Not Doughty. He increased his pace, wishing to be alone. His pursuer reached him and took his arm, stopping his progress.

"Mr. Ballam, please."

He turned stiffly to find Miss Amesbury breathing heavily from the exertion, holding his right arm, his ugly hand in plain view. She held his arm with both hands, but her grip grew lighter, and her hands lowered to his hand. His ugly, melted, horrible hand. She did not so much as look at it as she spoke.

"What I said in the gardens was flippant and hurtful. Please believe me when I say that I meant not a word of it. Mary—that is, Miss Redcliff—is much diverted by the advertisements, and I admit we've spent many an hour imagining the people behind them. It was her words I said, though they sounded far worse than she meant them. She's not like that . . . neither of us is. Truly, I'd hoped to find someone precisely like you. When I read your advertisement, I thought that I surely had. And now I know that I did. Please allow me an opportunity to show you who I am."

Her words implored so sincerely that he could not look away or dismiss her. Her tone, her face, her *everything* spoke to him and said even more than her words had. He thought back to the moment in the gardens before he'd stalked away. He'd left without hearing the whole of what she'd meant to say and before he'd listened to who she truly was.

He realized that her words hadn't been spiteful or dismissive . . . and she'd been quoting her friend, not expressing her own thoughts. Though now that he'd seen them both as they truly were, without masks of any kind, he knew that she was right; neither was as cruel as he'd imagined when he'd stormed away.

And now Miss Amesbury stood by him, alone and unafraid, holding his ugly hand without a thought. She looked at it briefly but did not recoil at the sight.

"I confess," she said, her voice lower now, "that I haven't stopped thinking of you since the masquerade. I haven't stopped berating myself for what I said. And I haven't stopped praying for the opportunity to both beg your forgiveness and to return this to you."

She reached into her reticule and withdrew, to his amazement, his black mask.

"Why—how—"

"It was all I had of you. I *had* seen your face before, though I didn't know it."

She'd remembered him from the Mayfair ball. The realization sent a river of golden warmth through his limbs. "I must confess that I've thought of your face ever since that night, and I wished it belonged to the amazing woman I met at the masquerade. I never would have guessed it did."

She held the mask out in offering. "Would you take this, with my sincerest apologies?"

For a moment, Charles could not answer. He stood there, amazed that she'd reached for his arm *after* seeing the ugliness of his hand. That she'd held his hand with generosity and kindness, without a hint of disgust. And now she stood here, speaking to him, not caring about what his hand looked like—not from curiosity or morbid fascination, reactions he'd seen countless times.

She saw *him*.

"No, I don't think I will take the mask," he said, though he touched the edge and let his thumb trail along it, wishing he could do the same to her cheek, her jaw.

Her face fell slightly at his words. "Oh. I apologize. I misunderstood. Good night, Mr. Ballam." She turned to go, but this time he stopped her—with his right arm out, gently touching her waist—with his bare hand. He'd done so without a second thought.

"Now you do misunderstand me," Charles said.

She looked up. "Oh?"

"Would you keep the mask for me? Put it in a drawer for safekeeping so I don't lose it again and will always know where to find it?"

"I could do that." A smile returned to her face and gradually spread to her eyes. "But you must make me a promise in return. I now know you're a man of your word."

Could there be a higher compliment? "Anything," he said huskily.

"Leave your card so I may call upon you?"

"I could do that," Charles said, echoing her words.

"There is more. Call on me. Take me on walks through parks. Read books with me. And—let's talk about things, become better acquainted."

"I believe that could be arranged," he said. "But not *A-la-Mode*."

"Never." She grinned.

Then, in a movement he could scarcely believe he was doing, he took her hand with his mangled right one and kissed the top of her glove. She did not cringe, gasp, or pull away.

"Miss Amesbury, I very much look forward to knowing you better," Charles said.

"And I you, Mr. Ballam." She stepped closer and wrapped her fingers around his melted ones. "Perhaps one day I may call you Charles and you may call me Clarissa."

He squeezed her hand gently in return. "God willing."

Annette Lyon is a *USA Today* bestseller, Whitney Award-winner, and 9-time recipient of Utah's Best of State Medal for fiction. She's published fiction set in the American West and the Regency and Victorian eras, though her most recent historical novel, *The Girl in Gray*, is set in the World War II era during the Finno-Soviet Winter War.

Her first foray into suspense, *Just One More*, was published by Scarlet Suspense in 2023. Annette has four adult children, one grandchild, and a flame-tipped Siamese cat with an attitude. She's represented by Jill Marsal of the Marsal Lyon Literary Agency.

Find Annette online:
Website: https://annettelyon.wordpress.com/
Blog: http://blog.AnnetteLyon.com
Twitter: @AnnetteLyon
Facebook: http://Facebook.com/AnnetteLyon
Instagram: https://www.instagram.com/annette.lyon/
Pinterest: http://Pinterest.com/AnnetteLyon
Newsletter: http://bit.ly/1n3I87y

UNUSABLE MATERIALS

Made in the USA
Middletown, DE
15 October 2023

40811429R00159